BOOKS BY HELENA NEWBURY

Helena Newbury is the *New York Times* and *USA Today* bestselling author of sixteen romantic suspenses, all available where you bought this book. Find out more at helenanewbury.com.

Lying and Kissing

Punching and Kissing

Texas Kissing

Kissing My Killer

Bad For Me

Saving Liberty

Kissing the Enemy

Outlaw's Promise

Alaska Wild

Brothers

Captain Rourke

Royal Guard

Mount Mercy

The Double

Hold Me in the Dark

Deep Woods

OUTLAW'S PROMISE

HELENA NEWBURY

FOSTER & BLACK

COPYRIGHT

PROLOGUE

This is my story.

It's about a big, scary, incredible biker they call *Irish*.

It's about Mac and Hunter and Ox and Viking and Mom (not my mom).

It's about a necklace and a promise. Family and loyalty. Sex and violence. Riding and sunsets.

I was going to start it with him saving me.

But to really understand it, we have to start with how I saved him.

1

ANNABELLE

Twelve Years Ago

I sat bolt upright in bed. What was *that?*

There was only silence, now, but I could still feel the sound echoing around my bedroom. The furniture in my dollhouse was still rattling.

I replayed the noise in my mind: a low growl, like a tiger getting ready to pounce. Then a crash of glass, a screech of metal and a final heavy thump.

And it had come from right outside my window.

I clutched my stuffed bunny, Perkins—just in case he was scared. He looked up at me with his one remaining eye and told me to be brave.

I strained my ears but the house was silent. Good. *He* hadn't woken up.

Very carefully, I crawled across my bed to the window and looked out.

Beyond the little field of wilted maize, the fence that separated our farm from the road was even more crooked than usual. Something big and dark had slammed up against it.

It moved. I ducked back down below the window, then cautiously peeked again. A man, bigger than my step-dad. Bigger even than I remembered my real dad being, and he was a big man. The man was trying to get up, but he kept slumping back down with a grunt of pain. His legs wouldn't support him.

He needed help.

I bit my lip and looked towards the room my step-dad shared with my mom. When I'd gone to bed, he'd been a good way down the bottle. Now he'd be in the heavy, coma-like sleep that would last until noon. If I woke him now, I'd be feeling it for a week. And I couldn't wake my mom without waking him.

I looked towards the window. It was down to me. I was only eight but there was no one else.

I took a deep breath, unlatched my window and crawled out onto the flat roof below, then down the wooden trellis to the ground. My bare feet sank into soft grass and the desiccated leaves the wind had stripped from the maize. The summer sun hadn't even started to creep over the horizon, yet, so I figured it must be the very middle of the night. Overhead, the sky was a glorious bowl of inky black dusted with a million stars.

I crept down the path, Perkins dangling from one hand. I could see the motorcycle, now, huge and gleaming, lying on its side near the fence like a wounded horse, one wheel still spinning. The road glittered with glass.

My steps got smaller and smaller as I approached the man. He seemed to have given up moving and just lay there on his back, staring up at the stars. I gawped at him, as fascinated as I would have been by an alien.

He wore boots, but not the plain, dirt-brown work boots men around town wore: these were black leather, studded with gleaming metal. He had a helmet, too, a metal bowl that hugged his scalp but left his face free. And over his white t-shirt he had a sort of leather jacket...but someone mean had cut the arms off of it. The badge on the front said *Hell's Princes*.

I took a step back. Mom said *hell* was bad, even though my step-dad said much, much worse words all the time. What if this man was dangerous? What if he was here to hurt us and I was out here on my own with him?

I squeezed Perkins' paw for courage. "Are you bad?" I asked the man. Because in my mind, however evil he was, he still had to answer truthfully.

His head whipped around and he groaned in pain. His dark brows rose in amazement as he saw me: three feet of white nightdress and frizzy red hair. "What?"

I already had my answer. His eyes weren't like my step-dad's, cold and gray and bloodshot from whiskey. They were blue like the sky when the storm clouds have just cleared and everything's fresh and new. Those eyes didn't want to hurt anyone.

Both of us looked up as a low growl vibrated along the road. The same growl his bike had made, but now it was a harmony. More than one of them. His friends?

He looked back at me in panic. "Go inside!" he snapped. "Go!"

No. Not his friends.

For the first time, I noticed he was pressing one hand to his side, as if he'd been running and he had a stitch there. But when he shifted his palm a little, I saw the red oozing out. And he looked towards the approaching engines when he did it. "They hurt you?" I asked.

He looked at me again, sighed and went to snap at me again. But he seemed to catch himself at the last second and his face softened. It didn't matter that he had black stubble all over his cheeks, which my step-dad said was for losers. It didn't matter that he was so big, with muscles as big as my head swelling his arms. I didn't feel that he'd ever hurt me, not even when he was mad. "*Get outta here,*" he told me. There was something odd about his voice, an accent that sounded like ancient, weathered rocks banging together to make silver sparks. "They might hurt you, too."

My stomach knotted and I crushed Perkins' paw in my hand and stepped back. I didn't want to get hurt. The sort of hurt they'd done to him looked worse than the kind my step-dad did. I took a few stumbling steps back towards the house.

Then I stopped. I didn't want *him* to get hurt, either.

I looked at the road. The approaching bikes were still out of sight, down at the bottom of the next valley, but the growl of their engines was getting louder.

I put Perkins carefully down on the ground, walked over to the man and took hold of one arm. Then I heaved. He twisted a little where he lay, but I couldn't lift him.

"What are you *doing?!*" he snarled, pain twisting his face. "Get out of here!"

I ignored his protests, stepped back and *thought*.

I've always known I'm weird. I'm too interested in how things work. Right back in elementary school, the teacher would have to shout to get my attention because I'd be staring at the door-closing mechanism, or looking at the construction machinery across the street. My mind just seemed to lock onto those things, the smoothly-sliding pistons and hard metal like ice cream and candy for my brain. My mom said I was like my dad, who'd designed engines. My step-dad just said I was stupid.

All I knew was, the man was too heavy to lift but I could see in my head how I might be able to drag him along the ground if I could just make him slippery. There was a big green sheet of waterproof sheeting in the tool shed and I fetched that, then unfolded it next to him. I took hold of his belt—it wasn't a leather belt but a shining silver chain—and used that to roll him onto the sheeting. He groaned as I did it and some Very Bad Words came out when his injured side pressed into the ground, but then he was on the sheeting and I bunched as much of it in my little fists as I could and started to drag him along the path to the tool shed.

The sheeting made him slide easily but he was still heavy. I was puffing and panting by the time we reached the shed, my bare heels digging into the dirt for traction. When I had him all the way inside, I left him there and hurried back along the path and out onto the road, picking my way carefully through the glass.

I'd never seen a motorcycle up close before—certainly not one like *this,* all chrome and black-painted steel. Tipping it up onto its tires was the hardest thing I'd ever done and I could barely keep it stable as I started to push it towards some bushes that hung out over the fence.

The bushes were only a dozen feet away but it felt like a mile. I sweated and heaved and tried not to think about how loud the engines were behind me. I distracted myself by staring at the bike: at its springs and levers and gleaming engine. A machine like that was pure heaven, to me. I wanted to run my hands all over it. I wanted to dissect it, to learn how every little part worked.

Then the front wheel hit the bushes and I let go, the bike's momentum taking it the rest of the way. By the time it slumped sideways against the fence, it was completely out of sight.

The engines were close, now. Too close. The growl had changed to a roar, beneath which lay heavy, overlapping *thump thumps.* As I started back towards the tool shed, I could hear the man cursing and calling for me. He'd managed to half-sit up, clutching at his side, and his eyes were wide with panic. He was scared for me, which was frightening...but made me feel warm, as well. I hadn't seen that look in years. My mom used to make it when my step-dad yelled at me but these days she just went quiet and looked away.

I was out of breath but managed to pick up the pace and run the rest of the way to the tool shed, plucking Perkins off the ground as I passed. I slammed the door behind me and sat down on the ground next to the man's outstretched feet.

The roar of engines built and built and the louder they got, the more frightened I got. As they crested the hill, the noise shook the shed, little bits of dust and dirt falling from the ceiling. It was too loud to talk, too loud to think...*what if they hurt me like they hurt him?*

Headlights blazed across the side of the tool shed, blasting through the cracks in the wood and painting white lines across the man's face. He looked down at me and his face tightened in anger: not at me but at the men outside. And he held out his arms for me.

That's when I realized I had tears in my eyes and was mashing

Perkins against my chest really, *really* hard. I flew into the man's arms and he cuddled me against his shoulder.

Then the shed went dark and the pitch of the roar changed as the bikes sped past. I slowly sat back down on the ground and we stared at each other as the noise faded away.

I fumbled around, found the battery lantern and turned it on. Its hard white glow gave me my first good look at his face. He was maybe seventeen and he had the blackest hair I'd ever seen, thick and lush and shining. His face was pale and he was sweating. "Thank you," he said. He closed his eyes. "Just let me rest a 'sec. Then I'll be out of your way."

That accent again, hard as rock and yet beautiful. "Are you Scottish?" I asked. "Like the Loch Ness Monster?"

He opened one eye and half-smiled around the pain. "Irish."

I thought about that. "Like a Leprechaun?"

"Yeah." The eye closed. "Like a leprechaun."

I stared at his side. The blood was steadily soaking across his white t-shirt, like someone had spilled blackcurrant on a tablecloth. "My mom says you should wash cuts. Or you can get ill."

He shook his head. "I can't go inside. Your parents might call the cops."

I bit my lip, considering. If he was scared of the police then he was bad and I was supposed to stay away from bad people. But...he didn't *seem* bad. Maybe he was *good* bad. Like Batman.

I got to my feet. "I can get stuff and bring it here."

He blinked up at me, then looked towards the house. "Will you get into trouble?"

"Only if I get caught."

He seemed to be about to tell me not to, so I ran over to the door before he could. Then I stopped, turned back and passed Perkins over to him. "Here," I said. "If it hurts really bad, you can squeeze his paw."

The man looked down at Perkins in amazement, then looked up at me and the sweetest smile I'd ever seen crept across his face. "Thank you," he said.

"Don't get blood on him."

"I won't."

Then I was running, bare feet slapping the dirt. I climbed back up the trellis, slipped in through my bedroom window and listened: nothing, not even snoring. I raided the bathroom cabinet for what I needed: I'd watched Mom patch me up and, once or twice, when my step dad's team lost a game, I'd helped her patch herself up. Then I went to the kitchen and grabbed a big bottle of water and some of my mom's banana loaf.

Back in the tool shed, the man had lifted his t-shirt and twisted so that he could look at his side. There were two long, straight slashes across his muscles, blood welling and running. He looked up as I entered as if worried I'd freak out, but I shook my head: I'd seen blood before.

At first he tried to get me to give him the supplies so he could do it himself, but it was too awkward and he soon gave up and let me do it. I washed the wound out with water and then antiseptic: he hissed but managed not to yell. Then I pressed a gauze pad against it and stuck it in place with tape. "Did *they* do this to you?" I asked, jerking my head towards the road.

He nodded. "I got away but they came after me. They were wearing me down and then I came off my bike." He ran his hand over his newly-dressed wound. "Thank you. I'm Carrick."

Carrick. I'd never heard that name before. A foreign name from a mystical land. "I'm Annabelle."

I passed him the water and the banana loaf. He stared at them for a second. "God bless you," he muttered, and devoured them.

Over the next four hours he drank the whole bottle of water, plus another I fetched him, and worked his way through four thick slices of banana loaf. He told me about riding his bike, about the motorcycle club who'd just made him a "Prospect"—a potential member—even though he was only seventeen. He told me about the —he had to think hard to find words suitable for my ears—*eejits* who'd cut him with a knife, a rival club. He showed me the *Hell's Princes* patch on the back of the sleeveless leather jacket he called a *cut*. Sometimes he'd doze, drifting off in the middle of a sentence. But each time he woke, his color was better.

When the sky started to lighten outside, he gingerly stood up. He was cautious at first, holding onto the wall for support, but he managed to stagger outside and retrieve his bike. As soon as he swung a leg over the saddle he seemed better, as if the bike and he had missed each other. "Will you be okay?" I asked.

He nodded, then looked at me. "Will *you?*" He looked around at our ramshackle house and the field of dried-out maize.

I thought about telling him my step-dad sometimes hit us. But my mom had always told me that I shouldn't disrespect him, and telling other people our secrets probably qualified. So I just nodded.

Carrick looked as if he wasn't satisfied. He reached under his t-shirt and took off a slender gold chain. "Have this," he told me. "For good luck."

It was a four-leaf clover in shining gold. I looked down at it in amazement as he settled it around my neck. It was the nicest thing anyone had ever given me.

"And I want you to have something else, too," he said. He felt in his pockets, found a gas station receipt and a stub of pencil, and wrote a phone number. "You saved me. Where I'm from, that means I owe you a boon. A favor. If you ever need me, you call that number. Okay?"

I nodded and clenched the paper tight in my fist. Then he started the bike and the heavy *thump thump* turned to a roar as he pulled away. I watched the big bike until it was out of sight and then turned and ran back to the house before someone missed me.

When I was fifteen, my mom died. I thought maybe our grief would bring my step-dad and me together but instead the resentment started to build. He'd invited my mom into his house but he'd never really wanted me.

And as I started to get older he started to look at me in a way he never had before. He never did anything. Not once. But the staring and the resentment built until the two were twisted together like choking ivy around a blackened, scarred tree. He hated me; he wanted me.

I'd long since memorized the phone number Carrick gave me but I didn't call. Calling the number would take its power away. As long as I held onto it, like a talisman, I could pretend that he could still come and rescue me.

He grew in my mind, becoming larger-than-life. I remembered those blue eyes and that hard, strong jaw: I'd only been a kid at the time but now I was sure he'd been gorgeous. As I got older, the fantasies changed: I thought of hard abs, of tanned biceps under a tight white t-shirt. Beneath the covers, I thought of that Irish voice growling *Annabelle* and I gasped his name in return.

Even when I hit eighteen I still couldn't move out: my waitressing job barely made enough to pay the bills and my step-dad kept reminding me that he'd put a roof over my head for years so I owed him. My grades were good but there was no way I could afford college.

But I found that my weird mind was good for something: I could fix things. People would bring me lawnmowers and chainsaws to mend. I was like a doctor with a patient: a machine that was out of whack *felt* wrong to me, the sound made me itchy and jumpy and I couldn't leave it alone until I'd fixed it. In my head, the machines just sort of came apart into shining pieces and I could sift through them and figure out what was wrong. I was happier around machines than around people: machines didn't laugh at how cheap my clothes were or make me feel like a freak. It brought in a little extra money but my step-dad was starting to run up debts with his drinking: first to bars, then to banks and then to loan sharks.

I didn't know how to talk to guys: I'd mumble and flush...and who'd want the weird girl from the farm way out of town, who still lives with her dad and has grease under her fingernails? I worked a seven day week as a waitress because at least that got me out of the house, then stayed up late fixing.

The years stretched ahead of me, inevitable and identical. I thought life couldn't get any worse.

And then, one night, it did.

2

ANNABELLE

Now

I came home to find my dad talking to a guy I didn't recognize: a biker. For an instant, my mind went to Carrick...but this guy was much older: forty or more, with a bald head and a thick, dark beard shot through with gray. The front of his leather cut had a shining metal spider the size of my hand on the chest, positioned as if it was scurrying upwards towards the man's face. It had been made with jointed legs so that it seemed to tense, ready to pounce, every time the man moved, the metal clinking and rattling. It made my skin crawl. The patches on his cut said *Blood Spiders* and *President*.

"Go upstairs," said my step-dad, as if I was still a teenager. But he had that drunk, *don't argue with me* tone, so I climbed the stairs, feeling their eyes on my ass the whole way. Instead of heading into my room, I hunkered down behind the handrail and listened.

"How many are coming?" my step-dad muttered.

"About thirty," the biker told him. "Enough you'll get a good price."

He's selling drugs, I decided. But I couldn't imagine him as a drug farmer. He had no knack for growing things. Meth? When would he cook? He barely left his armchair. He must have gotten hold of a package of something cheap and was hoping to sell it on....

My step dad's voice again. "Is that guy coming?"

"Let's hope so. I sent him the photo."

What photo? Why would he take a photo of drugs?

My step dad went quiet for a moment.

The biker's voice grew low and hard. "You got second thoughts," he said, "you tell me *fucking now.* People show up, there ain't no getting cold feet: there'd be a riot. And if *Volos* turns up and you try to back out, he'll kill you. He'll kill me, too. The guy's serious. *Protected.* You gotta be sure."

I heard my step dad knock back some whiskey. "I'm sure."

"Go get her ready."

Sometimes, your mind just refuses to go there. *Her? A car. He must be auctioning a car.* People sometimes called cars *her,* especially if they were old and valuable. Did he have something stashed in a barn I didn't know about?

The door banged as the biker left. A moment later, my step-dad came upstairs. I raced for my room and he found me there.

"Get changed," he said. "Put on a dress. Put on some make-up."

My mind finally started to swing around, like a boat pulled loose from its moorings by a whirlpool grown too powerful to resist. I sat there and gaped at him but my brain still refused to accept it. *That's insane. Things like that don't happen.*

I couldn't ask. Asking the question would make it real. Instead, I said, "I don't have a dress." I wore a uniform for waitressing and jeans at home. I didn't go on dates. I hadn't owned a dress in years.

"Wear that one your mom left you."

My stomach twisted. My mom had left me an old, bottle-green vintage dress that I'd always loved when I'd seen it on her. It was small on me and not really suitable for anything other than a vintage-themed ball—it was a keepsake, not something I'd wear.

Our eyes locked. I could feel mine going big, desperate. *Please don't let this be real. This can't be real.*

And for a second, I saw his eyes soften and he looked away in guilt. My stomach plunged down to my feet because suddenly I knew I was right.

"You can't do this," I told him. My voice had gone thick and hoarse. "You can't—You can't *sell* a person."

"I provided for you and your mom for years. Time you made a contribution."

I wanted to scream at him that I'd been the one paying the bills for years...but I knew it wouldn't matter. In his mind, I was still the unwanted kid he'd been stuck with. "You can't...." I shook my head, cold fear climbing my chest. I couldn't get my head around the concept. I hadn't known that things like this even went on: was I just naive? "Please!" I said at last, my eyes filling with tears.

"Get ready!" he snapped. Then he turned and left, slamming the door behind him.

I turned to my closet and took out the dress.

I wouldn't normally have let him drive when he was that drunk, but he was too riled up for me to risk arguing with him. So I clutched at the edges of the seat as we bounced and skidded on the dirt roads, cutting cross-country. At first I thought we were heading to Teston, the nearest big town, but we passed by and stopped on a country road a few miles beyond it.

It was a bar, but take off the neon sign and it could have been a barn. Basic and functional, a place for people who just want to get wasted, away from the prying eyes in town. The parking lot was already full of cars, a biker with a shotgun standing by the entrance to vet people as they arrived. I saw him turn some cars away, pointing to the sign above the door: *Private Function.*

Tonight had been organized. *Planned.* Everyone had known about it except me.

The cold fear that had started in my bedroom had spread to fill my whole body. *I am going to be sold.* To a man. I knew it would be for sex, either with him or....customers. I'd serve him, or I'd be on my back in some brothel until I was too old and then he'd kill me. I was so scared I thought I was going to throw up. *This can't be happening. I'm twenty years old. This can't be all my life is going to be.*

Our car stopped beside the biker—he too had one of those leather cuts with the spider on it. "This her?" he asked.

I tried to shrink in my seat. The biker's eyes trailed all the way down my body: ugly lust, the kind that makes you cross the street to get away. My mom's dress had looked great on her but on me it was too tight across the bust, the front too low cut for my larger breasts. Where it had flowed elegantly over her hips, it clung to mine, outlining my ass.

"Did Volos show up yet?" asked my step-dad, slurring a little. He was even drunker than I'd thought. Was he trying to block out the reality of what he was doing?

The name made the biker nervously scan the line of cars behind him. "Not yet. C'mon. Hay's waiting for you."

Who's Volos? The name sounded foreign. Whoever he was, he scared the hell out of even the bikers.

We were met at the back door by the guy who'd come to our house, the Blood Spiders President. I guessed he was Hay. "Put her in there," he said, nodding at a door. "We'll start in five, whether Volos shows up or not. The guys are getting impatient."

My step-dad gave me a push from behind. I stumbled—he'd insisted I put on heels and I wasn't used to walking in them.

I think the room was supposed to be a dressing room. A cheap bathroom mirror hung crooked on the wall. Outfits on hangers dangled from a washing line: lingerie and tiny skirts and tops, some of them latex and leather. The Blood Spiders must offer strippers or hookers here, when they weren't auctioning women.

I spun and grabbed my step dad's arm just as he turned to leave. "*Please!*" I begged. "Don't do this!"

Again, I saw that momentary softening. He knew this was wrong.

But then he looked at the floor. "It'll be okay," he muttered. "Pretty thing like you, you'll do okay."

I gaped at him. Did he really believe that? Did he really think any guy who'd *buy* his woman would treat me well? When he looked up and met my eyes again, I knew he was trying to convince himself as much as me. *"Please!"* I begged again.

He shook his head and pulled out of my grasp. "Don't have a choice," he told me gruffly, and pulled the door closed behind him.

Shit! I started to panic-breathe. *This is really going to happen. In five minutes, if I don't get out of here.*

I looked around: no windows. I opened the door a crack and peeked out at the hallway. To my left, it ended in a set of double doors that I guessed led to the main room. I could hear thumping rock music and the yelling of excited men. *I can't let them take me in there.* If I did, my fate was sealed.

I looked the other way, towards the back door. My heart sank: a biker was leaning against it, standing guard. *Shit!*

The only other door was directly across the hall. A cheap plastic sign read *Office.* That was my only chance. Maybe there'd be a window I could crawl through.

The biker standing guard lit a cigarette, then glanced up at the smoke detector in the hallway and cursed. For a glorious moment, I thought he was going to step outside to smoke. But he just inhaled, opened the door a little and blew the smoke outside, then turned back to the hallway. I felt sick with tension. I'd have to run across when he next turned away. I'd have *seconds.*

He lazily inhaled. My hand tightened on the doorknob....

He turned. I dashed across the hallway and through the door to the office. I stood there with my back against the door for a second, shaking...but there were no footsteps in the hallway. He hadn't seen me.

I looked around. The lights were off but enough light came from the crack under the door for me to make out a desk, a chair and some bookshelves. No window.

I wanted to cry. *Please? Just a little luck?*

I started to search the room for anything I could use. I was shaking, close to hysterical—

A phone. An old-fashioned corded one, the plastic cracked, the handset covered in peeling stickers. I grabbed it and held it to my ear, praying. *Yes!* There was a dial tone. I pushed the buttons for 911.

The noise from the main room suddenly rose in volume as someone opened the double doors. *Shit!*

The call connected. "911 Emergency." A woman's voice, calm and reassuring.

"Please help me! I'm in a bar outside Teston—"

My voice trailed off as I realized I was talking to a recording. "...and an operator will answer your call as soon as one becomes available."

No! I could hear voices in the hallway: the Blood Spiders President—Hay—and my step-dad. I crouched down behind the desk, but that would only buy me a few seconds at best. *Come on!* But the recorded 911 message just kept looping and looping. I hung up and stared at the phone's keypad in desperation. Who else could I call?!

The shamrock necklace swung forward and brushed my wrist.

It's been twelve years. He won't be there. He might be in jail or dead or—

I heard my step-dad open the door to the dressing room. "Annabelle?" he asked in puzzlement.

My chest went tight. I prayed...and dialed the number I'd memorized.

"Fuck!" said Hay from the hallway. I heard him stomp towards the guard at the back door. "You let her out to take a piss or something?"

The line connected and the phone at the other end started to ring.

"No!" It sounded like the guard was choking. "No one came outta there!"

The phone rang and rang. *Come on. COME ON!*

The door to the office swung open and I closed my eyes, trying to disappear. I heard Hay curse and his footsteps retreated: he hadn't seen me. But there were only so many places I could have gone. When they searched again....

The call was answered and my heart leapt...but it was a voice I didn't recognize. Another recording. "You've reached Hell's Princes," rasped the man. "Leave a fucking message."

More voices, right outside the office door: Hay, my step-dad and three or four others. "C—Carrick?" I stammered. "I don't know if you'll get this. It's Annabelle. I'm in trouble. I'm at a place outside Teston, a bar. There are bikers: Blood Spiders. They're going to—"—my voice choked up as I tried to say the words—"S—*Sell me*—"

The door burst open and the light went on. Heavy boots thumped across the room and then a biker with dirty blond stubble was looming over the desk. "*Got her!*" he yelled.

I scrambled back across the room away from him. I was still clutching the handset so the phone fell off the desk and crashed on the floor. The line went dead.

"Shit!" the biker said. He grabbed my wrist and hauled me to my feet. I tried to twist away and he slapped me hard across the face with a meaty hand. I cried out, seeing stars.

More men burst in behind him: Hay, my step-dad, a few others. "She was on the phone!" the blond biker told them.

"Who did you call?" Hay snarled. He grabbed me by the throat and lifted me right off my feet, his thumb digging into my windpipe. "*Who did you call, girl? The cops?*"

I clawed at the hand holding me but his grip was like iron. I couldn't breathe, my airway narrowed down to the width of a drinking straw.

"911," I croaked. "But...they didn't...answer."

He gazed into my eyes a second longer then tossed me: a piece of rubbish he was finished with. My legs buckled and I went down on my ass, only for the blond-haired biker to wind his fist into my hair and use it to haul me to my feet. "Auction's starting," he told me. "Let's go."

They marched me out of the office and down the hallway to the main room. As we approached, the noise of the crowd rose up like a wall to meet me. They opened the double doors—

And I entered hell.

3

CARRICK

I kicked down my bike's kickstand, switched off the engine and stretched, wincing as my shoulders complained. They'd been doing that a lot, recently, after a long ride. Felt like someone had been beating me with an iron bar.

But it didn't matter: I was home.

The clubhouse was lit up in front of me, amber light flooding out of the mesh-covered windows, flames licking out of the oil drum barbecue out front. It was ugly as hell but to me it was as comforting a sight as any picture-postcard mansion. Inside, there'd be women, cold beer and sticky slow-cooked ribs from the barbecue.

I needed it. I needed to lose myself for a few hours to forget what I'd just done.

I swung my leg over my bike and marched across the compound. The party was already spilling out into the warm California night: I saw members, swigging beer and talking business; prospects scurrying around bringing them fresh bottles; a couple of hangers on and, yep, some girls. The girls all looked the same: blonde, short denim shorts, tight t-shirts and big eyes. They gasped and nudged each other as they listened to the men tell them about shit they'd done. *Can you believe this,* their expressions said. *Real bikers!*

But when they saw me, they swallowed and backed away. That's the thing about being the club's enforcer, their scary fucker: you don't get to choose who's scared of you.

But there are always one or two girls who hear what I do and get excited, not scared. Right on cue, one of them slid her arm around my waist as I walked past. "You want to get me a beer?" she asked, all white teeth and lip gloss.

I could feel my cock swelling as I looked down her body from her fake tits to the jewel that glittered in her navel. But I knew it wasn't *me* she was after. She just wanted a taste of *bad,* wanted a lights-on, no limits, gasping, panting fuck they'd never forget. And who better to let between her thighs than the club's big Irishman, the angel of vengeance they unleash on their enemies? I'd be the ultimate act of rebellion.

"Get your own fuckin' beer," I spat, and walked on.

I was doing her a favor. Oh, sure, I'd be happy to toss her on a bed and pound her. It would help me put tonight's job out of my mind. But then, in the morning, she'd realize what she'd done and run a mile.

I'm the guy the outlaws call on when they need to teach someone a lesson. I'm the last resort of the fringes of society. Who'd want to be involved with *me?*

Better that people are scared. Better that they stay away. It keeps things simple.

As soon as I got inside, a hand grabbed my shoulder. I turned to see Mac, our President. "It's done," I grunted.

Two drug dealers had thought they could deal in our town. They'd both be waking up in the hospital and they'd get the hell out of California as soon as they could walk again. That's what I do: I protect the club's interests, whether that means intimidation, a beating or ending someone. It's what I'm good at. Maybe *all* I'm good at. Except...

Except...you scare people long enough, you forget how to do anything else. You come home too many nights and wash the blood off you in the shower, after a while it feels like it's still there.

Mac didn't say anything but I knew he could see it. The job was starting to get to me: I barely slept, I hardly talked. He knew I'd die for the club, knew I gave it everything I had...but he wanted me to take from it a little, too. He wanted me to lean on him and the other guys.

I stiffened, the anger blooming inside me. That's what none of them understood, not even Mac. This weight was mine to bear and mine alone. This job was my penance. I didn't deserve to lean on the rest of them. Not after what I'd done.

I shook off Mac's hand and walked on. I'd get blind drunk. That was all the fucking therapy I needed.

I was heading for the bar when I heard the clubhouse phone ring. The rule is, whoever's nearest answers and technically that was me. But the only people who ever called were jealous girlfriends, enemies with threats or cops with questions. Fuck it, I was thirsty.

I marched straight past and told the prospect tending bar to give me a beer.

"*Phone,* Irish!" yelled Ox from across the room.

They call me *Irish* on account of—oh, you get it. Ox...there's not much of a story there. Guy's big as an ox, introduced himself as Ox when he first joined and, since he won't tell anyone his real first name, we don't have much of a choice. He's a gentle giant...unless he gets riled.

You don't want to see Ox get riled. "They can leave a message," I muttered. Then I wrapped my hand around the slick glass and knocked back the beer in three long gulps. *Oh, Christ* that tasted good: cold amber heaven, meltwater hitting a river bed that's been dried up for months. I slammed the glass down and told the prospect to give me another.

I was sipping my second beer, making this one last, when I saw Ox finally get up out of his seat and walk over to the answerphone. I knew he'd check it: he's not the sort of guy who can leave something undone, even if it's someone else's job. That's why he makes such a good treasurer.

I found a seat on one of the couches and had just settled in when

Ox's huge boot kicked the cushions right between my legs. "It was for you," he told me accusingly. "Some woman."

I groaned. One of the girls from a previous party? "I'll listen to it in the morning."

"Listen to it *now,* brother." He jerked his thumb towards the phone. "She sounded like she was in trouble."

I sighed and stalked over there, taking my beer with me, then replayed the message.

"C—Carrick?"

My beer glass hit the floor. My spine snapped straight, every muscle coming to attention. The reaction was soul-deep and instant: I knew that voice and it wasn't one I ever wanted to hear scared. It cut through all the layers of gruff hostility I'd built up to protect myself, right through to my core.

"I don't know if you'll get this. It's Annabelle."

I fell. Straight down a thousand feet, plummeting into the past. I was lying on my back looking up at a star-filled sky and that same voice asked me, *"Are you bad?"* I automatically put my hand on the scars on my side, feeling the long-healed knife wounds burn and throb as they had that night.

Twelve years. I'd been seventeen, young even for a prospect. I was a different person, back then: innocent and...*good.* She must think I was still that guy. She'd barely recognize me, now. I barely recognized myself.

But she was a sweet kid. A kid who'd never done anyone harm her entire life. And she was—

"...in trouble. I'm at a place outside Teston, a bar. There are bikers: Blood Spiders."

My heart clenched tight as a fist. I'd heard rumors about that place.

"They're going to...S—Sell me—"

My hand crushed the phone so hard I felt the plastic creak. *No they're fucking not.*

I dropped the phone and ran for my bike.

4

ANNABELLE

When I saw the room, my legs gave way. The blond biker raised his hand threateningly and I tried to stand because I didn't want to get hit again, but my legs were like Jell-O.

Hay had said there would be thirty coming but there were closer to eighty men. They filled the whole room aside from the small stage. At least ten Blood Spiders were there to keep the crowd in line but that didn't keep them quiet. The noise was deafening: cheering and baying and stamping, all of it directed at me.

They were calling me every obscene name under the sun, already dissecting my body, my face, my red hair. It was almost a relief that they were all yelling at once because some of it was drowned out and—

"Good tits!"

—I could—

"She a natural redhead?"

—just hear—

"She take it up the—"

—fragments. I squeezed my eyes closed, trying to block it out, and felt myself dragged up onto the stage. Hay must have raised his hand for silence because the crowd went quiet.

"You know why you're here," he told them. "You know the consequences if you go running your mouth off. Let's get down to business." He pulled out a stopwatch. "Each of you gets sixty seconds to look her over. Ask what you want, but no touching until you buy her."

Buy her. Jesus, this is real. I opened my eyes.

The first guy who came up on stage had intricately-shaved stubble and a gold chain around his neck: a pimp? A gang leader? He moved so close that I could feel his body heat. I tried to back up, only to find the blond biker's hand on my back.

The guy began to walk around me. I could feel his eyes on my hips, my ass, my legs. He moved my long red hair out of the way to inspect my neck—apparently, that was allowed—and I felt the warmth of his breath on the sensitive skin there. Then he came around to the front and gazed for a long time at my breasts. I felt like an insect under a microscope. I wanted to run away and hide, wanted to scream at him to *stop looking!* But the blond biker was right there behind me, ready to discipline me. All I could do was stand there submissively and watch the bulge in the guy's pants swell as he imagined what he was going to do to me when he owned me.

"Time," said Hay, clicking the stopwatch.

I was shaking. I wanted to throw up. And that was only one man.

The next man wore a suit and pushed his glasses up his nose as he threw questions at me. Was I a virgin? *No.* Did I have any diseases? *No.* Had I ever had a baby? *No.*

The third man I was sure I recognized. He was in his fifties, with sandy-blond hair, and the too-tight shirt collar was familiar. My stomach twisted. *One of my teachers, from high school? God, please no.*

He grinned at me. He wouldn't stop grinning, whether he was looking down my dress or looking down the length of my back to my ass. That's when I remembered where I'd seen him: at a town meeting, fielding questions from reporters with a laugh and a wink.

He was Teston's chief of police. My heart sank: now there was no hope at all.

It went on and on. Some tried to touch me: the bikers yelled at them or threw them off the stage. When a man grabbed my breasts for the fifth time, the blond biker broke his fingers as an example to the others, and after that it mostly stopped.

There were loud ones and quiet ones. The loud ones weren't so different to the over-aggressive guys who yell at women in bars, the guys who sometimes won't take no for an answer.

The quiet ones were terrifying. I could feel the wrongness radiating off them. They'd lick their lips and look at me with a mixture of lust and absolute hate, as if I was responsible for every woman who'd ever belittled them. These were the guys you read about in newspapers, who keep a woman locked up in their cellar for years.

There was a third type. Just two guys out of the eighty or so, one in his twenties and one in his fifties. They looked embarrassed to be there and, when it neared their turn, they looked up at me with expressions that were almost shy.

It's funny how your perspective changes, when you're really, really scared. As each of those two guys examined me, I found myself smiling at them. When the second one accidentally touched me as he craned around me to look at my ass, he apologized and I said quickly, "It's okay."

Then I caught myself. *What?! No it's not! What am I doing?*

And that's when I realized *I wanted to be bought by one of them.* I was actually being nice to them, just because they were better than the alternative. I wanted to throw up. After just a half hour on stage, I was so scared that I was practically selling myself.

At that moment, two men in suits with identical, close-cropped hair walked in and climbed up onto the stage, ignoring the waiting line. "Volos is outside," said one of them.

The crowd went deathly silent. I saw my step-dad take a long, shuddering breath. Even Hay went pale and stepped back out of the way. Whoever this Volos guy was, everyone was petrified of him.

The men in suits grabbed my arms and walked me off the stage and down the hallway to the rear door. Both had the build of football players and bulges under their jackets I was pretty sure were guns. Who the hell was this guy, that he had professional bodyguards?

A biker held the rear door open for us, almost bowing his head in respect as we passed. A big, black car was waiting for us in the darkness, its shining paint reflecting the bar's neon sign. The rear windows were privacy glass, so I couldn't see who was inside, but something about it scared the shit out of me. I knew, on an instinctual level, that if I went inside that car, my life would be changed forever.

"No," I said in a strangled voice.

The men ignored me and kept walking.

"*No!*" I said again, digging my heels into the ground.

They lifted me into the air and carried me the rest of the way. Then the car door was opening and....

The man was normal from the neck down. Average body, smart suit, polished shoes. He could have been any businessman from anywhere in America.

But his *face....*

They say even babies recognize faces, that humans are hardwired to see eyes and mouths: that's why we see faces in clouds. But when it came to Volos's face, that same internal wiring made my brain lock up. His face was...*wrong.*

He wasn't scarred. His face had been twisted and distorted, as if the flesh had melted and then hardened again. I couldn't stand to look at him but I couldn't look away.

The men pushed me onto the rear seat next to him and slammed the door. In the sudden silence, I could hear my own panting. I wanted to throw open the door and run but I was frozen with fear.

Volos leaned towards me and I saw that he was wearing a mask. That didn't ease my fear...in some ways, it made it worse. What sort of man chooses a mask like *that* to conceal his identity?

All I could see of his real face were two tiny points of reflection where his eyes looked through slits. But they were enough to tell me that he was looking at me, his gaze running from the top of my head all the way down to my feet and then slowly back again. The parts of me he'd looked at immediately felt tainted. This wasn't just lust. He wanted me the way a spoiled child wants a toy.

He leaned closer and I shrank back against the car door. The hideous mask filled my vision, almost brushing my face. I went rigid, barely daring to breathe. I couldn't see his mouth but somehow I knew he was smiling. He *liked* that I was scared.

Then he lowered himself back into his seat and knocked twice on the window. Instantly, the door swung open.

"Fifty thousand," said Volos. His voice was a shock: so...*normal*. He could have been the guy who served you your latte or your boss at work.

The two men in suits nodded, grabbed my arms and hauled me out of the car. That's when it sunk in that Volos was going to buy me. I had no idea what women sold for, but surely I couldn't be worth fifty thousand dollars. I didn't feel like I was anything special. That meant that Volos would outbid everyone else...and then he'd own me.

"Don't worry," said Volos as I stared at him in terror. "I'm going to take very good care of you." And then the men were dragging me back into the bar.

Inside, the hush had changed to bad-tempered grumbling. They all knew that they'd likely be outbid, now that Volos had shown up. My insides went cold. *How often does Volos do this? How many women has he bought?!*

"We'll start the bidding at two thousand," Hay told the crowd.

As soon as the bids began to flow, it became real in my mind. I really was going to be sold. All I could hope was that I'd be bought by someone kind, maybe one of the two men I'd smiled at.

But as the bidding rose past ten thousand, the first of the two shook his head. When we hit twenty thousand, the other ruefully sighed and dropped out, too.

When they hit twenty-five thousand, the bidding slowed down. Hay glanced at my step-dad as if annoyed: I guessed that he was in for a percentage of my final sale price. "Come on, you fuckers," he yelled at the crowd. "Let's get it going!" But the bids began to peter out.

Hay snarled and grabbed the top of my dress, wrapping his thick fingers around the delicate beading at the neckline. Then, with one tug of his arm, he wrenched it down. I screamed as the stitching started to rip and a few buttons popped off—*No!* I tried to break free, desperate, but the blond biker grabbed my arms from behind. It wasn't just the thought of being exposed: the dress was one of the only things I still had from my mom.

Another wrench and both shoulder straps gave way. The dress fell to my feet and the crowd came alive, whooping and roaring, as I stood there in just my bra and panties.

The bids started to flood in. Thirty thousand, thirty-five, forty. Now I knew why my step-dad had done this: he'd be able to pay off all his debts and have money to spare.

At forty-five thousand, it was down to the man with glasses—the one who'd asked all the questions—and the two men in suits bidding on behalf of Volos. *Please!* I begged. *Anyone but Volos!*

Then the bidding reached fifty thousand. And the man in glasses shook his head.

"Sold to Volos for fifty thousand dollars!" declared Hay. And I knew my life was over.

Carrick didn't come. A ridiculous thought. Completely unfair. I'd called him only an hour before, on a number twelve years out of date. It wasn't *his* fault. But that logic didn't stop it feeling like a cold, iron spike was being hammered into my heart. The thought of him had kept me going through my darkest times for the last decade. Now I'd grabbed at my one, forlorn hope and found it was just an illusion, nothing but a childhood encounter I'd blown out of all proportion.

I had no hero.

The men milled around, grumbling at missing out. Volos's men passed an envelope no thicker than my hand to Hay, who extracted some bills and passed the remainder to my step-dad. *Is that it?* Just a handful of paper. A pathetic thing to exchange for a human life.

One of Volos's men grabbed my step-dad by the arm. "Volos wants to make sure you understand," he said. "He's not just buying her. He's buying you and your story. What's your story?"

My step-dad glanced at me just once, then looked away in guilt. "She went to New York, with some guy she met on the internet."

And suddenly I understood why I was worth fifty thousand dollars. I was a woman who no one would ever look for.

The two men grabbed my arms and started walking me towards the hallway and Volos's waiting car.

That's when the bar's door was kicked in with a crash that sounded like the end of the world. A man with a shotgun stepped into the light and I caught my breath as I saw his face.

"Nobody *fucking* move," said Carrick.

5

CARRICK

I saw her immediately: she was impossible to miss. But my eyes kept searching the room: I think I was still looking for a kid, because that's how I remembered her.

It took a few seconds before my gaze swung back to the woman in her underwear. I took in the long, silky red hair, the pale skin, those big, liquid eyes the color of moss.

It can't be. This was a woman, twenty or so. Annabelle was just a—

My brain knew the math was right but I just couldn't process it. I'd had over a decade of remembering her as a kid.

Then I saw the gleam of gold around her neck, the shamrock twisting and bouncing as she pulled against the men holding her. *It's her.* And God, she was *gorgeous.* She'd grown into a long-legged, full-breasted beauty, all luscious curves and smooth white skin.

And those bastards were going to sell her. The rage boiled up inside me and flooded down like lava to fill my limbs, every muscle hard and straining with the need to kill, to smash, to destroy.

I let out a roar that made the windows shake and stepped into the room. Everyone stepped back and the whole place went silent as a tomb.

When I speak, people listen. "Here's what's going to happen," I told them. I jerked the shotgun towards the two men holding Annabelle. "Tweedledum and Tweedle*fucking*dee are going to let her go. She's going to walk over to me. And then we're going to leave."

I saw a few people blink at my accent. I sound more Irish when I'm angry.

I was *very* fucking angry.

A big Blood Spider with a beard shook his head at me from the stage. "This is none of your business." There was a hint of fear in his voice. He'd seen my cut and heard my accent. Everyone had heard the stories about the Hell's Princes' Irishman.

I saw the President's patch on his cut and pointed the shotgun at him, instead. "I beg to differ," I snarled. *Bastard.* He had his MC *selling women?* I'd heard things about the Blood Spiders but I hadn't believed it until now. "Tell your boys to back down."

Out of the corners of my eyes, I could glimpse the other bikers shuffling, trying to surround me. I couldn't fight all of them. I needed their pres to get them off my back. I took two big steps and leapt up onto the stage. *"Tell them to back down!"* I roared, and shoved Caorthannach right in the president's face.

Caorthannach looks like someone's fever dream of a double-barreled shotgun. Her barrels are twice as wide as a standard one, the metal silver-green and covered in carvings showing lost souls being devoured. Her stock is solid Irish oak, polished glass-smooth by a century of hands. All good weapons deserve a name and I named her after a fire-spitting demon. She's scary enough that I rarely have to fire her.

The Blood Spider president looked down those enormous barrels and went pale. He made a gentle *down* motion with both hands and his men stopped moving. "Don't do this," he muttered to me. "We can work something out."

I shoved the gun right up against his cheek, pressing the metal into his skin. The temptation to shoot the bastard was almost unbearable. "Believe me," I snarled. "We can't."

I walked across the stage, pushing him ahead of me until we were looking down at the two guys in suits holding Annabelle.

Professional bodyguards, probably ex-military, from the look of them. Whoever they worked for had serious money...and from the looks of it, he'd bought her. Bought this sweet woman who'd never hurt anyone. The rage was expanding in my chest, swelling to fill every inch of me. "Let her go," I grated. "Or Blood Spiders MC is going to need a new president."

The two guys in suits looked at each other uneasily. The tension in the room built and built. I glowered down the barrels at the president and gave a low growl.

"Do it!" snapped the president. "He's crazy!"

The suits looked at each other again but then released her. Nobody wants the death of an MC's president on their hands. Annabelle ran to me, grabbed my arm and pressed her body tight to mine.

Damn. For a second, the rest of the room faded out. All I could think about was the way her warm skin felt against my bare forearm and the smell of her hair, like honeysuckle on a warm day. *This is Annabelle?!* She was the most gorgeous thing I'd ever seen.

I backed towards the door. The two guys in suits glared at me, eyes hard, lips pressed into tight little lines. "You've got no fucking idea what you've done," said one. "Volos will kill you for this."

Who the fuck is Volos? "He can join the fuckin' queue," I said.

I kept backing towards the door. Halfway there, I realized my mistake: distracted by the feminine wonder pressed against my left hip, I hadn't taken the president with me as a hostage. The further I got from him, the less threat I was. I could feel the bikers start to shuffle towards me as they realized the same thing. *Shit. Just another ten feet and we'll be out of here.* Five feet. Three feet.

Someone smashed a bottle over my head.

And then everything went to hell.

6

ANNABELLE

I'd convinced myself that my memory of Carrick was exaggerated. After all, when you're a kid, *everyone* seems big. So I wasn't ready for the size of him. I wasn't ready for his height, or the way his shoulders stretched the back of his leather cut to its limits: a back you could break a two-by-four across and he wouldn't even notice. I wasn't ready for the bulk of his chest under that tight white t-shirt, for the sheer intimidating *presence* of him as he yelled at the men holding me.

His voice, though...that was the same. Ancient dark rocks grinding together, each rough impact throwing out silver sparks. Except it had a whole different effect on me, now. The low, throaty rasp of it seemed to vibrate through my whole body; the sparks raced down my spine to finish in a silver crackle of heat that blossomed through my groin.

Then the men finally let go of my arms and I ran to him, crushing myself against the big, solid mass of him, like hugging a rock face to shelter from the elements. God, he was even bigger than I remembered and everything was so *hard:* his tanned forearms, criss-crossed with thick veins, were like warm steel. And the touch of him...it was so familiar, even after twelve years, and yet so new. I felt...*right,* pressed up against him, even with the hell we were still in. As if I was finally in my proper place.

I looked up at his face and my breath hitched. As a kid, I hadn't appreciated that he was *absolutely freakin' gorgeous.* I thought I'd invented that as a teen, twisted my memories into some idealized Irishman. But no exaggeration was necessary: that hard jaw covered in black stubble; those dark brows that gave him a brooding, *are you looking at me?* glare; the wide, full lips... He'd lost a little of the boy over the years and gained a whole heap of the man, and the result was the hottest guy I'd ever seen. Hot and *mean.* Savage and hard-bitten, one of those men who'd been hardened by years of fighting. I saw scars on his neck that didn't used to be there and the raw, violent menace rolled off him in waves, pushing even the bikers back. I'd never in my life seen anyone do *intimidating* like Carrick.

Then I looked closer and frowned. I still remembered his eyes from that night twelve years ago: the blue of a sky just after a storm has cleared. Now they were different, as if the storm wouldn't let go. I could glimpse the blue but it was struggling to pierce the darkness. The change made my chest ache: what had he been through, to lose that innocence?

Just as I thought it, he glanced down at me...and suddenly the blue seemed to open up, pushing back the clouds. For a second, he looked how he had that night. Was that...*me* that was doing that to him?

He shifted the shotgun to one hand and his other arm wound around my waist and snugged me protectively closer. It was just about the best thing I'd ever felt.

We backed up another foot. Then I screamed as I was showered with warm beer and shards of green glass. Carrick's arm was torn from my waist as he fell and then I was jerked away by one of Volos's bodyguards.

My head whipped around to look at Carrick. He was on his knees. As I watched, a biker kicked his oversize shotgun out of his reach, sending it spinning across the floor. The other bodyguard grabbed my other wrist and together they started to haul me across the room.

Panting with fear, I craned over my shoulder to watch Carrick. Bikers surrounded him: six or seven at least, blocking my view. Legs drew back and they started to kick him. My heart clenched into a tight little ball. *No!* They were going to kill him and it was all my fault! I'd drawn him into this!

I kicked and thrashed as I was dragged along but I couldn't get any traction. I was pulled into the hallway and towards the rear door. The whole time, I was staring back at Carrick, tears in my eyes. All I could see were bikers kicking him and raining down punches: he was still down on the floor. "*Stop hitting him!*" I sobbed. But they didn't.

Ahead of me, I felt a sudden, cool breeze. I turned to face front and saw a biker holding the rear door open ahead of us. Volos's car was waiting right outside, the door open and the engine running. *No!*

And then from behind us came the roar of a man who's reached his limit.

The room went silent. The men dragging me stopped and we all turned to look. The kicking and punching stopped and then the circle of bikers around Carrick all took a step back.

I saw Carrick's head emerge above the circle as he got to his feet. "*Is that the best you've fuckin' got?*" he yelled.

The room was so quiet, I heard one biker mutter, "*Shit.*" His voice had that sickly tone of someone who's just realized they've made a massive mistake.

Then Carrick picked him up by the front of his leather cut and flung him across the room, right at one of the men holding me. He went down like a skittle. The other man let go of my arm in shock and suddenly I was free.

I ran. I sure as hell wasn't going out the back of the bar, towards Volos, and there were too many bikers between me and the front door. The only hiding place was behind the bar. I dived behind it and huddled there, watching the fight play out in the mirror above the bottles.

When some men fight, it's almost like art: a ballet of spins and flips, punches and kicks.

Carrick was not one of those men.

He wasn't showy and he certainly wasn't elegant. He didn't fight like someone who'd trained in a dojo; he fought like someone who'd found himself in a barroom brawl every night of his life. And that was exactly what we needed.

He waded through the bikers like they were nothing: a headbutt, a punch, a knee to the groin and he was onto the next one. He was outnumbered but he *just didn't care*, too angry and stubborn to let something like logic get in his way. And while the bikers were just doing their job, protecting the bar and their president. Carrick fought as if he was fighting *for* something, like some ancient Celt warrior on a holy mission. As if he was fighting for—

His eyes met mine in the mirror and I swallowed.

But then I saw the men in suits draw their handguns and take aim at him. They didn't have a clear shot: the fighting was too close and chaotic. But any second now, they'd find an opening and Carrick would go down: even he couldn't survive a hail of bullets.

All I wanted to do was hunker down behind the bar and wait for it to be safe, but there was no way I was letting him die. I searched behind the bar, frantic: maybe there was a shotgun or a baseball bat. But there was nothing.

Then, as my desperate eyes ran over the bottles, my weird brain did its thing. The whiskey and vodka and rum stopped being drinks and became *chemicals*.

I grabbed a bottle of vodka, unscrewed the cap and rolled it out across the floor towards Volos's men, letting it glug a trail of liquid behind it. I hurled a bottle of rum as hard as I could and heard it smash against the far wall. I emptied the whiskey over the edge of the bar, making a spreading amber pool.

Then I found a matchbook, lit a match and tossed it towards the alcohol, shying away and closing my eyes as it landed.

There was a *wumf* and a barrage of cursing. When I looked in the mirror, half the bar was on fire. Volos's men were backing away, the floor in front of them a carpet of flame. "Fuck this," I heard one of them say, and they started to retreat down the hallway towards the rear door.

Carrick punched another biker to the ground. There were plenty left but the fire had broken up the fight. It was already licking up the wooden walls and the air was filling with thick white smoke. Some of the bikers started to panic and run for the nearest door.

I ran to Carrick and pressed myself to his side again. The instant our bodies touched, I felt better. I felt *not alone.* This time, I took hold of his bicep with both hands and clung on for dear life: no one was separating us again. He grabbed his shotgun as we passed it and brandished it again, swinging it towards anyone who came towards us. Then we were backing out of the main door and into the blessedly cool night air. Smoke was pouring out of the door in an almost solid stream. "Get on the bike!" yelled Carrick.

I would have recognized the big Harley anywhere. As a kid, I must have sketched it a thousand times in my school books. I'd dreamed of someday riding it and, even with all that was going on, I got a little giddy as I swung my leg over the saddle. It was only when my ass hit the leather that I remembered I was still in my underwear.

Carrick got on in front of me, his broad back filling my vision. He'd been patched in, now: his cut had lost the *Prospect.* The *Princes of Hell* skull grinned at me from the badge..

"Hold onto me," he growled over his shoulder. That accent. That growl. It made me resonate like a tuning fork, as if I'd been needing to hear it my entire life. I flung my arms around him, then swallowed as my palms brushed warm, washboard abs under soft cotton.

"Closer!"

I shuffled my ass along the saddle. My thighs opened a little more and my groin kissed up against his ass, the muscles hard through the denim. I leaned forward and pressed my chest against him. My breasts pillowed against his back. It would have been intimate even in clothes but I could feel my nipples stroking against his leather cut through my bra. I swallowed again.

He started the engine and the whole bike came to life, throbbing and growling like a beast. My whole life, I'd always known when a machine wasn't working properly: I'd gotten used to that edgy feeling I get when something's not quite right. I'd never known the flipside:

the sudden rush of deep satisfaction when you touch a machine that's loved and cared for, every gear meshing as it should, every piston smoothly pumping. And with the bike, the sensation was even stronger because I was *on* it, almost part of it. It was glorious.

Carrick twisted the throttle and we roared off into the night.

7

CARRICK

T o get to the highway, we had to ride right through the center of Teston: exactly where I didn't want to be. It was Blood Spiders territory and the word would already be getting out. Harleys aren't exactly stealthy and we were hard to miss with a half-naked woman on the back.

Half-naked. Every time I turned the handlebars, every time I changed gear, my back shifted in new and interesting ways against her breasts. *Jesus, that body!* I'd only had time for glimpses during the chaos of the fight but they were burned into my mind: full, ripe breasts bouncing and swaying in a black bra. Long, toned legs and that ass...my mind was already running through all the ways I wanted to fuck her.

Right. Like a sweet thing like her would want a monster like me. I felt the first stirrings of anger in the pit of my stomach, the sour regret at what I'd become. *If my life had worked out different....*

But that way lay madness. *Just get her out of town and drop her off somewhere.* My debt would be repaid. Then I could go back to the clubhouse and drink until I forgot those big, green eyes and that perfect pale body.

But by the time we hit the center of Teston, I could hear the thump of other Harleys. *Shit.* At the next intersection I throttled back, slowed to a stop and peeked around the corner into Teston's main street.

It wasn't good. I counted three—no, four Blood Spiders cruising up and down. They knew we had to cross the street to get out of the city. As soon as we did, they'd see us and chase us down. A few quick gunshots and the bike would be on its side, I'd be bleeding out and Annabelle....

Annabelle would be back in their hands.

My fingers tightened on the handlebars. *Not going to happen.* Whenever I thought of her being auctioned off, a deep, hot wave of protective anger flooded through me, so strong it almost scared me. I'd never felt anything like it before.

I hung back, waiting for something big to come by. When a cement truck rolled up at the intersection, I swung the bike alongside it, cozying up to it like a minnow next to a whale. Hopefully, the rattle of its engine would cover the throb of ours and the bulk of it would block us from view from one side. The other side? We'd have to hope we got lucky.

The truck moved off. I gunned the throttle hard and then backed right off, letting the bike roll across the street as quietly as a big Harley can. The cement truck hid us completely to my right. I checked to the left and caught my breath. One Blood Spider was heading away from us but another was just turning to come back towards us.

Sweat broke out along my neck. I could speed up and get off the intersection in time but make more noise, or I could keep cruising and hope he was too far away to make us out against the dark wheels of the truck. I felt Annabelle suddenly grip me hard: she must have seen the guy too.

I decided to keep going. We were nearly through the intersection. Another few seconds....

A shout went up. *Shit!* I gunned the throttle hard and we sped into the next street, but I could already hear bike engines behind us. I turned into an alley and then into a narrower one, only a few feet wider than the bike. We blasted through cardboard cartons and other trash, Annabelle pressing herself in tight behind me so she could use me as a shield. I turned another corner and then quickly killed the engine, rolling to a stop behind a pile of discarded cartons. I listened. Had they seen where we went? Would they follow us in?

The thump of bike engines came closer and closer. I heard at least two of them turn into the first alley. It was like listening to a couple of huge beasts approaching, the low throb of their engines like heartbeats that shook the alley walls. There was nothing we could do: if we moved, they'd hear us. Our best chance was to sit tight in the darkness and hoped they missed us, then escape when they'd gone.

I twisted around in the saddle to explain that to Annabelle but, as soon as I saw her, fuck me if I didn't forget how to speak.

It was dark in the alley but there was enough moonlight to make her pale skin glow, her black underwear adding to the effect. She was looking up at me with those big, moss-green eyes, willing me to get her out of there, willing me to know what I was doing.

It hit me like a sledgehammer. Fuck: she *believed* in me.

Her hands had slid from around my waist when I twisted around and now they were on my hips, cool fingers in the creases of my thighs. If she slid them forward even a few inches, she'd be caressing my cock and just the thought of it had me rock hard. If it had been one of the girls who hung around the club, I would have grabbed her wrists and damn well pulled her hands to my crotch myself. But just thinking about Annabelle grabbing me there made me feel guilty.

Since when did I feel *guilty?*

One of the bikes was getting closer. I tensed, ready to start the bike and tear off if the guy found our hiding place. Annabelle's eyes went wide and she grabbed hold of my upper arms, squeezing my biceps tight. *"Please don't let them take me!"* she said in a hoarse little whisper.

Jesus. She thought I was her hero.

Part of me gave a bitter little laugh inside. Another part grew harder and colder, like coal crushed into diamonds by the weight of everything I'd done. *She has no fuckin' idea.*

But there was one tiny, rogue part of me that flared bright, in all that darkness. One stupid, childish part of me that *wanted* to be her hero. Her words made that part of me swell with pride, like I was some medieval knight being given a quest by a princess.

Princess. A good word for Annabelle. A sweet innocent princess captured by the enemy, relying on her white knight to save her. She didn't realize I was dark as they come.

She was so goddamn beautiful, sitting there in the moonlight. That *hair!* I'd never seen anything like it: a gleaming, silken curtain of warm copper that hung right down to her mid back. I wanted to sink my fingers into it and wrap it around my fists. I wanted to stroke my hands down it and feel her naked skin beneath. And then I wanted to kiss her.

I couldn't remember the last time I'd fantasized about kissing a girl instead of just fucking her. *What's going on?!*

She was looking right into my eyes, waiting to see what I'd do next. Her breathing had sped up: I knew because, out of the corner of my eye, I could see those soft breasts rising and falling. *She's scared of me.* Yeah. That had to be it.

I didn't let myself consider the alternative.

At that moment, the sudden snarl of an engine split the air. One of the Blood Spiders was coming down the alley. Thanks to the shadows, he hadn't seen us yet, but he sure as hell would as he got closer. The pile of boxes we were behind only came up to our shoulders. They wouldn't hide us completely unless—

I swung my legs over the bike and twisted fully around so that I was straddling it backward, facing Annabelle. Then I clapped my palm over her mouth and pushed her down.

8

ANNABELLE

I fell back until I was lying on the seat, Carrick's body pressed to mine all the way from shoulder to groin. Our faces were just a few inches apart but it was dark, down behind the boxes, and his face was in shadow, unreadable. My lips worked against his palm as I panicked. *What the hell is he doing?!*

Then I heard the bike engine and understood. It came closer and closer, until the vibrations were rattling my teeth. My feet were off the ground but Carrick's were firmly planted and I could feel the low throb coming up through his legs, hips and groin and passing into me, both our bodies trembling together.

And then the biker stopped. Right on the far side of the boxes that screened us, no more than six feet away.

Oh. My. God.

I lay there, absolutely motionless, afraid to even breathe. If the biker saw us or heard us, I'd be taken back to Volos and Carrick would be killed.

The two of us were pressed so tightly together, I could hear every beat of his heart. I *had* to breathe, so I inhaled just a little through my nose...and felt my breasts lift and press against his chest.

I felt his heart speed up.

There was a scrape of rubber against concrete as the biker put his boot down to steady his bike. I imagined him looking around, searching the darkness. He was so close, I could hear his breathing.

Carrick slowly released the pressure on my mouth, lifting his hand a millimeter at a time. But as he did it, the moon hit a break in the clouds and I got a look at his expression for the first time.

As he looked towards the cartons and the biker they hid us from, he had that same look of furious, brutal determination I'd seen in the bar. He was ready to kill to protect me. But then his palm lifted just enough that only my lips were pressed against it, and when they finally broke contact it was almost a reverse kiss. I saw his whole body tense—

And when his gaze snapped back to me, he glared at me with such scalding lust that I felt the heat plunge straight down inside and turn to slick wetness at my groin. He looked as if he wanted to rip my panties off and fuck me right there on the saddle until I was just a twitching, gasping, limp mess. And he looked *furious* that I was tempting him into it.

I flushed deep scarlet. *But I'm not doing anything!* At the same time, my whole soul seemed to lift: after years of teenage fantasies, the idea that *he* might actually be attracted to *me* made me reel.

We stared at each other in the moonlight. I'd never looked at a man so closely in my life. I could have gazed at that face for years, like some professor in a museum who spends her entire career obsessing over one painting, one statue. He was a freakin' violent work of art.

Black hair turned almost blue by the moonlight. Skin tanned by the sun and wind as he rode. Those heavy brows and that brutal jaw: he could have been some war-painted Irish barbarian from a thousand years ago. But his face had beauty, too, in the high cheekbones and those hard-soft lips.

A metal clank from the other side of the boxes—the biker had put his bike's kickstand down. The rustle of leather as he dismounted. *Shit!* He was going to look around.

The hand Carrick had taken from my mouth started to move. My eyes locked onto it as it passed above my neck...my collar bone. I swallowed. Was he going to squeeze my breast? But he passed above it, then dipped down, reached across the bike for something fixed to its side by his leg—

His bicep brushed my breast, warm skin and hard muscle sliding against my pale skin. Unbidden, I felt my nipple pucker and harden. Both of us froze and we lay there, staring into each other's eyes. I watched that magnificent, muscled chest move with every slow, silent intake of breath...and then I felt his cock, hot and weighty, pressing higher and higher on my inner thigh as he went rock hard against me.

On the far side of the boxes, I heard the biker take a step towards us. Metal jangled—the Blood spider on his cut. *He's going to find us!*

Carrick leaned fractionally to the side, straining to reach whatever he was grasping for. His arm slid across my breast. I bit my lip to keep from crying out, streamers of pleasure rippling down from my pebble-hard nipple. Apparently, my body didn't care how much danger we were in.

I watched as Carrick started to ease his arm silently back up. When his hand reappeared, it was holding that insane shotgun I'd seen at the bar. It looked even bigger, up close, the carvings on the barrels gleaming in the moonlight. He brought it up and across me and pointed it at the stack of cartons, ready to shoot if the biker appeared around the side.

At that second, the throb of the engine was joined by another. *Shit!* In my fear, I grabbed for something, anything...and my hands closed on Carrick's shoulders. He tensed, too. The odds of us getting out of there were shrinking and shrinking.

The second bike stopped alongside the first, both of them keeping their bikes idling. The vibrations strummed through us, booming in my lungs, growling through my head, making it impossible to think. I could feel myself slipping towards panic. Even if Carrick could shoot both of them, the noise would bring every Blood Spider in the area down on us. My breathing started to speed up and, the more it did, the harder it was to stay silent.

"Anything?" One of the bikers, his voice horribly close.

"I ain't seen shit." The other one. I heard the snap of a lighter and then he took a drag on a cigarette.

"They're in here. I saw 'em come in."

"Yeah, well we'd better find them. I called the bar and Hay's going apeshit. That psycho Volos wants his woman. *Now.*"

Volos. I closed my eyes, trying to shut out the words, but it was too late. I could see the mask's twisted features looming closer and closer. I felt my whole body tense, my breathing growing ragged—

And then Carrick's warm fingers were stroking my cheek. It was clumsy, as if he wasn't used to tenderness. When I opened my eyes, he was glancing between the bikers and me, looking completely out of his comfort zone. He looked as if he'd happily start shooting, just so he could get away from comforting me. And yet....

And yet however awkward it was, it felt really freakin' good. I felt safe, and my breathing slowed a little.

"Fuck it," said one of the bikers. I heard him take a last drag on his cigarette and then the smoldering butt arced over the wall of boxes. It missed my ear by an inch and hit the ground in a shower of embers. "Maybe they made it past us. Let's check the streets. You take Roosevelt, I'll check Heatherton. Plenty of parking lots around there they could be hiding in."

"What if they're still in here? They could slip out behind us."

"We got guys watching the highway. If they do make it out of town, we'll run 'em down."

Both of them gunned their engines. The walls of the alley boomed and shook. The roar rose...and then died away as they sped off.

Carrick slowly straightened up. After what felt like an hour of having him pressed against me, I felt suddenly cold without him there. I straightened up as well, which left us sitting face-to-face with only a few inches between us.

That conflict in his eyes again, even clearer, now. Lust...lust so powerful it made my whole skin feel like it was on fire. But anger, too. *Frustration.* Anger at me, that I tempted him...but anger at himself, too. He was tearing himself apart. What the hell was going on?

He looked away, glaring off into the darkness. Then he shrugged out of his leather cut and handed it to me. "Here," he muttered. "You can't ride around like that."

I took it, but his hand kept its grip on the leather for a second, as if letting it go felt wrong. It hit me that the cut was something he treasured. And he was lending it to me.

"Thank you," I said.

He released it and I slipped it on. It felt good to have some of me covered, even if my legs were still bare. And the leather was warm from his body: it was almost like *he* was wrapped around me, keeping me safe. It even smelled of him, a little: leather and oil and the citrus tang of his cologne.

When I looked up again, he was gazing at me with such intensity I caught my breath. Not just lust. Something else. A breeze whipped my hair across my face and I brushed it back. "What?" I asked.

He shook his head. "Nothin'." His voice was gruff, almost deliberately so. He quickly climbed off the bike and climbed on again forwards, his back to me. "I can't get you out of here tonight," he said. "They're watching the highway. They could be on us before we saw them, in the dark."

I nodded, even though he couldn't see it. "So what do we do?"

He didn't answer for a second. Then, "We're going to have to find a motel."

9

CARRICK

I hunched over the handlebars as we rode, silent and stoic. But inside, I was unleashing a string of curses that would have made even the filthiest fuckers in the MC wince.

She liked me. I'd seen it in her eyes. Only she didn't like *me*: she liked the me she knew from over a decade ago, when I was still a good guy. When I didn't have years of club dirty work on my soul. Before *he* turned me into a monster.

I couldn't take advantage of her. Oh, Jesus, I wanted to. She was into me, and she was semi-naked and *grateful* and we were heading to a fucking *motel*.... The universe was handing me her on a silver platter.

But...something was going on. Something that twisted and wrenched at me from the inside. When she'd sat there wearing my cut, with that long red hair blowing in the wind...for the first time in years, I'd wanted something more than just hearing her moan and scream my name. Something I knew I couldn't have, anymore, not even from one of the girls who hung around the club. Certainly not from a sweet girl like Annabelle.

She made me want to be *with* her. She made me want to sling her on the back of my bike and head off for a long ride. A really long one: just get lost for a week or two. With sunsets and kissing and—

Jesus, what's the matter with me?

My life had been simple. Grim, but simple. The life I'd deserved. Only now Annabelle had brought home everything that I'd been missing and it was driving me crazy. I had to get the fuck away from this girl and instead I was going to have to spend the night locked in a room with her.

So I cursed. I cursed the Blood Spiders for locking their city down so tight.

I cursed Briggs, our former president, for turning me into this monster.

I cursed myself for suddenly developing a conscience instead of just fucking her.

I even cursed Ox for listening to that message. But as soon as that entered my head, I knew it wasn't true. However painful this was, there was no way I could have lived with myself if she'd been sold. And there was no way I was abandoning her now. I had to make sure she was safe.

They were expecting us to head for the highway so I took us the opposite way, finally stopping at a tiny village just outside Teston, little more than a gas station, a motel and a couple of stores. I asked the motel manager for a ground floor room and then wheeled my bike right inside with us, so it couldn't be seen from the road.

As soon as the door closed, I felt the tension start to build. She looked up at me with those big eyes....

I can't. Each beating I'd handed out had made me heavier, darker, until I was like a lead slug of chaos my MC could fire into an enemy, knowing I'd rip them apart. That was what I was good at: scaring people. Hurting them. That was all I was good *for*. And the last person I wanted to hurt was her.

Then it got worse. She shrugged my cut off her shoulders, folded it carefully and held it out to me. "Here. I know you want this back. Thank you."

I looked down at it...and her. The way she was holding it, her upper arms were squeezing her breasts together in her bra, like she was offering them up to me. *Sweet Jesus*. Didn't she know how gorgeous she was?

I took it. What else could I do? Tell her to cover herself, because the sight of her in her underwear was driving me insane? I grunted something that might have been *thanks*.

I tried to find somewhere to look that wasn't her boobs.

I looked down. That was worse. I was suddenly staring right at her groin, eyes locked on the little triangle of black fabric that was all that stood between me and the soft, warm folds I'd felt when she was pressed up against me.

I looked up. Even worse. Now I was gazing right into her eyes, so big and innocent, so...*good*. People say it's the bad girls who have all the fun but a bad girl's bad already and where's the fun in that? A good girl, one who's pure as driven snow, one you can *turn* bad...now that's a fantasy. And Annabelle was as good as they came.

Which was why I had to keep the hell away from her. What life would she have with me? Sewing up my wounds? Waiting to get the phone call that I'd been shot or stabbed somewhere? Getting tangled up with the MC, drawn into a world that would likely get her killed?

No. No way. She'd saved my life. Now I had to save hers...by getting her as far from me, the MC and my whole way of life as possible.

I tore my eyes angrily away from her face. Her arms. I'd look at her arms. Arms that were so soft and pale, arms that would feel fucking terrific wrapped around me on long, dark nights....

Legs. Legs were even worse. Jesus, they were so long, so perfectly shaped, firm yet feminine, legs I wanted to run my tongue all the way up. I wanted those legs wrapped around me, too, but in a whole different way....

I turned away from her. "I'm going to take a shower," I muttered, and stormed into the tiny bathroom. I had to put some distance between the two of us before I lost control and just grabbed her.

In the shower, I tried to convince myself that I was washing because I needed it, because I'd been riding all day and had road dust in my hair and oil under my fingernails. All of which was true, but....

But I hadn't felt like I'd needed to clean up...not until I saw her.

And I couldn't stop thinking about her. She was right *there,* on the other side of a thin sheet of drywall, pacing around the room, long, pale legs flashing in the light of the room's one bulb, all dressed up like a fucking Victoria's Secret model in underwear and heels, and all that red hair—

I was no expert but her hair color *looked* natural. Did that mean that, under those panties....

My cock slapped against my stomach, achingly hard. My hand moved towards it...and then my hands tightened into fists. *Fuck!* I was *not* going to start stroking myself. What was I, a teenager?

I angrily toweled off and pulled on my jockey shorts and jeans, then stomped barefoot and topless into the bedroom, steam curling around me. Annabelle was sitting on the bed and she looked up at me as I walked in. Instantly, the tension was back. The pull was so strong, I had to physically force myself to take a step back or I would have just dived on her, pushed her down on the bed and kissed her hard and deep. *Damnit! How the hell am I going to get through 'till morning?*

Just be gruff. Be surly. That's the answer. Don't even speak to her. Sure, it felt wrong, but it would keep me from doing something we'd both regret. I'd make myself hard and cold as fucking stone, she wouldn't even be able to—

"Thank you."

I blinked. "What?"

"Thank you. For saving me." She slowly stood up. "I didn't have a chance to say it before."

And suddenly, all my *cold stone* melted into warm Jell-O, like she'd taken a laser to me. "Yeah. Well." I looked everywhere except her face. "I owed you, didn't I?"

"I didn't know if you'd even remember me."

I stared at the TV. The remote for the TV. The little dish with the packets of sugar and Sweet n' Low. I wanted to say that when I'd heard her voice on the message, it had triggered something deep inside me. Without even having seen her, without knowing she'd turned into this beauty, I'd just known I had to save her. But I just grunted, "Yeah. Yeah, I remembered you." I meant it to sound throwaway, but it didn't come out like that. I wound up catching her eye at the end, and no matter how hard I tried, I couldn't look away. *Fuck!*

"They made you a member," she said, nodding at where my cut lay, carefully folded on the bed. "What else happened? What have you been doing?"

Scaring people. Hurting people. Sometimes, killing people. "MC stuff," I muttered at last.

Annabelle walked closer. Even in her heels, she was a little shorter than me: I had to look down into her eyes. "Thank you for getting me out of there." She was so close now that, when she breathed, her breasts almost brushed my chest.

"It was a fucked up scene," I muttered. "What happened, anyway? How'd you end up being..." I broke off. I didn't want to say it.

"Sold."

Just the sound of the word made me mad. That someone would dare to think they had the right to possess her. "Yeah. Sold."

She sat down on the bed. That made it a little easier to breathe but, immediately, I missed that closeness. "My step-dad," she said, staring at the floor. "He was in a lot of debt. I guess the Blood Spiders offered him a way out." She glanced at the window. "You think we're safe here?"

"Safe as we can be. I'll keep watch while you sleep. And tomorrow I'll get you out of here." I ran a hand through my hair. What I was about to say went against everything I was used to. "And then you should go to the cops."

She immediately shook her head, long red hair hanging down to cover her face.

"They can protect you—"

She lifted her head. "Teston's chief of police was one of the guys trying to buy me."

I felt my face fall. "Ah, *shit.*" Most outlaw MCs have some cops on the payroll. We do. But if the chief of police was mixed up in this, if he felt confident enough to be right there at the auction, it probably went even higher. Maybe the state police were in on it. Annabelle was dead as soon as she got in a cop car.

That only left one option. "You could go to the FBI," I said. I had trouble getting the word *FBI* out for two reasons. Firstly because the feds—ATF and FBI—are our worst enemies, always circling, waiting for us to screw up just once so they can take us down for good. And secondly because saying *FBI* took me straight back to that night: a crashed car by the side of the road and the smell of cordite and blood....

The room spun a little. I reached behind me and let one hand rest on the handlebars of my bike: I needed something to keep me grounded.

"It's not just the auction and the bikers," Annabelle said, her voice almost a whisper. "The man who was going to buy me, Volos...even they were scared of him. I heard the president of the Blood Spiders talking to my dad: he's protected."

I slowly sank to the bed beside her. *Protected* could mean a lot of things. Mafia, either ours or the Russians or maybe the Chinese? Or just friends in very high places? Either way, if that was true then we couldn't trust anyone. I sighed. "Then you need to disappear," I said. "If you stay quiet, they've got no reason to come after you, as long as they don't think you're going to the cops. You can go somewhere new, start a new life...."

She blinked at me. "We just let them get away with it?"

My heart sank. There's nothing like seeing wide-eyed innocence to make you realize how jaded you've gotten. She actually believed that bad guys went to jail. "Yeah," I said sadly. "We let them get away with it." Seeing the dismay break across her face, I wanted so bad for the world to be like she'd imagined it, for every last bad guy to be behind bars. Even though I'd be one of them.

I saw her shoulders rise, just once, like the tremor before an earthquake. Tears were close...and that made something stir inside me, something I hadn't been counting on. I wanted to rip what remained of her clothes off, sure, but this was deeper. I really couldn't bear to see her cry.

"Sorry," she said, starting to blink. "Just...I keep thinking about my step-dad. I lived under his roof for years, and all that time...that's all I ever was to him. He never loved me. I was just a *thing* to him, to be sold. *That's all I was!*"

The anger boiled up inside me: rage at her step-dad that felt all too familiar. I knew what it was like to be betrayed. Before I knew what I was doing, I had my finger under her chin and I was tilting her face up to look at me. "*Hey!*" I snapped. When she was looking right into my eyes, I said, "Listen to me. You're *not* someone's fucking property. You're worth more than your step-dad or the bikers or that Volos fucker, or anyone else. You're fucking priceless. And don't let anyone tell you different."

I was at least as surprised as she was by the steel in my voice, like I was telling some fucker to put his gun down. The thought of her crying had just brought it out of me.

But it worked. She blinked back the tears, nodded and gave a hesitant, embarrassed little smile. It hit me like a sucker punch in the chest: a smile that would make a man's whole day. *Damnit!* Why did she have to have one of those smiles? I could feel myself teetering on the very brink of self control. All I had to do was lean forward and my lips would be right on hers.

I stood up and turned my back on her. "Get some sleep," I grunted.

10

ANNABELLE

I nodded quickly, climbed into bed and pulled the covers over me. Then I lay there on my side facing the window, trying to get myself under control. I was a mess: part of me still wanted to cry; part of me was scared; part of me just wanted *him*. Despite everything that was going on, I was into him. *Really* into him. In fact, he might be the first guy I really *was* into. All through school, the other girls had chattered about clean-cut boy bands and then quarterbacks and then movie stars. And sure, some of them had been good looking but I'd always thought there was something wrong with me because they'd always left me cold.

Carrick? He set me on freakin' *fire*.

It occurred to me that maybe there hadn't been something wrong with me at all. Maybe I'd just been around boys—some of them grown-up boys, but still *boys*. Maybe I'd just needed to meet a man.

It wasn't just the muscles or the tattoos or even that gorgeous face. There was a confidence about him. Like he'd seen every horrible thing life could possibly come up with and nothing could phase him, anymore. Except....

Except when he looked at me.

When he looked at me, that coldness in his eyes disappeared for a second and he looked like the guy I'd first met. Did that mean I could help him regain what he'd lost?

I lifted my head just a little. He was over by the window, with his back to me. As I watched, he turned off the light and then lifted one corner of the drapes to look outside. The overhead bulb lit up the Hell's Princes insignia that covered his shoulders and the whole muscled hardness of his upper back. I could just make out another tattoo, as well, lower down, so small it was easy to miss: a shamrock. I found myself tracing the lines of his back.

When I closed my eyes again, my mind was filled by an image of his chest, the pecs broad and huge. When he'd strode out of the shower surrounded by steam, as if walking right out of hell itself, I hadn't been able to take my eyes off of it. Those smooth slabs of muscle looked so solid, so hard....

How had an Irishman come to be with a Californian MC? I knew almost nothing about his past. Even when I'd first met him, he'd only talked about the *now,* about riding and fights and bars, as if anything before that was off limits.

I couldn't figure him out. When he looked at me, it was as if he wanted to tear the clothes right off my body. I wasn't used to even thinking about sending out signals, but I was fairly sure I was sending out the right ones. Yet the closer we got, the more he gruffly pushed me away.

Me being me, it reminded me of opposing magnets. The way you can bring them closer and closer together and they'll push harder and harder apart, twisting and turning to avoid each other....

Until they get *too* close. And then one of them will suddenly flip around and they'll snap together so fast it scares you.

I knew I should be scared. He was a stranger and I was alone in a motel room with him. He was an outlaw, a criminal. And yet however hard I tried, I couldn't be scared of him. Not after he'd come for me like that, after twelve years. Not when he'd taken a beating to save me. Not when the man who *should* have protected me, my step-dad, was the person who'd started all this, and the police were tied up in it, too. I might never trust anyone again...but I trusted Carrick.

I thought it would be impossible to sleep with him standing there but, slowly, I began to sink down towards the blackness. I could feel him watching over me, a big, solid presence committed to protecting me. I'd never had that before and it felt wonderful.

I slept.

11

CARRICK

I woke disoriented. I knew something was wrong even before I opened my eyes. The bed was too soft to be one of the spare rooms at the clubhouse. At my apartment, I usually passed out on my couch in the early hours. Someone else's bed? Some woman I'd gone home with after a party? That sounded plausible. But I didn't have a hangover.

Then I became aware of a warm presence in front of me. I was lying on my side and a soft female ass was nestled against my groin. I was spooning her and she was pressed against me all the way from shoulder to toes.

I opened my eyes...and saw flame-red hair.

Shit!

Annabelle lay like a sleeping princess, her head slightly turned towards me, strands of her hair moving as she gently inhaled and exhaled.

Did we...?

No. I'd stood by the window, ready to raise the alarm if I saw any Blood Spiders coming, but by two AM the distant roar of bikes had gone. By then, Annabelle had long since gone to sleep.

I'd meant to keep watch all night but I was exhausted: I'd been about ready to drop when I arrived at the clubhouse, before this all started, then I'd had the ride to Teston and all the craziness at the bar. I had colorful bruises all across my ribs and back where the Blood Spiders had beat me but the worst thing was my shoulders: all the riding had turned them to cold, unyielding concrete shot through with jagged pain. The bed looked as soft and inviting as a cloud sent from heaven.

But *she* was in the bed. It was hard enough restraining myself when she was safely across the room.

Eventually, I decided I'd climb under the covers but not sleep. Hell, I can never normally get to sleep anyway, so staying awake wouldn't be a problem. I'd just lie there, not touching her, and rest my shoulders for a while and then—

And the next thing I knew, I was waking up spooning her and daylight was flooding through a crack in the drapes. Annabelle's soft, warm body must have had some kind of magical effect on me because I'd slept like a fucking log. I felt fully awake and rested for the first time in months.

Only now, I somehow had to climb out of bed without waking her. Not easy when I was tight up against her, and that lithe, ripe body was dressed only in a few scraps of black fabric—

I felt my cock respond to the thought, thickening and hardening against the crack of her ass. *Shit!* I tried to think of something: anything but her. Spark plugs. Exhaust headers. Pistons. Pistons pumping smoothly the way I'd pump between those pale, perfect thighs, Annabelle moaning under me as I—

My cock reared and swelled, pressing against her panties. Annabelle gave a low moan in her sleep.

I started to scooch back across the bed. That's when I realized my arm was wrapped around her body, my hand just under her breast. *Fuck!*

I lay there for a heartbeat, cock iron hard, body tense. A man can only take so much. All I had to do was flip her over on her back and wake her with a kiss like in a fairy tale. All my fantasies about her could become hot, panting reality....

And then what? Slap her ass and send her on her way, like one of the girls I'd fuck after a party? No way. She deserved better than that. What, then? A *relationship?* With *me?* No way. I couldn't bear to see her face when she discovered the blood I had on my hands.

I moved back across the bed, slowly withdrawing my hand from her chest. The top of my index finger was just brushing against the underside of her breast—*God* she was perfection. Just a little further—

She grumbled something in her sleep, grabbed my hand and pulled it back around her, clasping it to her.

My heart rose in my chest, a big expanding ball of warmth...and then it shrank down, tight and hard and cold. She felt protected by me. She thought I was some sort of fucking hero.

I went to extricate my hand...but the way she clasped it there felt so goddamn good. It was several seconds before I could bring myself to do it. Then I gently rolled off the bed and pulled on my jeans.

For her sake, I had to get her as far away from me as possible. And it started right now: I couldn't stay in that room a second longer, or I was going to do something fucking stupid, like dive back into bed and kiss her awake.

I pulled on my t-shirt and boots, threw on my cut—then stopped. The Blood Spiders might still be looking for us. They might have even passed around a description.

I slowly took off my cut. It felt like chopping off an arm. I folded it carefully over the back of a chair and then headed out.

My plan was to get us something to eat—I was starved and I knew she probably was, too. Plus, she needed something to wear. She couldn't ride around in her underwear in broad daylight. It felt weird walking instead of riding but when a couple of Blood Spiders roared past me I knew I'd made the right choice. I kept my head down, hands shoved in my jeans. Luckily, my t-shirt hid most of my ink.

There were only two stores in the village: a general store and a cafe. I tried the general store first, without much hope. *Yep:* everything from envelopes to saucepans but I couldn't see any clothes. I stomped over to the shop assistant. "You got anything to wear?" I growled.

She flinched and backed up a step, eyes huge.

Shit. Wasn't often I had to deal with people. I spent so much time being intimidating, I forgot to turn it off. These last few years, I'd almost forgotten *how* to turn it off. I tried to soften my voice. "It's for a woman."

The shop assistant swallowed and nodded. "We don't really do clothes. *But...*" She led me to the back of the store, her voice growing more confident with each step. "A local woman makes these so we keep a few in stock. We don't often sell one but they're *awesome.*"

Three dresses hung on the wall. I ran my hand through my hair. I had no clue about fucking dresses. They looked nice enough, though sort of old-fashioned.

"Is it for someone special?" the shop assistant asked.

I nearly laughed. I wasn't that guy: romance and dates and buying each other gifts. But the laugh died in my throat. With Annabelle, the idea didn't seem like something I wanted to laugh at. *Jesus, what's wrong with me?*

"Yeah," I muttered. I pointed at the blue dress. "That one."

I paid for it and then headed to the cafe. There I got two big takeout cups of coffee, a third of milk and a box of pastries. I took the whole lot back to the motel...and opened the door just as Annabelle came out of the shower.

12

ANNABELLE

I froze, my hair dripping down my back, the towel clutched around my naked body. The towel was small enough that keeping both my top half and bottom half decent required pinpoint positioning and absolutely no movement. For a second, Carrick and I just stared at one another as little drips of water pattered into the carpet.

"I bought breakfast," he muttered at last. Then he held out a bag. "And a dress."

"A *dress?*"

He put the bag down on the bed. He put the cups and cardboard carton he was carrying on the desk, next to where the Harley was parked. The entire time, his eyes didn't leave my body. I swore I could feel the water evaporating from my skin as those blue eyes scorched me.

"I should dry off," I said. "And get dressed."

He nodded, still staring at me. "Yeah."

"There's not much room in the bathroom. And the floor's wet. So I kinda need to do it in here."

He still didn't take the hint. He just kept staring, his eyes tracking an S-shaped path down my body, from the damp upper slope of one breast, down over the towel and back across my stomach to where the towel ended, dangerously close to my groin. "Mm-hmm."

"So, uh...could you turn around?"

He looked me in the eye and I almost took a step back. I'd never in my life seen such a look of raw, hot *need. I don't know,* his gaze said. *Can I?* As if he really might not be able to tear his eyes away, as if I drove him crazy.

I'd never driven a man crazy, before.

He turned around slowly, as if moving his limbs through wet concrete. His head was the last to turn, those blue eyes watching me until they absolutely had to let me go. Then his back was to me, the powerful muscles rising and falling as he breathed.

I swallowed and unwrapped the towel from me. Every square millimeter of skin tingled and throbbed. *He's six feet from me!* Close enough that I could hear his breathing.

"You want milk in your coffee?" he asked. He turned just a little to the side, towards where he'd put the cups. I caught my breath. All he'd have to do now would be to glance to the side and—

"Yep. Milk is good. Thank you," I croaked.

I bent to towel off my legs and feet, which meant taking my eyes off him. *Is he looking?* I could feel my breasts hanging down—was that his gaze I could feel on them, or just my imagination? My nipples started to pucker and swell. *Jesus....*

I straightened up. He was facing completely away from me, carefully stirring one of the coffees. *Oh.* I flushed, embarrassed...and just a little disappointed. He hadn't been—

Then I saw myself, reflected in the chrome of the Harley's gas tank. He was staring right at that little, distorted mini-me.

I caught my breath, found my underwear and pulled it on. I tried to do it matter-of-factly...but when you know someone's watching you, *nothing* is matter-of-fact. I felt like a stripper, only in reverse. *This is crazy. This is me, the geeky one. The one none of the boys were interested in.*

But *he* was. I could see the back of his head tilt and move, following every shimmy as I pulled my panties up my legs. I felt the heat begin to build, throbbing steadily down my body to pool between my thighs. *This is wrong. I should turn around, or tell him to stop watching.* But I didn't want to. I was getting hotter and hotter...and I felt oddly proud.

I reached for my bra, watching him watching me, his eyes locked on the sway of my breasts. I'd always thought they were too big, too *much,* when they should have been delicate and pert. But he seemed hypnotized by them and that only added to the warm glow.

I swallowed, put on my bra and grabbed the dress. It looked like something a girl might wear to her prom in the fifties: electric blue with a long, flaring skirt and a tight, low-cut bodice. But it was pretty, with stylized flowers embroidered on the front in silver thread. I pulled it on and zipped up the back. "Okay," I said. "I'm done."

He slowly turned around and looked.

And looked.

I felt my skin begin to prickle in an unfamiliar but very pleasant way. "What?"

"Nothin'," he grunted. He sat on the edge of the bed and offered the box. "Hungry?"

I hadn't eaten since lunch the previous day. When he lifted the lid of the box, the smell that rose up made my mouth water: sugar and caramel, the tang of berries and the thick, rich scent of butter pastry.

There were pain au raisins, the custard smooth and creamy, the fruit succulent and sweet. There were donuts, still warm from the fryer, puffed up and crispy on the outside, luxuriously soft on the inside. And there were my favorites, maple pecan twists, the nuts shining with syrup, the pastry flaking and melting in your mouth. We ate and ate, pastry shards around our mouths, sugar dusting our lips.

When we'd finished the box and drunk the coffee, I flopped back on the bed, arms above my head, grinning from the sugar rush. It was the best I'd felt since the whole nightmare had started. "That was amazing," I told him. I ran my hand over the too-tight bodice of my dress. "Good job that was the end of the box. Any more and I'd burst out of this thing."

I meant it as a joke but I caught his eye and saw the burst of ferocious heat there, as if he quite liked that idea. I flushed. Then he seemed to catch himself and stood up. "Time we got going," he told me gruffly.

I stood as well, dusting crumbs from my dress. "Where are we heading?"

He stared into my eyes for a second and I saw the frustration there, the battle he was having with himself. *What's going on? What isn't he telling me?* "My town," he said at last. "Where the Hell's Princes are based. Haywood Falls." He opened the motel room door and swung a leg over the bike. "Let's ride."

13

ANNABELLE

When we'd fled the bar the night before, I'd been too scared—and too naked—to enjoy the ride. This was a totally different experience.

Carrick stuck to quiet streets and back roads until we hit the highway. A few times we heard other bikes and he held back until they'd roared past. We had a nervous few minutes when we first joined the highway, but after a few miles it was obvious that the Blood Spiders who'd been guarding it in the night must have given up, probably figuring that we'd already slipped past them. It was still early and there was barely any traffic so Carrick opened up the bike and we roared along the deserted pavement.

I'd never felt anything like it. It was *nothing* like driving. In a car, you're cocooned in a metal box, your air filtered and the noise of the outside world muffled and mixed with talk radio until you're barely aware of it. When you ride, you're *there*: you lean with every turn, you feel the wind go from a gentle tickle to a full-on rush through your hair as the bike accelerates...it's more like flying than driving.

And I was doing it with *him*. My arms were wrapped around his waist, my breasts pressed against the warm leather of his cut. He sheltered me from the fiercest of the wind, unless I peeked out around his shoulder: just like in the bar, he was my mountain, my rock. My skirt whipped and billowed in the wind, demure one second and revealing the next, and I didn't care at all.

As we left the highway and started to descend a winding mountain path, it got warmer. Carrick throttled back and we cruised: long, lazy turns, the engine dropping from a roar to a throb. I'd already fallen in love with the Harley. Riding it—even as a passenger—was like a partnership, like being on a faithful horse who'll do your bidding as long as you treat it right. I wanted to get down on my knees beside the thing and just stare at it, fingering the mechanisms until I knew how everything worked. *God, I'm such a geek.*

At the bottom of the mountain, we rode into thick forest and followed a road that skirted a lake. As we came to a break in the trees, Carrick pulled over and nodded for me to look. I turned my head...and gasped.

Across the calm waters of the lake, nestled at the foot of the mountain, was a small town with wide, pretty streets and buildings that looked like they hadn't changed much in a hundred years. A waterfall started partway down the mountain and split into three separate falls just a hundred yards from the main street. The town faced onto the lake and the whole scene—the mountain, the forest, the town, the falls—was reflected in the surface. It was picture-postcard beautiful.

"Haywood Falls," muttered Carrick, trying but failing to keep the pride out of his voice.

I didn't say anything. I thought of Teston, with its grimy strip malls and shuttered, abandoned houses. Of my old house and its dusty field of failed crops. This was a different world.

Carrick twisted the throttle and the Harley's throb rose to a glorious, unashamed bellow, a joyful yell that echoed off the trees, announcing our arrival. It was impossible not to grin.

As we reached the edge of town, a sheriff's car fell in behind us. The man driving trailed us for a few seconds, then pulled alongside. The sheriff was in his fifties, his uniform stretched tight over his rounded stomach. He glanced across at Carrick and Carrick nodded a sober greeting, as if he knew the guy.

I saw the sheriff glance at me, then raise an eyebrow at Carrick and grin. He looked friendly...but then I remembered the chief of Teston police. *He'd* seemed friendly and trustworthy, too.

The sheriff pulled ahead of us and sped off. As we came into town, Carrick slowed and started pointing out places: a warehouse the MC owned, where they sold cheap clothing; the sheriff's office; the movie theater; the church. I didn't recognize the names on the stores. There was no Gap, no Walmart...not even a Starbucks.

We pulled up in front of a place that optimistically called itself a department store—if that was true, each department must be the size of my living room back home. "We'd better get you something else to wear," Carrick said as he switched off the engine.

I looked down at my dress. "What's wrong with this?"

He twisted around, which pressed his knee between my legs. His eyes met mine and I kind of gulped: I'd gotten so used to cuddling up to his back, I'd forgotten how close he'd be, when he turned around. For a second, he just looked into my eyes. Then his gaze tracked down over the low-cut front of my dress, over the tight bodice and down to where my legs were revealed by the skirt. "I've gotta stop in at the clubhouse and let them know I'm okay. I ran out on them last night. But if you walk into the clubhouse like that, you're going to start a riot."

I flushed. *Me?* But I followed him into the store.

He told me to pick out whatever I wanted. I settled on sneakers, a pair of indigo blue jeans, a couple of tank tops and two bra and panty sets and then went looking for a blouse to keep my arms out of the sun. With my pale skin, I had to be careful.

That was when the two girls found me. Tall, blonde and willowy with rich, even tans, both of them in shorts and tight t-shirts that showed off their perfect little upthrust breasts. Meanwhile, I was standing there in my weird, handmade dress looking like a top-heavy reject from the fifties.

One girl blinked at me. "Oh my *God*."

"I like your dress," the other one said, smirking. "Did you make it yourself?"

I felt myself redden. For a little while, riding around on the back of Carrick's bike, I'd felt proud, almost like some biker girlfriend. Now I was back to feeling like I had in high school: a freak. I'd developed a thick skin as a waitress and normally it wouldn't have bothered me but, after everything I'd been through in the last twenty-four hours, it was the final straw. I blinked, the room suddenly blurring....

Then I heard the thump of heavy boots behind me. Carrick stopped next to me, his shoulder almost touching mine. He didn't speak to the girls. He just looked at them.

I watched as both of them went pale under their perfect tans. They stared at me uncomprehendingly, as if praying they were wrong.

Carrick put a hand on my shoulder.

One of the girls whispered, "Oh *shit.*"

I saw the other girl gulp. She'd started to sweat, despite the store's air conditioning. "We didn't know," she croaked. "We had no idea. I'm so sorry!"

Carrick kept them pinned with his gaze for another few seconds. Both of them looked as if they were going to throw up. Then he jerked his head towards the door and they *fled,* dropping the clothes they'd been carrying in their arms.

I stood there for a second, open-mouthed. The hand on my shoulder felt good. The idea that I was under his protection felt fantastic. But...was this how he was seen around town? People were terrified of him? I remembered how the Blood Spiders' President had reacted to him, too. Whatever reputation he had, it carried between towns. He was *feared.*

I turned to look at him. He was gazing back down at me with a sorrowful look on his face.

This was why he kept pushing me away. His reputation...and whatever it stemmed from. I knew I should be grateful to him but all I could think was how lonely it must be, to be that feared.

I looked down at the clothes in my arms. "I can't pay you for any of this," I said awkwardly. "I mean, I'll pay you back, when I have the money...."

Carrick just looked at me like I was being silly. "If you ever owe me anything," he told me, "I'll let you know."

He paid for the clothes and I ducked into a fitting room to change into the jeans and a tank top. It was a relief to be in sneakers again after the heels. I felt like *me* again. Although, for just a second, I sort of missed the low cut, tight dress. The way Carrick had looked at me had been a thrill.

I sighed and stepped out of the changing room. And stopped.

Carrick was right outside, his arms folded across his chest, biceps bulging as he looked at me. I felt his gaze like a desert wind, scorching my face and then gliding down over my neck, my breasts, the swell of my hips.

It hadn't been about the clothes.

And that lit a warm glow in me, right in my chest, even as the heat soaked down to my groin.

"C'mon," he said. "We'd better get to the clubhouse." For a second, he seemed to have forgotten to be gruff with me. His voice was surprisingly gentle, like a bike engine just barely idling. Each throb, each syllable, was low but powerful, resonating through my entire body.

Getting back onto the Harley was easier, without the dress's long skirt. And I was modest, now, without all the leg showing: it shouldn't have felt like anything at all. Just two...*friends* on a bike together. But in my new, tight jeans, I seemed to be able to feel the hardness of his ass all the better on my inner thighs. And when I leaned forward and wrapped my arms around him, I discovered that the cotton tank top really wasn't very thick: I could feel the heat of him through his leather cut, follow the motion of his back as he breathed. If I held my breath, I could feel his heartbeat.

And I knew it wouldn't matter if I was wearing freakin' hockey padding. Riding with him was never going to feel like we were just friends, because we weren't.

We roared down the town's main street, the wind playing with my hair, the sun's warmth soaking into my bare arms. People turned and looked: some of them nodded to Carrick, most looked nervous and quickly turned away. But no one was indifferent. As someone who'd spent her entire life living in the background, I couldn't imagine what it must be like to have everyone know you.

We cruised to a stop in front of a big, sliding metal gate with razor wire looped along the top. Through the mesh I could see a long, low building with a neon sign atop it and bars on the windows. A couple of oil drums seemed to be on fire and there were bikers everywhere. My arms tightened in fear around Carrick's waist. *We're going in there?*

He reached down and rubbed my knuckles, reassuring me. Then a biker saw us, slid open the gate and we roared into the compound.

14

ANNABELLE

Bikers stopped what they were doing and stared as Carrick gunned the bike slowly past them. He seemed to fit right in: same sort of Harley, same leather cut, same badass attitude, so I didn't understand the shocked silence at first. Then I realized they were staring at me...or maybe Carrick *with* me. Why? He was freakin' gorgeous: it couldn't be that unusual to see him with a woman.

Now we were inside, I saw that the entire compound was surrounded with high fences and razor wire. There were a line of garages along one side and I could see a man working on a bike in one. In the far corner was a double wide trailer with smoke rising from the chimney.

But my attention was on the clubhouse itself. Low and squat with tiny windows: there must be barely any light inside. And the heavy metal door and barred windows made it seem like a prison. When Carrick parked the bike and climbed off, I actually sat there for a second just staring fearfully at the place.

"Come on," he told me. "It's okay." And he offered his hand.

I took a deep breath. He'd protected me this far. I took his hand and he led me inside.

The walls had been painted a deep scarlet. The little hallway that led from the door was hung with photos—some of them so old they were black and white—showing Hell's Princes from days gone by. Every member looked like a big, muscled badass. There were other mementos: a set of brass knuckles, what looked like an exhaust pipe and a framed set of rules that was fading and worn at the edges. There was a wooden packing crate on the floor, its lid ajar, and I could see baseball bats and crowbars inside, ready to be grabbed for defense. It was the most intimidating place I'd ever been.

We approached a big set of double doors, the scratched wood so dark with age it was almost black. I hung back, my arm stretching out as Carrick walked on ahead of me. I was remembering the doors that had led into the Blood Spiders' bar, all that noise rising up to meet me, all those eyes on me. My stomach suddenly lurched. The bike ride to Haywood Falls had taken my mind off what had happened but now all the memories of the auction were flooding back. What the hell was I doing with another group of bikers? Were these guys really any different?

Carrick squeezed my hand, reassuringly firm but gentle. "It's okay," he told me. "This is a safe place."

I looked again at the red walls, the weapons crate, then looked up at him with huge eyes.

"It's safe when you're with me," he clarified. He reached down and put his free hand to my cheek, brushing his warm thumb across my cheekbone, and immediately I felt myself calm a little. Then his thumb stroked slowly across my cheek again, as if he couldn't resist doing it one more time. Warm pleasure spiraled out from each brush of his skin: I wanted him to never stop. I looked up into his eyes and, for a second, he looked almost helpless.

Then he seemed to catch himself. He dropped his hand and looked away. He still held my other hand but the grip changed, loosening a little: friendly and protective but not as tight as before. Immediately, I missed it. Carrick shook his head as if he'd been dumb and pushed open the doors.

It was a big room but it seemed even bigger. The walls were the same dark red and I'd been right about the windows: there was hardly any light from outside. What there was came from big, old-fashioned light fittings, the bulbs throwing out an orange glow that didn't penetrate the shadows. It was daylight and even now I had to squint to make out the far wall. Rock music was pumping out of speakers somewhere but it was almost drowned out by the chatter of bikers.

Until all that chatter abruptly stopped and every single Hell's Prince turned to look at us. There were maybe twelve of them but it felt like a hundred, a sea of frayed cotton, tattoos, tan muscle and leather. *What the hell am I doing here?* These were real outlaws, one-percenters. They weren't fond of outsiders.

I nearly turned and bolted. Carrick must have sensed it because he put a spread hand on the small of my back to block me. Then one of the bikers, a huge brown-haired guy, tossed down his pool cue and marched over to Carrick. I shrank back in fear. The guy was so big the floor seemed to shake under his feet, his black boots at least twice the length of my sneakers. *Shit!* He grabbed hold of Carrick—

—and wrapped him into a bear hug. "*Carrick,* you dumb bastard," he rumbled. "Where have you been?"

I let out a long sigh of relief.

Carrick returned the hug, patting the big guy on the back. His voice was tight, as if his ribs were being crushed. "Had a little trouble."

"Trouble?" The biker who stepped up beside us wasn't anywhere near as big as the first guy and he wasn't loud—in fact, his voice was low and growly. But it was one of those voices that carried, even over the music, and he had presence. I checked the patch on the front of his cut. *President.*

"Nothing," said Carrick as the big guy reluctantly put him down. "Just a run in with the Blood Spiders in Teston. It's done, now." He rubbed his back, wincing just a little, and I winced in sympathy, remembering the beating he'd taken for me.

The president gave him a *don't bullshit me* look, patient but firm.

"It's *done.*" The Irish in Carrick's voice made it sound like a stone door slamming closed.

The president's look softened. I could see concern there, but he just nodded and thumped Carrick on the shoulder. "OK. Good to have you back, brother."

Then the president turned to look at me. "I'm Mac." He nodded at the big guy. "That's Ox."

Ox? "Annabelle," I told him.

Mac's gaze flicked up and down my body and I caught my breath, sudden heat rippling through me where his eyes had passed. The grin he gave me was absolutely wicked. It wasn't the brutish lust the guys at the Blood Spiders' bar had shown. This was furnace-hot and deliciously dark, like he wanted to take me by the hand and lead me down into temptation. With his thick black hair and the silver skull earring in his ear, it felt like being appraised by some roguish pirate captain.

I swallowed and looked to my side. And saw Carrick staring back at Mac, his jaw set. An instant later, Mac felt the stare and they looked at each other. I saw something pass between them: a warning, almost. *Not this one,* Carrick's eyes said. *Back the fuck off.*

Was he *jealous?!*

Mac blinked in surprise. He glanced at me again, this time with curiosity. He looked back at Carrick and nodded approvingly, a tiny but delighted smile on his lips. Meanwhile, I flushed right down to my toes. It felt like they were discussing me, even if they weren't doing it with words. And yet, underneath the embarrassment, there was a different kind of heat. I'd never been fought over before and the idea of Carrick claiming me as his started about a thousand filthy fantasies in my head. And *that* made me flush even more. *Don't be stupid!* Maybe he liked me—it sure felt like it—but every time I thought something was going to happen, he pushed me away.

To cover my embarrassment, I looked at the big guy, Ox. Carrick was big but this man was a monster, not just tall but wide: his shoulders must brush door frames. *How the hell does he ride?* Any bike would look like a toy with him on it. "You the one who called him?" he rumbled.

I nodded.

He rubbed his stubbled chin, which made a sound like someone sanding down a table. "Good. Sounded like some bad shit." For all his intimidating size, the look he gave me was gentle.

Carrick showed me around the rest of the clubhouse: the bar, the kitchen, the spare rooms where members could crash out after a hard night's partying. Then we passed a set of double doors, the dark wood elaborately carved. "What's through there?"

"Meeting room," he told me. "Members only."

I looked closer. The carvings weren't abstract: when they caught the light just right, I could make out a huge version of the Hell's Princes insignia.

He introduced me to the members, the prospects and the "hang arounds." Every guy seemed to be *big,* though there was no one else Ox's size. Most of them were thickly tattooed and not with the bland, meaningless patterns I'd seen in the outside world. Every bit of ink was part of their story and most of it seemed violent as hell. And everyone had a nickname. I kept wanting to ask the stories behind the names but it felt rude to do it in front of them. *Next time I get the chance,* I decided.

The more of them we met, the more I relaxed. Before I'd met Carrick, I would have shifted seats if any of these guys had sat down next to me. Even now, they were intimidating but what reassured me was how they treated each other: trading jokes, slapping backs. It didn't feel like a bunch of criminals. It felt like a close-knit sports team...maybe even a family.

And yet...the more I watched Carrick, the more confused I got. Everyone was friendly with him, they obviously loved him. But there was something different about the way he interacted with them, a distance the rest of them didn't have. Like he was keeping them all at arm's length. At first, I thought I was imagining it. But then I saw Mac watching with concern from across the room. He saw it, too.

We passed a phone and Carrick nodded to it. "It was Ox who answered the phone last night," he said. He slowed to a stop. "There was a party going on, but he came and got me...." His hand suddenly squeezed mine, back to that grip that was much more than *friends.*

My stomach lurched as I had the same thought he must be having: *what if he hadn't?* What if my tearful pleas had sat there on the answer phone, unheard, and Carrick had sat here drinking the night away? I'd be in Volos's car, now, while he did God-knows what to me behind the privacy glass, or chained up in some cellar.

I felt tears spring to my eyes and tried to blink them back. I spun, searching for somewhere safe, somewhere quiet, but there was nowhere: the room was too hot, too noisy, too dark.... I squeezed Carrick's hand as hard as I'd ever squeezed Perkins's paw when I was a kid.

He seemed to know instinctively what I needed. A muscled arm slipped around my waist and then he was walking me across the room, through the double doors and—

I gasped in relief as sunlight hit my face. I stood there and just panted for a moment. *Safe. I'm safe now.* My breathing slowed and the panic slowly started to fade. "Sorry," I muttered. I turned from him, letting my hair hang down to hide my face.

I felt hands on my shoulders, the palms warm against my bare skin. He turned me back towards him and then tilted my chin up, making me look at him. "You've got nothing to be sorry for," he told me. "It's the fucking Blood Spiders who should be sorry. But you're okay now. They're a long way from here."

I took a shuddering breath and nodded. I *was* okay. But it wasn't the distance from Teston or even the warm sun: it was the hand that cupped my chin and those blue eyes that gazed down at me. *They* made me okay. For just a second, they looked like they had twelve years before, clear and blue and free....

Then his hand dropped from my chin. "C'mon," he said gruffly. "I'll show you around."

Every time. Every time I thought we were about to get close, he slammed the door in my face.

The first stop was the workshop. A short, well-padded man in his sixties with a snow-white beard was kneeling beside a bike, deep in concentration, his coveralls so old and stained with oil they were more black than blue. "Scooter," said Carrick, "this is Annabelle. Scooter does all our repairs."

The man glanced up as we entered and nodded curtly. I gave him a smile, glanced around....

And I was *lost*.

There was an engine on a workbench, stripped down and separated into shining, perfect pieces. And thumb-tacked to the wall was a huge diagram of a Harley, six feet across. An *exploded* diagram, all the tiny parts separated so I could see how they slotted together.

It was like being inside my own head.

There were sets of wrenches and screwdrivers. There were boxes of obscure parts. There were maintenance manuals I knew I could happily disappear into for days at a time. I closed my eyes and inhaled: gasoline and engine oil. For the first time in my life, I felt like I was home.

"You alright?" asked Scooter.

I spun. They were both looking at me—not unkindly, but I was suddenly self-conscious. I was being weird again. "Yes," I said quickly. "Sorry." And I backed out of the workshop.

At that moment, a biker roared up on a Harley. He sat perfectly erect, more like a man on a horse than a biker, his black hair blowing in the wind. His skin was the deep, rich tan of a man who spends every day outdoors.

Carrick leaned close to me. "Hunter," he told me over the noise of the Harley. "Our Vice President."

"Why do you call him—" Just as I said it, the engine noise dropped to an idle and my voice was suddenly very loud. I flushed.

The man on the bike gave me a long, appraising look and then looked at Carrick and motioned for him to continue.

"He tracked down a cougar that was bothering the town," Carrick told me. "And he's pretty good at tracking people, too. Even helped out the sheriff, a few times."

I blinked at that. I thought outlaws and the police didn't mix.

I was about to say hi when I heard something - a *wrongness*. I stared intently at Hunter's bike.

"What?" asked Carrick.

"The timing's off," I thought. And then realized I'd said it out loud, and flushed again.

Scooter wiped his hands on a filthy rag and stood up. "I don't hear nothin'."

I shook my head. "I'm probably wrong."

"You know something about engines?" asked Scooter suspiciously.

"No! Not really."

Scooter muttered something under his breath and Carrick led me quickly away. "Don't mind Scooter," he told me. "He's good with bikes but he's a grumpy fucker. You like machines?"

I shrugged. "They just make sense to me," I said. "When you fix them, the parts fall into place and everything's just...where it's supposed to be." I felt myself turning red again. I knew I wasn't explaining it well. But, when I looked up into his eyes, he wasn't looking at me like I was a freak. Not at all.

He led me over to the double wide trailer. Someone had painted it eggshell blue and there were flowers in window boxes and more on the roof. It must have been sitting in the compound for years. "This is where Mom lives," Carrick told me.

I turned to him, astonished.

"Not mine. We just all call her that. She sorta...looks after us."

I slowly turned in a circle, gazing around. When we'd first roared up to the metal gate and the razor-wire fence, I'd thought this place looked like a prison. Now, thinking about the men I'd met inside and the ones I knew were in the world outside, it felt more like a protective fortress. And the clubhouse: those red walls and the dim interior still freaked me out a little, but I could see how the tiny windows and lack of daylight made it seem like a sanctuary, sealed off from the outside world. The one place these men would always be welcome.

I looked at Mom's trailer. Thought about the way the other members had welcomed Carrick home, even if he seemed to keep his distance a little. *It really is like a family.*

And something swelled up inside me: a *need*. I'd had so many years of living with my step-dad, soaking up his resentment. Before that, all the years of living with him and my mom, terrified of the violence he'd unleash. I hadn't had a real family, a place I could feel safe, since I was a little kid.

I was suddenly, irrationally, jealous. I wanted to belong to something too. I wanted somewhere I could return to where I knew people would hug me and ask me how I was doing. I hadn't realized until that moment how much I needed it.

Carrick looked down at me and frowned. "You okay?"

I nodded quickly and looked away.

He stepped in front of me, six-feet plus of unyielding muscle and black leather, blocking out the sun. "Annabelle?" He used *that* voice, pure iron dipped in Irish silver. It didn't permit any argument.

"Nothing! Just...it's nice." I made myself smile. "It's like a whole second family."

And then I saw something in his eyes. It was only there for a second, then he looked away to hide it, but I knew what I'd seen: a flicker of pain so strong it made me want to throw up. My jealousy evaporated. This wasn't his second family; this was his only family.

Maybe we weren't so different. I put a hand on his arm and he snapped his gaze to me again. "What happened?" I asked.

He shook his head. "Nothing."

"You lost them?" I asked quietly, thinking of my mom.

"Let it go!" He sounded more Irish the more angry he got. He shook off my arm and stalked away.

I chased after him, catching him next to the clubhouse. "I just want to help."

"Don't," he snapped. "Just stop it."

"What?"

"*Fuck!*" He spun and slammed his fist down as if whacking a table. "Being fucking nice to me!"

We stood there staring at each other for a moment. Then he took a deep breath, closed his eyes and said, "I'm not someone you're nice to. I'm not someone you're friends with. I'm not someone you *like*."

And there it was. That last sentence hung in the air between us. His eyes finally opened and stared into mine, begging me to leave it alone. I almost gave in. I could feel the mood shifting: pushing more could be dangerous.

But then I thought of the night we'd first met, how he'd ordered me to go back into the house...and how I'd stubbornly ignored him.

"Don't I get to make up my own mind about liking you?" I asked.

"*No!*"

That threw me, but only for a moment. "Well...too bad, because I already did." And I lifted my chin in defiance.

He stared at me, furious, shaking his head.

My voice quavered. "'I'm not very good at this stuff," I said, "But traditionally, I think this is where you say you like me, too."

He gave a growl, grabbed me by the waist and slammed me up against the wall of the clubhouse, my feet only just brushing the ground. "Of course I fucking like you!" he snapped. "That's why—" He sighed and shook his head. "That's why you need to get a long way from me."

I thought of how scared everyone was of him. Even the Blood Spiders president had known him by reputation. "Carrick...what is it you do for the club?"

He shook his head, as if he'd rather lose me than have me know. "I'm not who you think I am," he said at last.

Stop pushing, screamed a warning voice in my head. *Let it go.* But I was so determined to help him. "You saved me," I reminded him.

"Yeah, so now we're even."

"Or maybe that means it's my turn."

He stared into my eyes and I could see the battle going on there, the hard, cold gray fighting with the blue. I was sure he was going to relent but then he shook his head. The anger seemed to drain from him, to be replaced with tiredness. "You're way too late for that, darlin'." He put me down and grabbed my wrist. "Come on."

I followed, frowning. "Where are we going?"

"Bus station."

I stopped dead in my tracks, my heart plummeting down to my feet. *"What?"*

"There's a bus to Sacramento at noon." He took out his money clip and pulled out the entire wad of bills. "There's about four hundred there. Take it."

I took it. I was too stunned not to. "You're sending me away?" I croaked.

"This isn't the place for you. The town, the club....*me.*"

I stared at him, speechless. I'd pushed too hard. I'd forced his hand. *Shit!* I've never wanted to take back a conversation more in my life. But it was too late.

He swung his leg onto the bike and, numb with shock, I climbed on behind him.

15

CARRICK

She wrapped her arms around my waist for the very last time. It wasn't like before. She was as stiff as a mannequin and I wondered if she was crying. *Shit.* But it'd be much, much worse if I let her get in any deeper.

The frustration was boiling up inside me. I was mad at myself for hurting her feelings. I was mad at the world for being fucking unfair.

Yeah, well, life isn't fair. Guys like me don't get a happy ever fucking after. We wind up dead in a ditch by the side of the road. Hell, I'd already be there, if it hadn't been for her helping me, all those years ago. I was fucking lucky that someone like her had crossed my path twice in one lifetime, once so she could save me and once so I could repay the debt.

She was like a butterfly: when one of those lands on you, you don't try to grab it or you'll just crush it with your big, clumsy hands. You just drink in how pretty it is and then let it fly off to be with its own kind.

I knew all that. So why was it making me so mad, all of a sudden? Because she liked me as well? Because she had some delusion that I was a hero...and I wanted it to be true?

I was an idiot. I'd always known that I'd have to say goodbye to her. I'd meant to just drop her somewhere safe, as soon as we'd got out of the auction. But then there'd been the motel and that night together and breakfast and then the ride to Haywood Falls and buying her clothes and introducing her to the guys....

I'd gotten lost in the fantasy. I'd forgotten, for a morning, how much blood I had on my hands.

I told myself I was putting her on the bus for her own good, because she deserved way better than a life with someone like me. But I knew the real reason: her questions had made me realize that, if she stayed around, it'd only be a matter of hours before someone told her what I did for the club. And I couldn't take seeing her eyes when she found out. She'd never look at me the same way again. Or worse, she'd want to help.

I didn't share that load even with my brothers in the MC. No way was I going to taint *her* with it. It was my path to walk and mine alone.

I twisted the throttle and we roared out of the compound and along Main Street. In the mirror, I could only see Annabelle's red hair streaming out in the wind, her face hidden as she sheltered against my back. I could guess her expression, though, and it made me screw my own face up in disgust. I knew this was the right thing to do. So why did it feel so wrong?

The bus station was a low brick building, not much more than a ticket office and some restrooms. It was ten to noon when we got there. Ten minutes until she was gone from my life forever.

She bought her ticket and then we stood there facing each other silently. There was so much I wanted to say. I wanted to tell her how fucking beautiful she was. I wanted to explain to her that she deserved a good life with some guy who wore a suit and came home every night at six. I wanted to explain that sleeping next to her had given me the first peaceful rest I'd had in years.

But I've never been much of a talker.

"Take care of yourself," I said.

She nodded. And started to do those fast little blinks women do when they're about to cry. "Yeah, you too."

There was something I had to get out. "I meant what I said," I muttered. "You're fuckin' priceless, girl. Don't let anyone tell you different."

She bit her lip and nodded. Both of us turned to go—

Her body hit me with a *wumf,* right in the chest, and then she was hugging me even harder than Ox had.

I felt it all rise up inside me: the pain at seeing her go, the frustration at what I had to do, the anger at myself for the path I'd chosen. When I'd first met her, I'd been almost as innocent as she was. Why couldn't I have stayed that way? I could have met her again now and we could have built something....

I screwed my eyes closed and let out a long breath, stroking the back of her head like it was *her* I was trying to calm. Then I leaned down and allowed myself just one kiss on the top of her head. I drank in the smell of her hair, the soft silk of those copper strands. I'd have to make that memory last the rest of my life.

She released me, moving slowly at first and then fast, turning quickly away to try to hide the fact she was crying. I watched her walk away towards the restrooms. I'd never felt like such a worthless son of a bitch in my entire life.

But if I wanted her to be happy, to have a life instead of some fucked up thing with me, this is what I had to do.

I turned around and walked away.

16

ANNABELLE

I couldn't see where I was going: the sign for the restrooms was just a blur. But I didn't want to wipe at my eyes or he'd see. So I just kept putting one foot in front of the other, letting the tears spill down my cheeks and drip to the floor. Thankfully, the bus station was nearly empty but I passed close enough to one woman to glimpse the sympathetic look she gave me. Then she looked over my shoulder at where Carrick must still have been, and glared reproachfully at him. *Don't hate him,* I wanted to tell her. *He's the one who helped me. He hasn't just dumped me.*

It just felt that way.

I blundered through the door and into a deserted hallway. Three doors. I had to stop and wipe the tears away before I could see which was male, which was female and which was the rear exit. I made it through into the female bathroom, grabbed hold of the sink and *then* I finally let it all out. The animal fear at what had happened to me. The deep, wrenching shock at finding out that the world was an even shittier place than I'd thought, that the auctions and people like Volos really did exist. But most of all, the knowledge that I was on my own, now.

I'd felt like I was on my own ever since my mom died. But now—

briefly—I'd felt what it was like to have someone, whether I was snuggled against his back on the bike or just sharing pastries with him in a motel room. Most of all, I'd gotten used to feeling someone's hand in mine.

At last I sniffed, wiped my eyes and looked at my red, tear-stained face in the mirror. *Idiot!* Why had I pushed him? I had no clue about this stuff. *This is what happens when you're more comfortable around machines than people.*

If I'd stayed in Haywood Falls, could I have helped him? Could we have built something? I fingered the shamrock necklace.

It didn't matter now. I was never going to see him again.

I splashed some cold water on my face, dried off with a scratchy paper towel and took a deep, shaky breath. I needed to run if I was going to make the bus. Plus, hurrying would stop me thinking: if I kept thinking, I was going to start crying again.

I pulled open the door...and ran right into a wall of solid muscle. A white t-shirt. A leather cut. *Carrick!* He'd come back for me! A warm bomb went off in my chest.

Then my fingers touched something unfamiliar on the front of his cut. Metal. Eight legs.

I looked up.

"Hello, Annabelle," said the blond-haired Blood Spider.

17

CARRICK

People in Haywood Falls tend to steer clear of the Princes anyway. When it's *me,* the Irish enforcer who hands out beatings? They cross the street. So when they saw me storm out of the bus station, my face like thunder, they got the *fuck* out of the way.

I'd never regretted something more. Not sending her away: that had been the right thing to do. It was the choices I'd made, years ago, that tore me up. Because if I'd made better ones, maybe it wouldn't have to be this way.

Goddamn you, Briggs. I wished he was still alive so I could have the satisfaction of putting a bullet in his head.

I swung my leg over my bike. *I'm going to get drunk,* I decided. Absolutely shitfaced. Proper wake-up-in-another-state drunk. Maybe when I sobered up, it wouldn't hurt so bad.

I started the bike up and checked over my shoulder before I pulled out, just to make sure a semi-truck wasn't about to pancake me. Then I revved the throttle and—

I stopped and frowned, then turned and looked over my shoulder again. I'd glimpsed something in my peripheral vision. It took me a while to find it again....

There.

Two Harleys parked side by side in an alley, almost invisible from the street. Not ours. The custom paint job was red and black.

Blood Spiders.

I climbed off my bike, the shock making me slow. *Here?* Clubs are fiercely territorial. They don't stray into another club's town, not without a damn good reason.

I looked at the bus station...and started to run, fear clutching at my chest. *Be wrong,* I prayed. *Be wrong....*

I was halfway there when a dirty white van tore out of an alley and sped off down the street. As soon as I saw it, I *knew.* Then I saw the blond-haired Blood Spider from the auction follow it out on foot and race across the street to get his bike. He saw me, slowed to a jog and grinned at me victoriously. Why was the bastard grinning?

That's when the second Blood Spider, the one I hadn't seen, slammed his fist into the back of my head. As I fell, he followed it up with a vicious boot to the temple. I slumped to the sidewalk, everything spinning. I heard the echo of his boots as he joined his buddy, then the roar of their bike engines. As they turned to follow the van, the blond one swung wide so he could pass by me. I tried to get to my feet to take a swing at him, but I couldn't get my arms and legs to work.

"Too bad, Irish," he called. "Hope you had time to fuck her before we all do." Then he twisted his throttle and roared off.

I stared at his bike as it grew smaller and smaller. *Get up!* But every tiny movement made my head pound. *Get up!* I tried to push at the sidewalk but my arms felt like wet cardboard.

She needs you! Get up!

I gave a low growl and *heaved,* sucking in air as the pain washed over me. I climbed to my knees, then to my feet. I stumbled towards my bike, moving faster and faster as the adrenaline started to kick in. By the time my ass hit the saddle, my head was almost clear.

And I was *pissed.*

"Irish?" a voice from the sidewalk. I turned and saw Tailor, one of the prospects, a paper bag of groceries in his arms.

"Get everyone!" I yelled. "Tell them to catch us on the highway!"

I started my bike. In my mirror, I saw Tailor drop the groceries and sprint off down the street towards the compound.

Already, the van was out of sight. I twisted the throttle and roared after them.

And prayed I could get her back.

18

CARRICK

I roared down Main Street, weaving through the traffic. The light at the next intersection changed to red. I hunkered low on the bike, redlined the engine and sped across, drawing angry beeps. I wasn't stopping for anything. *This is my fault* kept going through my head. If I hadn't tried to send her away. If I hadn't been such an evil bastard in the first place, so I didn't have to....

If I got her back, I wasn't letting her go again. I'd keep her close, keep her safe, even if I couldn't be with her, even if it drove me fucking crazy. Because the thought of her in their hands—

I snarled and twisted the throttle all the way, blasting towards another red light. By the time I saw the bus coming across the intersection, it was too late to stop. I *prayed*...and flashed by just in time, the bus missing my back wheel by no more than a foot.

As we reached the edge of town, the road became twisty and I started to make up ground. Both the bikers were good riders but this was my turf: I knew every corner, knew exactly how fast I could push it. With every bend, they came a little closer. The fear was turning into anger, now, building and building the nearer I got.

I saw them turn their heads at the sound of my engine, then stare at me in shock. *Yeah, that's right, you bastards. I'm coming.*

Both of them fumbled for guns. *Amateurs,* I thought viciously. It's not like in the movies: it's hard to ride *and* shoot, especially at something that's moving. I could already see them wobbling as they tried to aim with one hand and steer with the other.

There's a reason I wear a chain as a belt. I reached down and unfastened it, then slid it out of the loops. The nearest biker turned pale as he saw me bearing down on him, the chain dangling from my fist. He raised his gun and fired once, but his hand was shaking. Twice, but I veered and the bullet sang past my head. Then I was on him, swinging the chain. It caught him in the side of the head and he tilted, then the road grabbed hold of him and he and the bike went spinning along the pavement.

I went after the blond biker next, whirling the chain in circles around my head. He scowled at me and pulled out around the van. I pulled out to follow him—

And saw the truck thundering towards me in the oncoming lane. I swayed right and it flashed past me, so close that the slipstream sucked the air from my lungs.

I pulled out again and bore down on the blond biker. He tried to avoid me by pulling in ahead of the van but the chain whipped out and I caught him on the hand. He cried out and slewed off the road and into a ditch, alive but with a handful of busted fingers.

As we hit the highway, I looked back at the van, eyes wild with fury. There was one Blood Spider driving and another in the passenger seat. Behind them, I could see shapes moving in the rear: two more bikers, maybe three? And all probably armed. Even if I could get the van to stop, I was going to be seriously outnumbered.

That's when I heard the end-of-the-world rumble behind me, a bass throb that grew to a roar. First one bike then more and more shot past the van and formed up alongside me. Mac. Ox. Hunter. Viking. More and more members joined the group, until we were five thick and three deep, blocking the road.

"They've got Annabelle!" I yelled to Mac over the deafening roar.

Mac nodded and then looked across at Hunter. He pulled a hunting knife from beneath his cut and throttled back.

The guys in the van had been forced to slow, the driver wide-eyed and pale. As Hunter dropped back alongside him, he swung sideways, trying to run him off the road. But Hunter effortlessly swayed out of the way and, as he passed close to their front wheel, the knife flashed in the sun. The tire exploded, pieces of scorching rubber arced through the air, and the van driver had to slam on the brakes as he started to skid. Three tons of metal slewed across the highway towards us, but everyone managed to dodge out of the way. The van spun a full one-eighty and finally came to a stop facing the wrong way in the center of the highway.

I got to the driver's door just as he opened it and drove my fist into his face as hard as I could. On the other side, Ox was hauling out the guy in the passenger seat and hurling him to the ground.

The rear doors flew open and three Blood Spiders jumped out, pulling guns. But they were swarmed by members before they could get a shot off, punches raining down on them. I pushed my way past the fight and jumped into the rear of the van....

And there, lying on her side on the floor, was Annabelle. The bastards had put duct tape over her mouth and tied her wrists behind her back but she didn't look hurt. I freed her hands, then carefully peeled off the tape, wincing along with her as it caught on her skin. "You okay?" I asked, as soon as it was off.

In answer, she threw herself into my arms, burying her head in my chest. I held her there, my hand on the back of her head. I didn't want her to ever move. "I'm sorry I sent you away," I told her, my voice tight.

She clutched me even harder. "Don't do it again," she managed.

I viciously shook my head. I wasn't losing her again. Not this girl. Even if keeping her safe meant being around her—but not having her—twenty-four seven. Even if it drove me crazy.

I knew what I had to do. If the Blood Spiders were after her, she needed more than me. She needed the whole club. The last thing I wanted to do was draw them into this but I didn't have a choice.

I looked up to see Mac standing with his arms folded, waiting for an explanation. And I could hear the wailing of sirens in the distance: some terrified driver must have called the cops.

"We're going back to the clubhouse," I told Annabelle. "You're under our protection, now."

19

ANNABELLE

The next few minutes were a blur. The Blood Spiders were left by the side of the highway, bloodied and bruised: hopefully the cops would pick up at least some of them. The Hell's Princes and I continued on down the highway, staying just out of sight of the cops, then turned off down a country road and circled back to Haywood Falls.

It was the first time I'd ridden in a pack and it was terrifying...and wonderful. The bikes roared along well above the speed limit, but so close I could have reached out and touched them. We were all one slip away from a horrific pile up but they were all so practiced, so confident, that we swung around each bend in perfect unison, leaning in so far that I thought my long hair would brush the pavement.

Carrick and I were at the very center of the pack. The engine noise was deafening but I'd never felt more protected, a princess surrounded by her knights. The air around me was warm, heated by fifteen blistering-hot exhausts and scented with leather and smoke.

I was still trembling from how close I'd come. They'd been talking, in the back of the van, about how they'd hand me over to Volos. But not before they'd taken their frustrations out on me for escaping. They'd planned to take me back to their clubhouse, throw me down on the pool table and—

I squeezed my eyes closed and tightened my arms around Carrick's hard body.

Pulling into the compound felt different, this time. The fences felt good—*safe*. Even the clubhouse felt solid and secure, not claustrophobic. Carrick and the others marched straight to the carved wooden doors of the meeting room and pushed them open. I caught a glimpse of a huge table surrounded by chairs.

"Wait out here," Carrick told me over his shoulder. And then the doors closed behind them and I was alone in the main room, standing in sudden silence.

I knew it was some sort of private meeting but I figured they must be talking about me. I crept closer but the doors were thick, heavy wood. I could hear the rumble of deep male voices but no words.

I crouched in front of the doors and pressed my ear to the wood. That was better. I could make out Carrick's Irish-tinged voice and just the sound of it made me go weak. He sounded so *mad,* so utterly determined to protect me. He was telling the others what happened the night of the auction—

A hand grabbed my shoulder, hauled me to my feet and spun me around.

I was suddenly face-to-face with a woman in her sixties, with long silver hair that fell almost to her ass. She was wearing blue jeans, a soft plaid shirt and she looked *pissed.* "What in God's name's going through your head, girl?" she asked in a fierce whisper. "You can't listen to that!"

She hauled me across the room to the bar to put some distance between us and the door. Then she let me go and I stumbled to a stop. The woman let out an exasperated breath and glared at me, but then her eyes softened a little. "What goes on in that room is damn near sacred," she explained.

I nodded quickly. "Sorry." Then I realized something. "You're....Mom."

She smiled. "And you must be the one Carrick brought back from Teston." She looked me up and down. "Yeah, now I see why."

I flushed. What was *that* supposed to mean? I glanced at the door to the meeting room. "I don't want to cause them trouble," I mumbled. "I feel like I've dragged them into this. That's why I was listening."

Mom raised an eyebrow. "Girl, if those boys have decided they're going to protect you, you'd better thank your lucky stars and accept it, 'cause you ain't gonna change their minds." She paused. "Carrick, especially. Once that one sets his sights on something...." She trailed off but kept staring at me and I flushed again. Then she jerked her head towards the main doors. "Come outside. You look like you could use some tea."

Moments later, we were sitting in the double wide trailer Carrick had shown me. At least half of it was filled by a huge kitchen, with eight propane-fueled gas burners and enough counter space to plate up a meal for twenty. There was a snug little bedroom, a bathroom and the rest was the living area. I sat facing Mom on an old, very comfortable purple couch. Mom caught me frowning at it. "You're not crazy," she told me. "It *is* too big to get through the door. The boys took the whole side of the trailer off for me, slid it in and then bolted the place back together."

It had been worth it. It was the sort of couch you disappeared into. I could feel myself relaxing...and then it got even better. A gorgeous gray cat leaped up onto the seat next to me, padded onto my lap and curled up there, claiming it for his own. His collar read *Mr. Fluffy*.

I put my hand on his back: he had the softest fur I'd ever felt. Stroking him was addictive and rewarded by purrs. I felt myself relaxing even more...and I suddenly got the feeling that a lot of people had sat there before me, telling Mom their problems. "Carrick said you look after them?" I asked.

"I feed 'em, fix their clothes, hear their woes. Tell them what to do when they fall for the wrong one, or get her pregnant. Most of these boys ain't got much in the way of family."

I frowned. "But how did you wind up here?"

She grinned and leaned close. "I'm *Ox's mom,*" she whispered. "But the big lunk doesn't like to be reminded of it."

I blinked. *Ox?* That walking wall of muscle?

She handed me a cup of honey-sweetened tea. As I sipped, she said, "Carrick's quite a catch."

I coughed and spluttered tea everywhere, then flushed beet-red. "I don't think I've...um...caught—"

"Oh, heavens, girl. That boy's got a hard on the size of a ballistic missile for you. And the way you keep going red every time I mention him, you've fallen for those Irish eyes, so *that's* not the problem." She folded her hands in her lap and peered at me. "He's not letting you in? He's pushing you away?"

I nodded.

She put her cup down. "You realize he's doing it to protect you?"

I gave a noncommittal shrug. Then, "I know it's to do with what he does for the club. But...I mean, how bad can it be?"

She fixed me with a look and my stomach turned over. *Pretty freakin' bad.*

What if Carrick was right not to tell me? What if he told me and I couldn't handle it? What if it made me want to run?

But if he *didn't* tell me, if he kept trying to protect me, he'd be pushing me away forever.

"It takes a special kind of woman to love these guys," Mom said. "You gotta understand them. Understand the club and why they love it the way you do, because you can't ever come between them and it. And the bad stuff they do? You gotta look inside them, where it matters, and see that the angel outweighs the demon."

"Angel?"

Mom shrugged. "Even Satan started out as a fallen angel." She pressed her lips together. "But it ain't just about you and accepting what he does. Carrick's harder than most to get to know. He's loyal to the club—maybe *too* loyal. He carries a ton of weight for them but he never lets them help him. Didn't you wonder why he rode off to Teston alone to save you?"

I blinked. I hadn't thought of that.

"He loves these guys, but he's afraid to lean on them," said Mom. "I don't know why. I know it drives Mac crazy. He's certainly never let a woman get close...hell, he doesn't even let girls ride on his bike. Not until you."

Now I knew why everyone had stared when we'd rode into the compound together. My heart started to crash in my chest.

"A special kind of woman," Mom repeated, watching me carefully.

I nodded to myself and sat there stroking Mr. Fluffy as I thought. I tried to wrap my brain around my feelings, but they were too deep and too strong to get a proper hold of. Why couldn't this stuff be simple, like gear ratios?

Then I saw something on a kitchen shelf that I *did* understand. I gently lifted Mr. Fluffy off my lap and stood up. "Can I borrow this?" I asked, picking up the little glass bottle of almond oil.

"Of course you can," said Mom. "What are you going to do? Bake him a cake?"

"Something like that," I mumbled, flushing again.

20

CARRICK

I slammed my fist down on the table. "We got to ride to Teston. Wipe the fuckers out."

The meeting room was so quiet, I could hear the scratch as Mac rubbed at his stubble. "We can't just wade in there," he said slowly. "There's too much we don't know."

"We know enough!" I snapped. I was leaning forward in my seat, shoulders tensed like I was about to drive my fist through the table. I could hear the Irish coming out thick in my voice. "Jesus, they came right into town, *our town,* and they took her like she was theirs!"

Mac gave me that sad, solemn look I'd seen so many times before when one of us gets riled. I'd never been on the receiving end, before. "I know you're pissed," he told me. "We'd all be pissed if it was our girl."

"She's not *my girl*," I ground out.

Everyone just looked at me. What the fuck was the matter with them?

"They'll be back," I snarled. "We can't just wait around until they try again."

Mac held up a calming hand. "We won't, brother," he said softly. "But we need to know what's going on. Something's not right here.

They took a big chance, coming into our town. They knew they might run into us—that's why they sent so many guys. Why go to all that trouble? Why not just grab a different girl?"

Because she's one of a kind, I wanted to say. But what Mac said rang true. Life was cheap to the Blood Spiders. A woman was replaceable. Why risk war with the Hell's Princes to get her back? I sighed and ran a hand through my hair. "I don't know."

"What about the cops?" asked Hunter.

Everyone looked uneasy. Hunter used to be on the other side of the law—kind of—when he was a bounty hunter. He still distrusts them, but not as much as the rest of us.

"We solve our own problems," Mac told him.

"This is serious shit," Hunter pressed. "*Human fucking trafficking?* We should talk to the feds!"

Mac shook his head. "The feds always want something—nothing's ever free. Plus, we get a fed sniffing around here, they could get wind of the guns. I can't risk the club."

Now Ox spoke up. "Hunter's right. That auction is *messed up.*" I could hear the anger building in his voice. Ox has a slow-burning fuse, but once he goes off.... "We can't let that go on."

"It's not our town," said Viking.

"I don't care if it's not our *state!*" Ox slammed his palms down on the table and, with his bearlike strength, it was enough to lift the opposite table legs off the floor. "No one's selling women on our watch!"

Shit. This was going to end in a fight. Normally, Ox and Hunter were the calm ones but this thing was putting them on a collision course with Mac. *And it's all my fault,* I thought, the frustration tight in my chest. *This is why I never let the club get involved in my problems!* I forced myself to calm down. Now I *had* gotten them involved, I needed to support my pres.

"No one's saying we let it stand!" Mac growled. "We'll stop the auctions. But we need to know what's going on. We need to get hold of their President and ask him some questions."

Ox slowly nodded, though he looked far from happy, and lifted his hands. The table settled back onto all four legs.

"Their pres is a guy called Hay," I said, forcing my voice to be calm. "Mean fucker but not brave. We put a gun to his head, he'll talk."

"We need to get hold of him away from their clubhouse," said Mac. "Make sure we have him outnumbered and outgunned."

"I'll go over there tonight," said Hunter. "Sneak around and find out where he's going to be."

No one argued. Hunter does *stealthy* like no one I've ever met. He can be standing a foot behind you and you won't know he's there.

"Okay, then." Mac stayed standing, maybe to remind us who was the boss. "We'll meet up tomorrow morning, Hunter will tell us the place and time, and we'll move." He banged the gavel to end the meeting and everyone started to filter out. Ox was still muttering to Hunter about the auctions and I knew he'd be in a mood for days. Mac sighed in frustration.

I stayed behind until everyone had left. "Sorry," I muttered. I thought back to how I'd reassured him, when I'd first brought Annabelle to the clubhouse. *It's done,* I'd said. "Didn't mean this to turn into your problem."

Mac came around the table stood in front of me, slowly shaking his head. "We got your back, brother. When are you gonna figure that out?" He cocked his head to one side. "Why didn't you ask us to go with you, when you rode to Teston to rescue her? We all would have come."

I stared at the table. I knew he was right: they all would have rode out with me and stormed the Blood Spider's bar. We could have put a stop to the auctions right then and there and maybe the Blood Spiders wouldn't have come after Annabelle. It would have been easier, safer, *saner.* But....

But I couldn't accept their help. I'd die for this club but I wouldn't let them put themselves at risk for me. I gave, but I wouldn't take.

Until Annabelle came along. She was the one thing I'd bend my rules for. They'd already helped me save her on the highway and now

I was letting them go up against the Blood Spiders again. I hated it but I had no choice.

I stood up, shoving my chair back. I pulled Mac close and slapped his back. "I love you, brother."

He thumped me on the back. But when we separated, I could see the concern on his face. We used to be *tight,* him and me. When we first set up our gun-running operation, it was me who he'd trusted to go with him to the Black Sea to meet the Russian mafia guy who'd be supplying us. But as the club bonded closer and closer, I'd always stayed a little way apart. Me having to accept help, this one time, had just made it even clearer that I normally *didn't.* He wanted me to stop keeping the club at a distance. And I couldn't.

As I walked out, I clenched my fists. *This has to end. Tomorrow.* I needed to finish this thing...and I'd kill that bastard Hay, if that's what it took. Then Annabelle would be safe and things could go back to normal.

Outside, I found Annabelle standing in the sunshine, hand shielding her eyes as she looked up into a cloudless sky. She was facing away from me and I took a second to admire her body. My eyes traced a lazy "S:" over the pale, bare shoulders I wanted to grip and kiss and bite as I thrust into her from behind, down the elegant curve of her spine, *in* to the little dip at the small of her back, the smooth skin revealed by the gap between tank top and jeans, then *out* over those ripe ass cheeks, my eyes doing what my hands longed to. God, she was perfect. Her long red hair was billowing out in the breeze and, as I walked closer, the very tips of the strands just brushed my face. I stopped, closed my eyes and inhaled, smelling her. Honeysuckle shampoo coupled with that warm, feminine scent that drove me wild. I could have stood there all day.

I heard her turn and opened my eyes, but for a second I couldn't say anything. This is why I was letting the club help: I was crazy about this girl.

"We're going to fix this," I told her. "We'll make sure they don't come after you again. But for tonight, we need to keep you safe." I looked over my shoulder at the clubhouse. "I was going to say you could crash in one of the spare rooms, but...it gets quiet here at night, when there's not a party on. And I don't want you here alone."

When I looked back at her, she was staring right into my eyes. We both knew what I was going to say next.

"You're sleeping at my place tonight," I told her.

21

ANNABELLE

To get to Carrick's place, we cut through the center of town. As we cruised up to the intersection on Main Street, I watched the sunset turn the lake orange and gold. It was a beautiful place. I still couldn't wrap my head around the Hell's Princes being here. They were criminals, right? And I associated criminals with grimy cities. This place was as small town as it got.

The light went red ahead of us and Carrick slowed to a stop. As cars pulled up alongside us, I saw the drivers turn to look at us. Most quickly looked away. Some gave a quick nod of respect.

"Things work different, out here." The deep, Irish rasp startled me. Carrick had twisted in the saddle to look at me. He jerked his head towards the nearby Sheriff's office. "The cops don't have the manpower to look after things. So we do."

A guy in a sheriff's uniform was sipping coffee in the parking lot, watching the sunset. He nodded at Carrick, who nodded back. I realized it was the same guy we'd seem when we first rode into town. "Sheriff Harris is a friend," Carrick told me. He lowered his voice. "Turns a blind eye to most of what we do. In return, we make sure the streets stay clean. No hard drugs in town, no trouble."

I looked again at the drivers around us. The Hell's Princes, I realized, were like a band of rowdy swordsmen who slayed the local dragons and protected the town. People didn't necessarily *like* them. But they needed them.

Then the light changed and we roared off, the sudden acceleration making me clutch his waist tight.

Carrick's house was a small, one-storey place on a big lot: one of those quirks of town planning where there isn't quite room to fit two houses but there's way too much space for one. Most people would have built onto the house, or put up a garage or a deck or *something*, but Carrick had left the empty land as knee-high grass, as if he wanted space between him and his neighbors.

Inside, there was just one bedroom, a tiny kitchen and bathroom and a living room that was barely big enough for a couch and a TV. The place didn't seem big enough to contain a man like Carrick. He glanced around sullenly. "Don't entertain much," he muttered by way of explanation. Then he flexed his left shoulder and winced.

That reminded me of my plan. "Sit down," I said. "I'm going to take care of your shoulders."

He turned and stared at me. "What?"

I showed him the little bottle of almond oil. "I'm going to massage you."

He made a face as if I'd suggested painting his toenails. "I don't need that."

"The hell you don't. I've felt your shoulders: they're like concrete. *Sit down.*"

He glared at me and I could see it in his eyes: the frustration mixed with barely-contained lust. I swallowed.

"Please," I said. "You've done so much for me. Let me do this one thing for you."

He kept glaring, the broad slabs of his pecs rising and falling under his white t-shirt as he drew in deep, slow breaths. I felt the mood shift. *What the hell are you doing,* his eyes asked.

I swallowed again and looked at him defiantly. *It's just a massage.*

He took off his cut and laid it carefully over the back of the couch. Then he grabbed the hem of his t-shirt and peeled it off. I stared at the tan ridges of his abs: God, every part of him was hard, chiseled by a hundred bar room brawls and a thousand hours twisting and leaning in the saddle.

And sex. Don't forget that. I could imagine him using all that coiled power in his midsection to lunge and thrust, to control my thrashing body. I followed the hem of the t-shirt as it rose over his chest. The cotton had to stretch almost to breaking point to clear his powerful shoulders.

I looked up and found his eyes challenging me. And that's when I realized what was going on in his head. He thought this something else. He thought this was me trying to seduce him, to drive him beyond the point of control.

"T—Turn around," I stammered. "Sit backwards on a chair."

He stared at me a second longer then silently turned around, grabbed a kitchen chair and straddled it. I stood there staring at his back, at the Hell's Princes tattoo and the network of thin, raised knife scars he'd picked up over the years. My mind was whirling. How did I tell him he'd gotten the wrong idea? I looked down at the bottle of oil in my hand. *Shit, what am I doing?!* But it was too late to back out now.

"You really know how to do this?" he muttered.

I swallowed. "Sure." And I meant it. I'd never massaged anyone before, but bodies are just complicated machines. I looked at his back and I could see where the muscles ran, where the tissue was stretched tight with worry and stress. It was just mechanics and pressure. I uncapped the bottle and squirted a stream of the amber liquid over his shoulders, watching it trickle down his back. *Just mechanics and pressure. That's all this is.*

Except...suddenly, I was second-guessing myself. Was he *right?!* *Was* I trying to seduce him? I wasn't like that! I didn't *have* any goddamn feminine wiles!

A little voice inside me laughed.

I watched the oil trickle further and further down his back. If I didn't act fast, it was going to stain his jeans. I took a shuddering breath, stepped forward and put my hands on him, my thumbs either side of the tiny shamrock tattoo.

I wasn't ready for how he felt. I'd pressed up against him on the bike enough times but palms and fingertips are a lot more sensitive. I could feel the softness of his skin and the hardness of the muscle beneath. He was so *solid,* so unshakably, unquestionably *there,* larger than life and hotly alive, all my fantasies made flesh. I slid my hands slowly up his back, the oil collecting and pooling along the tops of my fingers and thumbs. Behind my hands, I left him shining and glistening, the room's lone, weak bulb turning his muscles into a study of light and shadow.

He drew in his breath and I could feel his lungs fill beneath my palms. I gulped. I'd never been so in touch with another person. I swore I could feel each beat of his heart....

I glanced away to try to get myself together but as soon as I saw the couch, an image flashed into my head: me on my back, jeans balled around my ankles, him between my thighs....

Then my hands reached his shoulders and I could feel the pain and the tension. I dragged my mind back to what I was supposed to be doing. I'd started this with good intentions; I had to finish it. I pressed my thumbs into the muscles: God, he really *was* knotted up there. He felt like a hunk of rubber that's been twisted and twisted until it's as hard and unyielding as iron. I pressed hard and he groaned.

"Does that hurt?" I asked, worried.

"Yeah," he spat. Then, after a second, "Keep going."

Encouraged, I worked my thumbs outward, stretching him like dough. He groaned again. I dug in circles, kneading and pulling. At first, there was no change except for him occasionally wincing and tensing. But gradually, I felt things ease, almost imperceptibly at first but then faster and faster. The frozen rubber started to thaw, becoming pliant. It turned to taffy and then melted taffy.

"You're good at this," he muttered.

I smiled. "Thank you."

As I kept working at his muscles, something started to happen. As he unknotted and unwound, everything he'd been pushing down deep started to rise towards the surface. The silence in the room grew and grew. I could feel him getting ready to tell me. And I needed to hear it because I knew we were never going to get any closer until that happened. But I'd learned my lesson: I wasn't going to push him this time. I'd massage all night if I had to.

He'd saved me. Now I had to save him.

I dug my thumbs in and drew them slowly outward in circles and he suddenly took a deep lungful of air and said, "*Feck!*"

I froze. It was the most Irish I'd ever heard his voice, hard and dark and beautiful. Not quite the same as *fuck*. Softened for my benefit.

He closed his eyes. "When the club has a problem," he said, "I solve it." He opened his eyes and they met mine in the mirror. Clear blue, just like they'd been a decade before. Wanting *so much* to be that man again, without all this weighing on him. "Sometimes, it's just scaring people. Sometimes, it's a beating. And sometimes, I have to end someone."

For several seconds, the room was so quiet I barely dared to breathe.

"How many?" I whispered.

His eyes were still locked on mine. "Too many."

My hands were still locked on his shoulders. However hard I tried, I couldn't get them to move.

"Fucking say something," he grated.

I wanted to. But my mind was still spinning. I'd known it was something bad, but *this*.... I was trying and failing to square the tenderness I'd seen him show me with the violence he was describing.

I felt his body shift under my hands. He was about to get up. Disgusted at how I'd reacted, he was going to walk off and we'd never get this close again—

It was his eyes that decided me. The pain in them, the guilt. I didn't know what *evil* looked like: evil would be someone who did it for fun, or someone who hurt and killed and just plain didn't care. But I knew that wasn't Carrick. He carried the weight of everything he'd done. He was a soldier forced to fight, not a psychopath.

I slid my palms up to the top of his oiled shoulders and pressed down. It was ridiculous, given how big he was. He could have easily just muscled his way past me.

But he didn't. He just met my eyes in the mirror again: suspicious but with just a trace of hope.

"Who were they?" I asked, trying to keep my voice level. Then I shook my head. "No, wait..." I wasn't sure I wanted to know. "Did they...."

"Did they deserve it?" he finished for me.

I nodded.

He drew in a slow, shuddering breath. "All but one."

And I knew that was it: the secret beyond the secret. One killing, one particular job for the club that had been tearing him apart ever since he did it.

All I wanted to do was make him feel better. Without thinking, my hands slid forward over his shoulders, down his chest—

In one quick movement, he grabbed my wrists and whirled around, standing as he did it. The chair fell over with a crash and then we were standing there, both of us panting from the suddenness of it. Less than a foot separated our bodies.

I realized he was holding my hands high above my head, and swallowed.

"You don't want this," he told me savagely. "You think there's some light left in me: there isn't. Not for a long time. I'm not a good man, just because I saved you."

"Maybe—" I had to fight for breath and my heart was hammering in my chest. "Maybe that's *why* you saved me. Because you want to be again."

He shoved his face closer to mine. Close enough, almost, to kiss. "*You don't want this,*" he told me again. "You're fuckin' perfect. You deserve a good fuckin' life with a good fuckin' man. A nice place. *Kids.* I'm a long way past saving and you're not going to change me."

I opened my mouth to protest but he cut me off, the Irish thick in his voice. "Don't. *Don't.* 'Cos every time you open those lips I want to kiss you. Every time you speak, I want to carry you off somewhere.

Every time I look at you, I'm seeing us *together*." As the words washed over me, setting off scorching explosions deep inside, I saw how hard his body had gone, every muscle taut and straining with the effort of holding himself back. "I've destroyed so much, Annabelle. So fucking much." He squeezed my wrists in time with his words. "I *won't*. Destroy. You."

And before I could argue, he was gone, releasing my wrists and stalking away. "Sleep on the couch," he told me. And he strode into the bedroom and slammed the door behind him.

I was left there panting, trying to process everything that had happened. I knew now why he thought he was unsaveable, why he was sure he could never go back to being that man I'd first met. What if he was right? And how did I feel about him, now I knew what he'd done?

The only thing I knew for sure was, tonight had changed things forever. Now I knew the truth, we couldn't go on like this for even one more day: there was too much tension and not enough holding us back. Like those magnets I'd imagined back in the motel room, tomorrow we'd either snap together...or break apart for good.

22

CARRICK

I barely slept. I told myself it was because I was used to passing out on the couch but I knew I was kidding myself. The real reason was, the bed felt empty. There was this big, cold gap where Annabelle should have been.

I'd gotten used to her, after just one night.

When it was finally morning, I showered and dressed. But when I checked the couch, she was still asleep. She'd stripped down to her bra and panties and found the blanket and pillow I use when I crash out. I knew from experience that, with them, the couch was a lot more comfortable than my worn-out bed.

Her hair was spread out across the pillow, a blaze of color. In some places thick red locks shone and gleamed, in others the strands were spread so thin over the white cotton they looked like copper-colored smoke.

I crouched down to study her. Those silken lips I'd fantasized about so many times were slightly parted and she had a tiny frown on her face as if she was working on some problem in her dreams.

My stomach tightened. Was she trying to fix *me*?

I hadn't meant to tell her what I did. Her hands had just been so...*calming.* At first, I'd been convinced she was trying to tip me over the edge, to make me grab her. It had worked, too: I'd been rock hard and aching in my pants as soon as she started touching me. But as it went on, I'd felt something...*let go.* I couldn't remember ever feeling that relaxed. And then it had all just come spilling out.

I'd been dreading seeing her face when she found out I was a killer. In some ways, it had been worse than I'd thought; in some ways, better. She'd looked horrified, but it hadn't felt like it was aimed at *me.* More at what I'd done.

Which was bullshit, because they're the same thing. We *are* the things we've done. I'm a killer. Simple as.

As I studied her sleeping face, she frowned deeper. My heart sank. *You can't fix me! Stop trying!* But I knew it was useless. Just like when she'd been a kid, dragging me along the ground. She didn't know when to quit. And that made something rise and...*open* in my chest. It had been a long time since anyone had given a shit about me.

Telling her what I did had been hard...and horribly, horribly easy. Addictive, almost. I could imagine coming home to her each night and *talking.* I never talked but I could imagine it, with her. Getting all of the bad shit I'd done out, then sleeping peaceful as a baby in her arms. *Christ,* that sounded good....

She grumbled something in her sleep and rolled onto her back. The covers fell away, revealing her sleeping body down to just below her bra. I had a sudden urge to kiss her. God, it would be so *easy,* like slipping into a hot bath: a slow kiss on the lips to wake her up, then I'd work my way down her neck. We'd tumble around on the couch, still warm from her body, the blanket half on and half off us. The first time would be slow and gentle: morning sex. But then we'd go for a second round and it would get fast and dirty, her sitting astride me as I lifted her by the hips, or her bent over the arm of the couch....

I realized I was leaning towards her. My lips were only a few inches from hers.

I stood up. *You fuckin' idiot! What's wrong with you?* Sure, she was still deluding herself that I was some sort of good guy, or could become one, but I knew better. Even if she could accept what I did, could I really drag her into this life? And there was all the stuff she didn't know. The story that began when I was just a kid and ended by the side of a dark road with a gun in my hand. *That* I could never share with her.

I had to shut myself off. Last night had been a mistake. I had to focus on getting the Blood Spiders off her back and shutting down the auctions. Then she'd be free and, when I was sure she was safe, I'd convince her to head to Sacramento or maybe San Francisco. She'd fit in well in San Francisco.

I grabbed a frying pan and slammed it down on a burner. I knew I was doing the right thing but the thought of her leaving stung.

Behind me, I heard her stir. I forced my voice into a growl. "Bathroom's all yours."

I heard her get up. I knew she wanted to talk, to resolve all the stuff we'd started last night. I could imagine her wrapping the blanket around her shoulders and standing there, studying me, but I kept my back to her, not showing any weakness. *Stay cold. Shut yourself off.* That was the only way to get through this.

I heard her pad to the bathroom and then the shower started up. I fried some eggs, threw some bread in the toaster and brewed coffee. Then my phone rang.

"Get to the clubhouse," Mac told me. "Hunter's back."

I told him we'd be right there. I poured two mugs of coffee and was putting the eggs between slices of toast when Annabelle emerged. I faltered for a second when I saw her. She was wearing a sea-green tank top that made all that soft, pale skin and red hair look all the more intense. Damn it, why did she have to be so beautiful?

I pressed a sandwich into one of her hands, a mug of coffee into the other. "Drink that, then eat on the way. We gotta go."

She nodded, staring up at me with big eyes over the rim of her mug. She was being patient, giving me time instead of stubbornly pushing me. I didn't think that was possible, for her. She was changing, trying to meet me halfway. Maybe, if I just talked to her....

No. Maybe she could change but I couldn't. I stared right back at her and sipped my own coffee. *Stay cold. Lock her out.* It was the smart thing to do, the only thing to do.

So why was it so hard?

Mac was waiting outside the clubhouse when we roared up. "We're just waiting for Ox," he told me. I saw him glance at Annabelle as she climbed off the bike, then look questioningly back at me. She'd spent the night at my place, after all....

I gave a minute shake of my head.

He looked at me as if I was insane. Then his expression changed to—

Fuck you, Mac. I don't need your pity. I climbed off my bike and turned away, pretending I was watching the gate for any sign of Ox. But being mad at him felt wrong, just like staying away from Annabelle felt wrong. We never used to fight. Not until she came along.

To my relief, Scooter ambled over. But it wasn't me he wanted to talk to.

He came to a stop beside Annabelle and looked her up and down suspiciously. "Last night," he told her, "I stripped Hunter's bike down. Just to prove you wrong."

Annabelle blinked at him, flushing.

"I don't know how you knew," Scooter said, "but the timing *was* off." He crossed his arms and stared at her grumpily for a few seconds, then seemed to make up his mind. "You want to give me a hand fixing it?"

Annabelle's eyes lit up like a kid's on Christmas morning. Scooter led her off towards the workshop.

I heard the gate rumble open and turned to see Ox finally arrive. Mac nodded towards the clubhouse. "Let's do this."

Moments later, we were sitting around the table as Hunter told us what he'd learned. "The Blood Spiders are dealing coke. They have an old sawmill outside Teston where they cut and repackage it. Only three guards. Their pres, Hay, stops by there once a week."

"How the hell did you find all that out?" asked Ox.

"Their clubhouse has a meeting room too. Gets real stuffy, so they open a skylight to let some air in. I was lying on the roof next to it. Heard everything they said."

I shook my head in wonder. I could imagine him lying there, patient and motionless as any army sniper, soaking up every word. His skills would be scary if he wasn't on our side.

"Hay will be there today in about two hours' time," said Hunter. "We should move."

We took seven men, enough to ensure we outnumbered Hay and the guards but not so many that we couldn't be quiet. We rode in a pack, silently eating up the miles, all of us brooding on what needed to be done. There's no better feeling in the world to me than riding but something felt wrong. Something was missing. I was riding next to Ox and he wasn't happy either, his mouth turned down in a scowl I didn't often see. Any Blood Spider who got in his way was going to have a very bad day.

Every few miles, I had to loosen my fingers on the handlebars because I was crushing them too tight. I couldn't help it. I kept thinking about how Hay had put Annabelle up on stage, stripped her down to her underwear and tried to sell her. Now I was finally going to see the bastard again.

Hunter led us to the sawmill and showed us a side road where we could hide our bikes. We crept the final hundred yards on foot, approaching over the crest of a hill. The sawmill sat beside a river, a crumbling red brick place with holes in the roof. If I hadn't known better, I would have thought it was abandoned.

Hunter crept down for a closer look and reported there were only three guards, just as he'd promised. Twenty minutes later, Hay rode up on his Harley. My chest tightened as soon as I saw him, the rage boiling up inside me, but I forced myself to stay calm. A beat-up car pulled up behind Hay and his blond-haired VP got out. I was satisfied to see that one of his hands was bandaged from where I'd hit him with the chain. It must have really dented his pride to be driving instead of riding.

We waited until everyone went inside, then burst in. I was the first one through the door, smashing it open so hard that it knocked the guard behind it flying. I brought a fist up under the chin of the second guard, knocking him on his ass. Meanwhile, Mac and the others burst through the rear door. One punch from Ox's ham-sized fist and the final guard went down like a puppet with its strings cut.

That left Hay and his VP. I stormed over to them and they both backed up against the wall, faces going white. I gave a low growl and—

Mac sprinted forward and got in front of me. "I got this," he said quickly. "Back off."

For a second, I just stood there panting, frowning at him in confusion.

He glanced down.

I followed his gaze and saw I was holding Caorthannach up and ready to fire, the barrels pointed right at Hay. Shocked, I slowly lowered the shotgun and nodded. Mac slapped me on the shoulder and I stepped back to let him interrogate Hay. *Jesus, I was about to— What's wrong with me?* I never normally lost control like that.

"Why did you come to Haywood Falls?" demanded Mac. "Why did you come after the girl?"

Hay was sweating and pale, his eyes flicking between Mac and me. "It's not us," he said.

Mac just glared at him.

"It's *not!* We don't give a shit, she's just one girl, nothing special—"

The rage bloomed inside me again, a silent explosion. I gripped Caorthannach's stock, fighting to control myself.

"Look," said Hay desperately, "We can work something out. Give her back and I'll cut you in."

I could feel the chains of my self control snapping tight and heating, glowing cherry-red.

"You want a girl for your clubhouse, I'll get you one," said Hay. "I'll get you two. Just give me the redhead."

And suddenly, I lost it. I marched forward, shouldered Mac out of the way and swung my shotgun up until the barrels were pressed against Hay's forehead. "I should have done this in the bar, you sick son of a bitch," I told him. My fingers tightened on both of the gun's triggers at once—

The cold barrel of a pistol pressed against my forehead. I glanced left to see Mac standing there. "Back down," he told me. His eyes were flickering between fury and sadness.

"This bastard deserves to die!" I snapped.

Mac's gun didn't move. "Yes he does. But we need to talk to him."

I looked back at the sweating, terrified Hay. "Fuck that."

"I am your president," said Mac. His voice was low but it filled every square inch of the sawmill. "And I am telling you to *put your gun down.*"

A breath. I stared into Hay's eyes and thought of how terrified Annabelle had been. Another breath. I thought of how she'd looked at me, when I told her what I did. How she'd look at me when I came home, if I told her I'd killed Hay. A third breath—

I lowered the shotgun. Mac's gun eased away from my head. I stepped to the side, eyes on the floor. If I looked at Hay again, I knew I wouldn't be able to control myself.

Mac got right in Hay's face. "Talk fast," he said. "You said it wasn't you who came after Annabelle. What the fuck did you mean?"

Hay's voice shook as he spoke. "We would have let it go! But he wants her bad. Keeps going on about her red hair."

"*Who?*" snapped Mac.

"Volos! That psycho who bought her!"

Mac and I exchanged stunned looks.

"So tell him to go fuck himself," said Mac.

Hay shook his head. "You don't know this guy. He's a first grade *fucking* nut job. You get in his way and they never find your body. Everyone's scared shitless of him. And he's got money, serious money. He picks out the best girls and sells them to some guy in Europe. He's *connected.* Said he'd bring the law down on the club if we didn't get the girl back—maybe even the feds."

And suddenly, it all made sense. The Blood Spiders were just hired thugs. It was Volos who'd been pushing them. And if I'd gone ahead and killed Hay, we would never have known. The shock made some of the anger drain away and what I'd done started to sink in: not just nearly killing Hay but defying my president. I looked at Mac just as he started to lay it out for Hay. I might do *intimidating* better than anyone, but I'm a blunt object. When it comes to fear through razor-sharp words, there's no one better than Mac.

"The auctions stop *now*," said Mac. "We already burned your bar. You run another auction, we'll burn everything you have. We know about this place and the coke dealing. You want your shipments to start going missing?" He leaned closer. "We got more men than you. We got more guns than you. We will dedicate our lives to *fucking you up*. And when every last shred of your club is gone? I will lock you in a room with Irish and let him take you apart."

Hay blanched. Swallowed. He looked around for support, but his VP was being held at gunpoint and all his guards were out for the count. He finally wilted under Mac's glare. "Okay!" he said at last. "The coke's worth more to us than the auctions. But what about Volos?"

"You tell him it's over. Annabelle stays with us. And if he has a problem with it, he can come see me," Mac told him.

We filed out. Mac and I trailed behind everyone else and walked in silence all the way back to our bikes, not even looking at each other. I kept replaying the scene in my head. What the hell had gotten into me?

I stopped beside my bike and turned to Mac. "I'm sorry," I said.

He stared deep into my eyes. Mac was always so damn good at reading people—that's what made him such a good leader. "You ever do that again," he told me, "I'll put you down. And then I'll take your patch."

I nodded. "I know." Then I shook my head. "I don't know what got into me."

Mac sighed. "I do." He grabbed me and pulled me into a hug, holding me tight and slapping my back. "And you'll figure it out too."

He got onto his bike and roared off, leaving me alone.

I swung my leg over my bike and settled in the saddle, but didn't start the engine. That was the second time I'd defied Mac in as many days. Yet he and the club were the most important thing in the world to me....

Until now.

That's when it hit me. I'd been fighting so hard to stay away from Annabelle because I knew I couldn't change. But she'd *already* changed me. She'd gotten deep inside me, right down in my soul, and I couldn't get her out no matter how hard I tried. Without her, there was no way I would have lost control like that and no way I would have defied Mac.

But there was no way I would have left Hay alive, either. It was thinking of Annabelle that had stopped me pulling the trigger. She was becoming my conscience.

Keeping my distance from her wasn't an option anymore. Things couldn't stay as they were.

I started my bike and gunned the throttle.

I knew what I had to do.

23

ANNABELLE

I was in heaven. Scooter had shown me how to disassemble the engine and now it lay in gleaming pieces around me as I sat cross-legged on the floor. He'd been cautious at first, maybe having second thoughts about letting a woman into his precious workshop. But the more we talked, the more he relaxed. The language we talked wouldn't have been intelligible to anyone else: it was pressures and ratios, cycles and strokes. He had the knowledge but I had the enthusiasm and I soaked up everything he told me like a sponge. By noon, he trusted me enough to leave me tinkering while he wandered into town to get us a couple of sandwiches.

And yet despite being exactly where I wanted to be, despite all the wondrous, shining parts around me, I couldn't fully focus on the engine. I couldn't stop thinking about Carrick and what he'd told me. Could I be with a man who did things like that? A criminal whose job it was to scare, to hurt, even to kill? I remembered what Mom had told me: did the angel outweigh the demon?

As the hours passed, my thoughts changed. *They've been gone too long. What if he's been shot? What if he's—*

I closed my eyes for a second, trying to push that thought away. What made it worse was knowing that any danger he was in was because of me. I felt something hard between my fingers and realized I was stroking the shamrock necklace.

I wished I'd asked Mom how to cope with this part of it. I tried to imagine never seeing him again and couldn't. Just the thought of it made my chest ache. I remembered the feel of his body against mine, when he'd first rescued me at the auction. The way he'd told me I was priceless, his tenderness all the sweeter because he was normally so gruff. The way he'd pushed me away so hard, just to protect me....

And suddenly, I knew.

It wasn't that I didn't care about what he'd done. The violence sickened me but...it was part of him. The club was part of him. The demon came along with the angel.

And the angel was worth it.

At that moment, I heard the roar of a bike. My heart leapt and I ran for the door but I didn't even make it out of the workshop before Carrick pulled up right outside and jumped off his bike.

For a heartbeat, we just looked at each other. Long enough for me to see in his eyes that the battle was over...and for him to see in mine that I wanted him, demon and angel together.

Then we ran at each other, our bodies slammed together and his lips came down on mine.

24

ANNABELLE

I was panting. I couldn't stop panting. It was the adrenaline of finally kissing him after all this time: we'd kiss and then come up for air and I'd barely have time to gulp in oxygen before we kissed again.

His lips were demanding, forcing me open, as strong and determined as he was in everything else. But my lips were at least as desperate as his, open to drink in as much of him as possible, then closing to kiss him back, my softness against his hardness. He growled low in his throat, stroked both hands through my hair and kissed down into me, tilting my head back. His tongue traced my lips and then sought me out, finding my tongue and dancing with it, and I moaned. I'd been dreaming of this kiss for years and it was even better than I'd imagined.

Those big hands that had refused to touch me for so long swept under my ass and cupped me and I let out a shriek as he hoisted me effortlessly into the air. He pulled me close, my legs wrapping around his waist, my breasts mashing against his chest, and I went weak. His hands stayed on my ass as he kissed me and kissed me, squeezing and kneading. His whole body was tight and hard with lust: I stroked down the backs of his arms and I could feel every vein throbbing, every muscle tensed. His heart was thumping against my breast, his breathing as fast and urgent as mine.

He broke the kiss and looked around the workshop. I let out an audible gulp when I realized he was looking for a place to fuck me.

I followed his gaze and I could see it running through his head. The stool? Too unsteady with two of us on it. The floor? Covered in shining engine parts.

He looked at the workbench. Then walked us over to it and set me carefully down on the edge. Without speaking, he grabbed the hem of my tank top and yanked it up to my armpits.

I was reeling from how fast it was all happening, after so long waiting. The sexual tension had been winding tighter and tighter, storing up energy, and now it was all being released. I glanced over his shoulder. "*Door!*" I squeaked.

He glanced behind him. The workshop had a metal shutter-style door big enough to drive a car through and it was still open. I could see clear across the compound to the clubhouse and members were strolling around in the sunshine outside.

Carrick glanced back to me and there was such a melting look of sexual hunger in his eyes, I actually thought he was going to shake his head, too turned on to stop, and just fuck me with half the club able to see.

But then he turned from me, stalked over to the door in three big paces, grabbed the handle and hurled it down towards the floor. He didn't even wait for it to close. The clattering of the door drowned out even the thump of his heavy boots as he came back to me. He pushed between my legs just as the door slammed into the ground with a sound like the end of the world. And in the soft silence that followed he stood there, hips between my knees, body hulking over me as I sat, and he spoke to me.

"I'm going to kiss you. All over. Every inch of that soft skin. Your shoulders, right down your back, your ass...everywhere. I'm going to slip my fingers deep inside you and feel you as you come."

I let out a high little groan.

"But right now," he told me, "I've got to see you."

He moved back just a little, grabbed the tank top that was still up under my arms and hauled it over my head and off.

With the door closed, the only light came through a skylight, a solid pillar of sunlight that lanced diagonally down through the darkness and lit up the workbench where I sat. It bathed my skin like a spotlight.

Carrick gave a low growl of satisfaction. He drank in the sight of me and then stepped close again, running his palms up my sides and then over my bra. I swallowed. I knew he'd already seen me naked, when I was changing into the dress, but—

And then he bent and kissed the top of each breast, his lips firm against their softness, and I gasped and forgot my nerves. His mouth felt so good there, the pleasure crackling across my skin and throbbing through my entire chest.

Then his hands went behind my back and my bra suddenly went loose. He drew it off my shoulders and I was topless before I knew what was happening, nipples throbbing at their sudden exposure. But before I could even catch my breath, his mouth was on me, engulfing me, tongue swirling over my hardening bud and the soft pink around it. I arched my back and groaned, feet twisting in the air behind his back.

He buried both hands in my hair, stroking through it, fingers toying with the strands, as he bent and licked at my breasts, alternating between them. One second, his tongue would sweep across a nipple or swirl around the edge of my areolae. The next, his mouth would be gone and the cool shock of the air on my slickened skin made me catch my breath. The pleasure was already climbing inside me, spiraling higher, filling me.

He stepped back and shook his head as if to say, *enough.* He reached for the belt of my jeans.

But *I* shook my head, too. I had to see *him.* I pushed at his cut and he got the idea, pulling it off and dropping it on the bench next to us. Then together we hauled his white t-shirt up and over his head.

He stepped close again and now it was skin on skin, him hard and tan, me soft and pale. My breasts pillowed against his pecs and both of us drew in our breath.

"You're filthy," he whispered, stroking his thumb across my cheek and showing me the dark smear.

I realized my hands were oily from working on the engine, and that I must have rubbed my face at some point. *God, I must look a mess!* I flushed.

He grinned a wolfish grin—the first time I'd seen him smile since he'd rescued me. "I fuckin' love it when you blush," he told me, and kissed me again, hot and deep. I groaned and wrapped my arms around his body, knowing I was probably leaving dark handprints on the muscles of his back and not caring.

We only managed to keep the kiss going for a few panting, frantic seconds before he grabbed for the belt of my jeans again. I pressed my palms into the wood of the workbench and lifted my ass to help him, and my jeans and panties slid down my legs. He dragged my sneakers and socks off, too, and suddenly I was naked.

He didn't let my legs go right away. He captured my ankles in one big hand and hoisted them high in the air, then kissed all the way down the outside of one leg to my hip. Then, as if he couldn't wait any more, he let me down and knocked my knees apart, stepping between them. He reached for the belt of his jeans, both of us staring down at the same spot, our heads almost touching. I watched him slide the buckle free and pop the buttons one by one. Then the jeans fell and he hooked his black boxer briefs down—

I swallowed as his cock came into view. A thick, long shaft with a perfect arrow-shaped head, soft curls of black hair around the root. It brushed my inner thigh and I melted inside as I felt the heat of it, the solid, loaded, weight of it.

He grabbed my naked hips and pulled me to the very edge of the workbench. As I slid forward, my knees had to open wider to pass his hips and I felt myself flower open.

He reached down between us, warm fingers stroking through the copper curls of hair and then over the lips of my sex—God, I was soaking. "I kept thinking about what you'd look like," he told me, gazing down. "You're perfect."

I watched as he rolled the condom on and kicked his boots and jeans away. Then his hands were on my inner thighs, steadying me, and he was pressing forward....

I threw my head back as he touched me, the heat of him throbbing through me. He glided up and down my lips a few times and then drove in. My head came forward: I had to see, had to watch as his cock spread me, breached me—*God*—gliding up into me—

I clutched at his back, fingers digging into his shoulders as he filled me. My knees squeezed tight against his sides and for a few seconds we just stayed there, panting at the feeling. I ran my hands up and over his shoulders and down his chest, wanting to feel every inch of him, my fingers drawing oily marks on his chest. Every time I looked down and saw his muscled, tanned hips tight between mine, a new burst of heat exploded in my chest and sank down to my groin. I'd imagined this so many times but the reality was so, so much better.

Each perfect silken slide sent a new wave of silver pleasure rippling outward from my groin. His size stretched me just right, both of us catching our breath as he went deep. It was slow at first but the rhythm built quickly until he was slamming into me.

My legs rose and wrapped around him, my heels at the backs of his knees. With each thrust, tight waves of pleasure crashed outward and then contracted down into a glowing, white-hot center, quickly slipping out of control. My hands frantically searched his back, unable to get enough of him, sliding over every hard muscle from his shoulders all the way down to his tight, thrusting ass. I could feel myself rushing towards the edge....

His mouth came to my ear, lips nuzzling me before he said, "I dreamed about doing this," he muttered, never slowing. "Looking into your eyes when you come."

The accent, the words, the heat of his breath in my ear...all of it took me closer. And then he pulled his head back just enough to look into my eyes. When I saw the clear blue there and that hunger to watch me, it was too much: I let out a cry and shot over the edge, spasming around him. With two more hard thrusts he buried himself and I felt his ass contract as he shot inside me.

When I could breathe again, he lifted me and laid me gently down on the floor, knocking engine parts out of the way with his feet to clear a space. The concrete should have been shockingly cold but its coolness was exactly what our heated bodies needed. We cuddled and kissed, rolling around, getting filthy and not caring at all. We only stopped when I rolled on top and Carrick suddenly cursed and half sat up.

"What?" I asked in panic.

He dug under him, pulled a shining metal gear from under his ass and tossed it across the room. I laughed and, for the first time ever, I heard him laugh, too.

25

CARRICK

Annabelle's eyes bulged as she gazed towards Ox. I'd never seen eyes so wide.

"Trust me," I said under my breath. "It's meant to be that big. He's a big guy."

She shook her head in wonder. "But how can *one man*...it's so much *meat!*"

It *was* a lot of meat. The waitress had to use both hands to set the platter in front of him. It's not often you see a double rack of ribs. But, as I said, Ox is a big guy: *big* big, not fat-big. And this was his traditional dinner when we came here.

We were at the diner in Haywood Falls, about fifteen members plus a few old ladies and hangers-on. The meals had become a weekly tradition for a year or so, now. An actual meal made a change from the drunken parties at the clubhouse and Mac thought it was good to show our faces around the town and demonstrate we were the good guys, or at least not the bad guys. It was a respectable, family place and the owners had been tight-lipped the first time we'd showed up, but Mac had promised to kick the ass of anyone who caused trouble. We'd been nothing but good customers and heavy tippers and now they welcomed us.

Annabelle and I sat side by side near the middle of the big table, with Mac, Hunter and Ox facing us. It was two days since the sawmill...and since I'd finally gotten together with Annabelle. I was in heaven: the sex was the best part but waking up each morning to find her wrapped in my arms came a close second. I'd never slept so good. We *talked,* which was all new to me. I'd even gone down to the lake with her and spent a lazy few hours just walking around, soaking up the summer heat, though with her pale skin we'd had to stick to the shadier paths. It was idyllic.

True, there was stuff I hadn't told her, the stuff from my past that was too toxic to tell anyone. But I'd convinced myself that was okay.

She'd insisted on ordering a huge chocolate milkshake. When it arrived, it came with two straws. I stared at it, confused.

"Like in the movies," she explained. "We share it."

I looked at her. Looked at Mac. He was trying not to laugh.

"Um..." I said.

Annabelle thrust a straw at me.

I felt my ears heating up. Fuckin' hell, was I *blushing?* I fingered the straw as if it was an unexploded bomb and glanced across the table again. Now Hunter was close to losing it, too, and he *never* laughs.

"Go on," said Annabelle. She lowered her head and drank, then stopped. "It's *romantic,"* she told me.

I looked across the table again. Ox was silently quaking, too, all three of them loving it. A whole stream of curses flew through my head....

But I couldn't refuse her anything. I lowered my head and drank the damn milkshake, with my brothers almost busting a gut, they were laughing so hard. I heard at least one of them snap a picture of the notorious, stone-cold Irish sharing a milkshake.

But it was worth it. When she looked up at me with those moss-green eyes and smiled, it was worth it. When we'd finished, she grabbed her straw. "Souvenir," she said. "Our first date."

I sighed and rolled my eyes. She was really into the romantic stuff —maybe because, from what she'd told me, she'd missed out on it all in high school. It was stupid, of course. It was only a damn milkshake.

When no one was looking, though, I grabbed my straw, and stuffed it into the pocket of my cut. Just in case she lost hers. Then I hooked an arm around her waist and pulled her onto my knee. "When we get back to my place," I whispered in her ear, "How about—"

There was a crash of breaking glass and Annabelle screamed.

For a few seconds, there was total panic. What started as one scream from Annabelle grew and grew, spreading through the restaurant. Some people were jumping to their feet, others were ducking down in the seats. I looked from left to right, trying to figure out what the fuck had just happened.

The window near the end of our table had a fist-sized hole in it. Annabelle was holding her face. Drinks had been knocked over and were soaking across the tablecloth and trickling onto the floor. Three of the members down near the window were on their feet, guns drawn, trying to see out of the window. The guns were what had started most of the screaming: families were quickly deserting their tables and moving towards the exit. Others were seeking shelter, thinking it was a sniper. But the hole in the window was too big for a bullet.

"Let me see," I told Annabelle, but she had both hands up to her face. "It's okay," I said, forcing my voice to be gentle. "Let me see."

She cautiously took her hand away and my heart twisted as I saw the long slash across her cheek. It didn't look deep but I wasn't surprised she'd screamed. Another inch and whatever it was would have taken her eye out.

I stared at the table, still trying to figure it out. That's when I saw the rock. The white paper wrapped around it blended in with the tablecloth: that's why I hadn't seen it, at first. Someone had hurled it through the window and either window glass or one of the smashed glasses on the table had hit Annabelle.

The owners of the diner raced over. Mac was on his feet instantly, trying to calm them down and snapping at the guys who'd drawn their guns to put them away. But the damage was done: half the restaurant had cleared out. Mac started counting out bills to pay for the window and the trouble, but we wouldn't be welcome back here. All his careful work to keep the town on our side had just been undone.

I grabbed the rock and unwrapped the paper from it. A handwritten note, just one sentence.

Give up the bitch or I'll tear your club apart.

26

CARRICK

"How do we find the bastard?" I snarled as I marched into the meeting room. I was the last to arrive—I'd stopped in with Annabelle at the medical center.

"She okay?" asked Mac.

I nodded. The doctor had dressed the cut but it wouldn't need stitches. "It's Volos," I said savagely. "He wants her. He's not getting her. So how do we find him?" My voice shook with rage.

Mac put his hand on my shoulder. "Easy, brother." He looked me in the eye. "Damn right, he's not getting her." He looked around the table and everyone nodded. "We'll protect her."

I grimly nodded my thanks but inside I was knotted up. I'd thought this was all over after we confronted Hay at the sawmill. Now the club was taking the heat again and it was all down to me rescuing Annabelle. I didn't regret what I'd done, not for a second...but I wished it was me catching the fallout, not them.

Mac turned to Hunter. "I talked to Sheriff Harris. He's looking into Volos for us but he didn't sound hopeful. You have any luck with your friends?"

Hunter still had some contacts from his bounty-hunting days. "Guy's a ghost," he said. "Most of the people I called thought he was just a myth. No one knows his real name. People agree he's powerful, though: money and connections." He looked between our faces. "Being blunt: we're small time, compared to him."

There was a round of cursing. Great. We'd made ourselves a brand new enemy. I almost wished for the Blood Spiders back: at least we knew where to find them. And however much I'd wanted to kill Hay, at least he was just a scumbag crook. Volos...he thought he *owned* Annabelle, that he'd bought her body and soul. That made me want to rip his throat out.

"Everyone be careful," said Mac. "We don't know what this psycho will do, once he realizes we're not giving her up. Nobody rides alone. Keep your eyes open." He banged the gavel and I went to find Annabelle.

I found her with Scooter in the workshop, wheeling out Hunter's rebuilt bike. We all watched as he climbed on and gave it a test run around the compound, then nodded approvingly. Annabelle grinned like a proud mom but I could see the fear she was trying to hide. She'd thought this whole thing was over and now it had found us again. I felt a wave of deep, protective rage wash through me. I stalked over and pulled her to me, wrapping my arms around her and kissing the top of her head. No way was he ever going to hurt her again. No *way*.

Somehow, I had to find a way to end this. And I had to do it without putting the rest of the club at risk.

27

CARRICK

"You want to *what?*" I asked slowly, sipping my coffee.

"Ride. I'm learning all about bikes but I've never actually ridden one."

I scratched at my stubble, still half-asleep. Despite the comforting press of Annabelle's body, I'd had a lousy night's sleep. I'd kept waking and pacing the house, peeking out of the windows for any sign of trouble. What if Volos had found out where I lived?

It was the first bad night's sleep I'd had since we'd gotten together. *I used to be like this all the time. Did I always feel this bad?* I was starting to realize what a mess I'd been, before I knew her. Now, I couldn't do without her. Part of me hated the idea of letting her loose on a Harley. But all of me knew how good riding felt. I couldn't deny her that.

Plus, ever since the diner, the fear had come back into her eyes. She'd thought she'd escaped Volos and now the psycho was back. This was about more than just learning a new skill: I figured it was her way of taking control.

"Guys'll be weird about it," I warned her. Outlaws aren't the most progressive bunch. Women ride on the back of bikes, not in the saddle.

"I don't mean *be a biker* or join the club or anything. I just mean learning to ride. I just want to know what it feels like."

I sighed. "You've gotta do exactly what I say," I warned, trying to kid myself I had some shred of control over the situation.

She nodded obediently and grinned. I nodded *okay* and then sighed again. How was it that I could snarl and make a whole roomful of muscled badasses back down, but a red-haired girl who only came up to my shoulder could wrap me around her little finger?

~

At the compound, I started to have second thoughts. She looked so small, on my bike. I jammed the helmet on her head, feeling like a worried mom. "*Slow,*" I growled. "Don't do anything I don't tell you to do."

She nodded silently, eager but breathing fast with nerves.

I slid into the saddle behind her. There was some good-natured chuckling from the members who were watching and I gave them my best scowl.

It was the first time I'd ever ridden on the back. It felt *weird,* not being in control of where we were going. *This must be what it's like for Annabelle.*

There were advantages, though. My groin was pressed right up against the warm swells of her denim-covered ass. I felt myself harden immediately. Then she started the bike up and squirmed a little in the saddle as the vibrations throbbed through her, and that made it even better. *Maybe this isn't so bad.*

"*Slow,*" I reminded her. "Okay, put the stand up. Take a minute, get the feel of it." I helped her, balancing the bike with my feet, but I barely needed to. Within just a few seconds of swaying, she'd got the big machine's balance point. "Now feed her a little throttle," I said. "Just ease her out."

Her pale hand twisted the throttle and we started to creep jerkily forward. I could feel the tension in her body: arms rigid, spine stiff. It took me back to my first time. But by the time I'd guided her through a few big, lazy turns, looping around the clubhouse and Mom's trailer, she was starting to relax and the bike was responding to her. "Now a little faster," I told her.

That's when things started to go wrong. She had an instinctive feel for the machine but she hadn't yet developed the muscles you need to wrestle a big bike back into line when it misbehaves. We suddenly found ourselves weaving unsteadily right towards the workshop. Annabelle let out a wail of fright.

I put my hands over hers and used my bulk to bring us back in line, then eased her hand off the throttle and slowed us to a stop. Annabelle was panting a little. "Sorry. I thought I had it."

I *shh-ed* her and brushed her hair back from her face so I could kiss her neck. "You *do* have it. You're a natural. You just need to build up the strength to go with that big brain."

She flushed. "I don't have a big brain," she muttered.

"Are you kidding? You're the smartest person I've ever met. You know more about mechanical stuff than I ever will. Scooter's impressed and he doesn't impress easily. And you'll get this, too." I kissed her again. "I believe in you."

She nodded silently. Then, as I climbed off the bike, "Carrick?"

I turned back to her.

"I believe in you too."

I stood there staring at her for a second, unsure what to say. But at that second, Mac burst out of the clubhouse and yelled at us to follow. Other members flooded out after him: the whole club. I quickly climbed onto the front of my bike as Annabelle scooched back to make room. "What's going on?" I yelled.

"The warehouse!" shouted Mac. "It's burning down!"

28

ANNABELLE

Carrick had explained how the warehouse was the club's one legitimate business, a place where they sold cheap t-shirts and jeans. The first job of a Prospect was usually to pull a few shifts there, with local teenagers making up the rest of the workforce. True, they used the profits to cover up their shadier business of running guns, but in itself it was a genuine money-making enterprise and popular with the locals: everyone living within the town was given a discount and it provided some of their kids with jobs. It had been Mac's idea and he was rightly proud of it.

So when we pulled up outside, my heart sank into my feet.

Tongues of flame were leaping up between the sheets of metal that formed the roof. Thick white smoke billowed out of the doorway. Cardboard cartons of clothes were strewn on the ground, some scorched and smoldering. Every few moments, a Prospect ran out of the smoke, threw down another box and ran back inside. They'd gotten all the civilian workers out of there: four teenage girls were standing terrified a safe distance away.

"*FUCK!*" snapped Mac. He jumped off his bike. "Where's the fire service?"

Tailor, one of the Prospects, shook his head. "We called, but—" he broke off as coughs wracked his body. "They haven't showed," he managed, wheezing.

Mac cursed and ran inside. "Everybody save what you can!" he yelled.

Carrick started forward but then turned and grabbed me. "You stay here."

I shook my head. "No way. You've all done so much for me. Let me help!"

He started to argue so I just dodged around him and ran for the door. Inside, the place was *big:* rows and rows of shelves all laden with piles of clothes. The fire had started on one side and was spreading fast: more than half the stuff that was on display was gone, but the storeroom at the back was still intact and that was where the Prospects were grabbing stuff from.

Carrick ran up behind me and grabbed my arm. "Get out of here!"

I pulled my arm out of his grip. "No! Please: let me do this." I looked up into his eyes. "*Please.*"

He huffed and I saw that protective need in his eyes, the look that made me warm inside. But there was something else there, too: respect. "Stay *right beside me,*" he said.

I nodded. We ran to the storeroom and I grabbed a carton of t-shirts. Carrick grabbed one under each arm and we turned, only to almost run into other members coming in the door. We squeezed past and ran outside, dumped the cartons and went back for more, but now *we* had to wait for people coming out. Everyone was spending all their time running from the door of the warehouse to the storeroom at the very back....

I stopped running and narrowed my eyes. In my head, the army of leather-clad bikers became oil in a too-narrow pipe. *Inefficient.*

I grabbed Mac as he raced past. "Mac!"

He spun to face me, incredulous. "*What?* I'm a little busy!"

"We need to make a human chain. It'll be quicker. We'll save more of the stock."

Mac stared at me, eyes blazing with anger. I got why he was pissed: the warehouse was important. But why was he pissed at—

Then I got it. It wasn't a coincidence that this place had caught fire, the day after Volos's warning. I felt like I was going to throw up. *This is all my fault. I brought this down on them.*

I swallowed. "It'll be quicker," I said again, my voice thin.

Mac stared at me a second longer...and then nodded. "Make a line!" he yelled to the others. "Pass the boxes out!"

I shoved my way into the line as it formed, more determined than ever to help. There were tears in my eyes and not just from the smoke. Carrick put his arm around me and gave me a reassuring squeeze which helped, but my guts were still churning with guilt.

We started passing the cartons of clothes along the chain, working as fast as we could. Soon, we had a continuous flow going: my hands were never empty for more than a second. We worked like that for several minutes as the flames crept closer and closer and then: "Enough!" yelled Mac. "Everybody out!"

He herded us all out the door, staying behind to make sure no one was left behind, then joined us in the fresh, clean air. We all stood there, hunched over and coughing painful, rasping coughs. Carrick found my hand and squeezed it and I squeezed back. Mac caught my eye...and nodded his thanks. He even looked a little guilty for snapping at me. But that didn't make me feel better: *he's right to be pissed at me. This is all my fault!*

At that moment, a fire truck pulled up, its crew cursing as they jumped out. "What took you so long?" Mac yelled, then descended into coughing again.

The firefighter in charge looked both pissed and defensive. "We got the call," he said. "Then we got another one from the state police, saying they'd caught you trying to burn your own place down, and there *was* no fire."

"Sonofabitch," muttered Mac.

I was reeling, too. *Volos.* He'd tried to ensure the fire would burn as long as possible. Either he really did know people in the state police, or he'd convincingly faked the call—neither was a good sign.

The firefighters went to work and quickly brought the fire under control but the stock left inside was ash and the building was a burned-out wreck. Between the efforts of the Prospects and the human chain, we'd managed to salvage maybe half the stock but the club had still lost tens of thousands of dollars...maybe more.

Then it got worse. Sheriff Harris pulled up and headed straight for Mac. He pulled him to one side, but I managed to overhear some of the conversation. "Arson?" was the first word out of the sheriff's mouth.

"Yeah," said Mac bitterly. "But we can't say that. The Feds would come snooping around. Write it up as an accident."

"You won't be able to claim on the insurance," said the sheriff. "The investigator will spot the signs—hell, I can smell the gasoline from here. They'll know someone burned it down."

"I know," growled Mac. "We won't claim."

Shit. This could bankrupt the club.

"This ain't good," said Sheriff Harris, looking at the gathering crowd. "Everybody's still freaked out about what happened at the diner. I got questions from the State boys about what happened on the highway. I'll keep looking into this Volos asshole for you, but you guys gotta stay off the radar or I can't protect you."

Mac slapped him on the shoulder and walked off. I really felt for him. Carrick carried the weight of all the bad shit he'd done but Mac had the future of the whole club on his shoulders.

Carrick slipped an arm around me. "You did good," he told me. "You helped us save a lot of stuff."

But none of it would have been burned if it hadn't been for me. If Carrick hadn't rescued me, if the club hadn't protected me...

I looked around at the Prospects, at the members, at the teenagers who worked there. Mac was reassuring them he'd cover their wages until they reopened, but now their parents were beginning to arrive, angrily pulling their kids into their cars. They'd never let them work for the club again. The club's reputation was in tatters: no one believed the fire was an accident, not when an MC was involved. And it felt like they were all looking at me: the MC, the civilians, even the firefighters. Was I imagining it, or did they know this was somehow my fault?

Carrick must have picked up on my mood. For a guy who pretended to be gruff and unfeeling, he was scary good at reading me. "C'mon," he said, pulling me away. He showed me over to where Mom was standing next to an ancient blue station wagon that matched her trailer. "I got to stay for a while. You get out of here. I'll see you later." He looked at Mom. "Can you run her back to the club?"

Mom nodded quickly. "Come on. You can help me fix a meal for when everyone gets home."

I bit my lip. I didn't want to run off when everyone else was helping but I could feel people's eyes on me. Maybe some of it was my imagination, but not all of it. They'd volunteered to help me, but they couldn't have known this would be the cost. I figured I should make myself scarce. I hugged Carrick and the feel of his hard, warm chest against my cheek was fantastic. "Don't be long," I begged.

He squeezed me tight, his chin resting on the top of my head. "I won't," he whispered.

I got into Mom's station wagon and he slammed the door. *I'll see him in a few hours,* I told myself. *It'll be okay.*

I was wrong. I was so, so wrong.

29

CARRICK

I t took hours to clean up, even with everyone helping. We had to separate the clean stock from the fire-damaged stuff and then we had to move everything. I love bikes like nothing else but one thing they're useless for is moving loads. We had to get the van from the compound before we could start ferrying stuff back.

The mood was somber. We'd completely underestimated this Volos guy. No one was making any noises about giving Annabelle up, not for a second. But everyone was pissed off. Losing the warehouse would really hurt the club. *And I brought this to our door.* I had to find a way to make this right, to protect both Annabelle and the MC. But where do you even start looking for a guy like Volos?

On the way back to the clubhouse, I was thinking on it so hard that I didn't notice the big red SUV at first, not until it was six feet from my rear wheel. Some guy in a suit was at the wheel. I could have easily outrun him but I wasn't in the mood. I waited for him to overtake but he didn't, just sat there on my tail. *What the fuck?*

Then he pulled alongside me and sat there next to my shoulder until I looked. That's when I saw the badge he was holding up to the window and its three blocky blue letters. *FBI.*

Oh *fuck.*

I throttled back and pulled over. But I kept my bike running.

The guy got out and sauntered over. He was in his thirties and well dressed for a fed, with a sharp suit. I figured he was some trust fund kid who'd disappointed his parents and wound up working for the government. He walked around in front of my bike. "Carrick O'Harra," he said with great satisfaction as he took off his sunglasses. "Been waiting a while to meet you. Thought we could have a nice quiet chat."

I looked around. We were on a quiet country road that led into Haywood Falls: I'd taken the scenic route to give me some thinking time. There wasn't much traffic. No one would see us. But if he thought I was going to keep this from Mac and the club, he was crazy. If any of us get approached by a fed, the first thing we do is tell the others. Otherwise, people think you might be cooperating.

I gave him my coldest stare.. "I got nothing to say to you."

"It's Agent Trent, by the way. But you can call me Marcus." He looked over his shoulder. In the distance, we could still see the smoke rising from the smoldering remains of the warehouse. "Seems like you really pissed someone off."

I sat back in the saddle and narrowed my eyes. The fire only started a few hours ago. How did the FBI hear about it so fast? Sheriff Harris wouldn't even have written up his report yet.

"Oh, we've been watching the Princes for some time," Trent told me. "Waiting for the right opportunity. Then we heard you were making enquiries about Volos and that really got our attention."

My jaw dropped. "You know about that psycho?"

Trent nodded. "And he's not someone you want to piss off. He operates on a whole different level." He sounded almost impressed. "You are way, way, *way* out of your depth, O'Harra."

"But you're going to bring him down?" My pulse was racing. I hated the idea of working with the feds, but if they could get Volos off our backs....

Trent threw back his head and laughed. "Oh, Jesus, no! Are you kidding? Volos is practically a legend. No one's even gotten close to catching him. Half the FBI think he's a *myth*. No, no, no." He paused for effect. "I'm here for the guns, O'Harra. I want to put the Princes away for running guns: Mac, Ox, Hunter, all of them."

I blinked at him. "*What?* Fuck you! I'm no rat."

He grinned and folded his arms. "You haven't heard what I'm offering."

I leaned forward and twisted the throttle, revving the engine. I was ready to ride straight over him if he didn't get out of the way. "I ain't interested." My foot went to kick the bike into gear—

"Annabelle."

My foot missed its target and I clumsily rocked on the bike. I slowly looked up at him.

And then I killed the engine and the silence of the forest swelled up to surround us.

Trent stepped right up to my bike and put his hands on the handlebars, leaning in until our faces were only a few inches apart. "Volos is going to destroy your club. It's a plaything to him, an amusement. He's like a cat with a mouse. You'll watch your friends die and then he'll kill you and take Annabelle back. It's just a matter of time. But if you were to help me...well, then I'd have to put you in witness protection. You *and* Annabelle. You'd testify and then disappear. Fresh new lives. Even Volos wouldn't be able to find you and he wouldn't be targeting the club anymore. Some of your friends would go to jail for a while but they'd *live*. And the Hell's Princes would survive."

I stared at him, unable to believe even a fed would stoop this low. Mac's words came back to me: *they always want something.*

"I'm offering you a life," said Trent. "You could leave it all behind, O'Harra. The killing, the violence—oh, I know what you do for the club. In a few months, you could be on the other side of the country with a new name and your girl by your side. All you've gotta do is give me the club."

We stared at each other. *Say something,* I screamed inside. But I couldn't find the words.

Trent smiled.

"Go fuck yourself," I spat. But my voice was thick and hoarse. I started up my bike again.

Trent plucked a business card from his pocket, slid it into a pocket on my cut and tapped it meaningfully. Then he stepped back out of the way before I could run him down.

As I tore away, I was almost panting with rage. *He thought I'd rat out the club?* I'd heard of some pretty dirty deals from the feds in my time, but this was a new low. Volos sold women and this guy was prepared to practically side with him to get what he wanted. *I should have punched him out. Hell, I should have shot him. I should have—*

But as I sped around the next bend, I knew my anger wasn't really at him. Feds are feds. Making dirty deals is what they do. I was pissed at myself. Because when he'd made the offer...I'd hesitated. I hadn't been able to tell him to fuck off. Only for a few seconds, but when my loyalty to the club was being questioned, that was a fucking ice age.

I hadn't been able to tell him to fuck off because a little part of me had been tempted.

A little part of me had seen an image of Annabelle in a summer dress, walking hand in hand with me. Happy. Safe. Together forfuckingever.

And I hadn't been ready for how fucking hard that image tugged at me. Being able to look in her eyes and not see that fear there. Being able to set her free from this whole nightmare, permanently.

I'd never, ever rat out the club. But that image of Annabelle had actually made me consider it and that scared the shit out of me. And Trent had seen it, too: that's why he'd smiled.

I leant low into the next bend, my anger pushing me to ride faster and faster. *I have to fix this.* Not by ratting out the club. Not with the club's help, as Mac would want me to do. The club had suffered enough. I had to do this myself.

And suddenly, it was all clear to me. I had to kill Volos.

Violence and killing were what I was good at. Kill him and all my problems went away. My hands tightened on the handlebars. All I had to do was find him. But how did I do that when even the FBI couldn't catch him?

I had the bike pushed to its limits, now, leaning hard over to make each turn. I had to find someone who'd know something. The Blood Spider's President, Hay, had known almost nothing. Someone else....

My hand slipped from the throttle and the bike began to slow. I feathered the brakes and brought it to a stop, right in the middle of the road.

There was one other person who might know something. Someone I'd happily take apart to get the information out of him.

Someone who deserved to die.

I made a tight turn and then blasted back the way I'd come, heading towards Teston.

30

ANNABELLE

B ack at the compound, I chopped onions and fried off chunks of steak with Mom. But once the chili was slow-cooking for the members' return, there was nothing else to help with and she chased me out of the trailer and told me to go enjoy myself.

With most of the members helping clean up after the fire, the compound was spookily deserted. Every hour or so, the van would return to drop off another load of rescued stock, but Carrick was never in it and the faces of the Prospects driving were grim. The guilt ate me up. I checked with Scooter but there was nothing that needed fixing so I couldn't even help out that way. And the last thing I wanted to do was sit around.

Eventually, I borrowed the spare bike members used while theirs was being fixed and practiced riding. It was much harder without Carrick to guide me. He was right: I didn't have the muscle to haul the big bike's weight around. But I'd never get stronger unless I tried.

I gritted my teeth and started riding in slow circles and figure-8s around the compound. It took all my concentration, which was a blessed relief: it took my mind off Volos. *I'll tear your club apart,* the note had said. Now it had begun. What if they couldn't stop him? What if it got so bad that they decided to—

I shook the image from my head. *Stop it!* Carrick and the club had promised to protect me and they would. I had to trust them. But if they wouldn't give me up...how much would they lose?

The bike teetered and it took all my strength to keep it upright. *Concentrate!*

After a few hours, my thighs burned and my arms ached but I welcomed the pain: I felt like I deserved it. I only stopped when I heard the throb of approaching engines. I climbed off the bike and ran over to the clubhouse as the members rode up. But Carrick wasn't among them. When I asked, everyone said he and Hunter had been the last ones to leave. I waited...but still he didn't show.

Then Hunter rode up, a crate of beer strapped to the back of his saddle. "Have you seen Carrick?" I asked immediately. I was starting to get a bad feeling.

Hunter frowned. "Weird thing," he said. "He was ahead of me. I stopped to get beer and then I saw him race past the store the other way, heading out of town."

"What's out that way?"

Hunter shrugged. "The highway," he said. "Teston."

I walked away, completely confused. Could he be going to the Blood Spiders? Why? To try to track down Volos? They'd already interrogated the Blood Spiders' President. And there was nothing else in that direction, aside from—

I stopped dead.

Aside from my house.

I spun and raced back to Hunter, catching him as he climbed off his bike. "We have to go after him!"

"Why? What's the matter?"

I unstrapped the beer and climbed onto the bike behind him. "He's going to question my step-dad," I said breathlessly. I looked him in the eye. "Hunter, he'll kill him."

Hunter nodded grimly. "Hold on tight."

We roared off. And I prayed we'd be in time.

31

CARRICK

The drive to Annabelle's farm was like stepping back in time ten years. I could still remember every twist and turn of the approach...hell, I'd even been on the same bike. Except, back then, I'd been looking over my shoulder for the bikers chasing me, feeling the blood soak slowly through my t-shirt. I'd lost control right outside her house. Right...*here*.

I slowed to a stop alongside the fence. There was still a sagging section where my rolling body had smacked into it: twelve years, and Annabelle's step-dad still hadn't gotten around to fixing it. *There:* that's where she found me. There was the tool shed, where she'd dragged me. Where she'd saved my life by hiding me.

My hands tightened on the handlebars. And how had I repaid her? I'd left her with a necklace and a promise. I'd left her alone for twelve years with...*him.* I hadn't known, of course. I'd had no idea how much of a bastard her step-dad was. I hadn't known he'd do something as unthinkable as selling her. But that didn't stop the knowledge from knotting me up inside.

I knew *now*.

I climbed off my bike, unstrapped Caorthannach and brandished her in both hands. The rage built with every step I took towards the house, like I was soaking up all the evil in this place through the soles of my boots.

I realized I was going to enjoy this. I was going to enjoy beating the information out of him.

Ten years ago, the fields in front of the house had been full of dusty, dead maize. Now they were barren dirt. This was barely even a farm, anymore, just a slowly rotting house in a dead plot. I opened the screen door...and then, on instinct, I tried the door handle. It turned and the door swung open. I caught my breath, hands curling into fists, waiting for him to run at me...but no one appeared.

I stalked inside. Had he heard me approach? Was he lurking somewhere with a gun? I checked the living room: nothing. The kitchen: nothing. Upstairs, then.

I crept up the stairs as quietly as I could, wincing at every creak. But still no one appeared out of the shadows. The afternoon sunlight was lancing through windows, pinning motes of dust in midair. It was eerily quiet.

I checked each room I came to. One of them, I figured, was his bedroom: it stank and the bed looked used. But it was as empty as the rest.

Eventually, there was only one room left. *Annabelle* was hand-painted in big, blue and red balloon letters on the door, together with a butterfly. The whole thing had been painted over at some point, but whoever had done it had only used one coat of white and the colors still showed through.

I slowly pushed it open, holding my breath. I was expecting to find the step-dad holding a shotgun.

No one. He wasn't home. So why had the front door been unlocked?

The closet was wide open. Inside, there was nothing but empty hangers swaying in the breeze from the open window. That made no sense, either. Annabelle hadn't taken anything with her to the auction: I'd had to buy her new clothes. The drawers were empty, too.

Pretty much all that was left in the room was a bookshelf on the wall: some very old books on engineering and—

I frowned at the thick book someone had carefully covered in paper and then in plastic to make it last. A Harley had been sketched on the spine, every line lovingly hand-drawn in pencil. I pulled it down and opened it at a random page. It took me several pages to realize I was looking at her diary.

She hadn't written in it every day. She'd saved it for the really good times and the really bad times: the ones she wanted to remember and the ones she wanted to cleanse from her soul by trapping them in ink.

There were a lot more bad times than good times. I could tell the really bad ones by the circular stains that marked her tears.

Every page I turned notched the anger inside me higher. I knew reading it was wrong but I couldn't stop.

I read about her mom dying, my chest growing tight.

I read about her step-dad hitting her and then letching after her, my fingers gripping the pages so hard I almost tore them.

It wasn't just what had happened to her; it was how she dealt with it. Maybe she hadn't even known she was doing it at the time, but she'd doodle things in the margin: motorbikes, leather cuts, even a good rendition of the *Hell's Princes* logo. I could imagine her sitting there, tears in her eyes, drawing to work up courage to describe her day. *I'd* given her courage. Memories of me. I'd been her escape.

But it was worse than that. *Carrick,* it said, just after each bad day. Like writing it was her way of drawing a line underneath. *Carrick. Carrick, Carrick, Carrick.*

I'd been her rescue plan for twelve fucking years.

The rage was so strong, I could barely breathe. At first, my name was in elaborate balloon letters. As she got older, it became brutal and hard: dangerous and exciting. When she was in her late teens, it became sensual and flowing. And when she was an adult...it started to get smaller and smaller.

She'd given up hope.

I swung at the closest thing: the bookshelf on the wall. My fist snapped off the bracket that supported it and the whole thing tumbled to the bed, spilling a flood of books.

I'd been her knight in shining fucking armor. And instead of being there to save her, I'd been off in Haywood Falls, dealing out vengeance to the enemies of the club, getting darker and darker, less of a hero each day. *Why didn't you call?* I could have rescued her a year before, five years before....

I tossed the diary onto the pile on the bed, panting with rage. I'd failed, back then. I hadn't known she needed help.

But I knew now.

I stomped down the stairs, no longer worried about making a noise. A good thing her step-dad wasn't home, with what was going through my mind. I'd track him down, though, make him tell me where Volos was—

As I passed the living room, a noise made me freeze in the doorway. A kind of groan. I raised Caorthannach and stole forward.

There was an armchair that faced away from the door. And sprawled in it, hidden from the doorway by its back, was Annabelle's step-dad. His mouth was slackly open, a bottle of whiskey nestled to his chest as if for comfort. He was so thoroughly passed out, he hadn't even been aware of me.

I walked around the chair, never taking my eyes off him. The rage was white-hot, now, searing away thought and leaving only emotion. This was him. This was the man who'd hit her, who'd made her live in fear for so many years. This was the man who'd lusted after her. This was the man who'd sold his step-daughter.

I've dealt with a lot of despicable people in my life, but I've never hated a person so much.

I fingered Caorthannach, her engravings familiar and comforting. God, it would be so easy, so quick. One squeeze. Both triggers. He'd be *gone*. But I needed answers.

I didn't want to have to speak to him. I hated him so much that it was almost worth losing out on the information, just to avoid it. But if I wanted to help Annabelle, I needed to get it out of him.

Alright, then.

I marched back upstairs to the bathroom and started the bath filling with cold water. Back downstairs, I took one last, disgusted look at him...and then grabbed a handful of his shirt and hauled him out of his chair.

He weighed almost nothing. The booze had turned his muscles to fat and then melted the fat away to leave him skinny and mean. He came awake as I dragged him across the living room. "What?" he slurred. "What do you want?"

I ignored him and dragged him up the stairs, his ass and legs bouncing off each step. He was grabbing at my hand, now, trying to free himself, but he didn't have anywhere near the strength he needed.

We reached the bathroom and I dragged him over to the tub. I took one last look at his drunken, uncomprehending face....

And then I heaved him into the tub and pressed him down under the water.

He woke up *fast*. Water exploded out of the tub in white plumes as he thrashed but my arm was like iron, pinning him down to the bottom. The aim wasn't to kill him. The aim was to sober him up, scare him and soften him so that he'd talk.

I waited three seconds and then loosened my hand a little, letting him rise towards the surface.

And then I remembered a phrase from her diary: *purple flower*. Back when the other girls had still played with her, Annabelle had gotten caught up playing and had come home too late to do her chores. Her step-dad had beaten her and the next day bruises Annabelle called *the purple flower kind* had risen all over her stomach and chest and she'd had to claim she had her period so that she wouldn't have to get changed for gym class.

My hand pushed down until her step-dad was on the bottom of the tub again. As he realized I wasn't letting him up, he began to kick, his boots hammering on the porcelain.

My hand loosened again. He rose until his face almost broke the surface....

I think maybe he has a spy hole, Annabelle had written. *Or a camera. I don't know. But I can feel him watching me, when I'm getting changed.*

My hand pushed down again. And this time, it stayed. There were too many pages of misery in that diary. He'd done too much wrong.

He deserved to die.

32

CARRICK

Footsteps downstairs, then running up towards me. Not the heavy footfalls of a man.

Annabelle burst into the bathroom, her face deathly pale. *"Stop!"* she yelled.

I looked at her, looked at her step-dad under the water...and didn't move. *This is what I do. This is vengeance.* Not for the club, for once. For her. And maybe it was wrong but I was way past the point where I was going anywhere except hell. So I might as well take him with me.

"Carrick, *stop!*" She grabbed at my arm, but I was keeping that fucker pinned with everything I had. *"Stop!"*

Her step-dad's struggles were slowing, now. "He deserves it." My voice was rough with emotion.

She grabbed hold of me, crying, pulling at me. *"You're better than this!"*

Her step-dad's limbs were going limp. I shook my head at her. "No. I'm not."

She pushed her tear-streaked face close to mine. "But *I want you to be!*"

I stared at her for three long heartbeats. I remembered what she'd said, back at the compound. *I believe in you too.* She still believed I could be her hero.

I hauled her step-dad out of the tub and hurled him down on the tiles. He drew in a huge lungful of air, coughed up some water and then lay there groaning.

Hunter appeared in the doorway. "You two go downstairs," I told them.

Annabelle looked at me with huge eyes.

"I have to find out where Volos is," I told her. "But I won't kill him." When I glanced at her step-dad, it took everything I had to say it, but I said it: "I promise."

She nodded, biting her lip, and took Hunter downstairs. I picked up her step-dad by the neck.

"Now, you sick son of a bitch. You and me are going to have a conversation where I ask the questions and you tell me exactly the fuck what I need to know." I paused. "I promised I wouldn't kill you. But I am hoping, fucking *praying* that you try to hold out on me because then I get to beat it out of you. Understand?"

He nodded, terrified.

"Then let's begin."

∾

A half hour later, I came downstairs. Hunter and Annabelle were sitting on the couch in the living room. Annabelle looking scared and Hunter was giving me a reproachful glare—probably for taking off on my own again.

"I'm done with him," I told them. I held out my hand to Annabelle. "C'mon. Let's get anything you want from your room." I figured she wouldn't want to ever come back here again.

Upstairs, she slowed as we passed the closed door to the bathroom. A faint groan came from inside. She swallowed and continued along the hallway.

In her room, she stopped and frowned at the empty closet. "Don't worry," I said. "I know where your clothes are."

She turned to the bed and started gathering up the books. Then she froze as she saw the diary lying on top of them. Her gaze snapped to me, first accusing and hurt and then ashamed.

I opened my arms and she ran to me, slammed into my chest and nestled there. "I'm sorry," I told her as I wrapped my arms around her. "I shouldn't have read it. I couldn't stop." I squeezed her tight as she started to cry. "But that bastard can't hurt you anymore."

I held her like that for a long time. The press of her warm body made me feel human again, after the cold violence in the bathroom. After what I'd nearly done.

When she moved back from me, she gathered the books into a pile and hefted them, then added a framed photo of her and her mom from the wall. We both looked around. The room was pretty much empty. "Anything else you want to keep?" I asked.

She looked into the empty closet again. And then, bending, she pulled something from the shadows down at the bottom. The brown, threadbare rabbit from when she was a kid. She clutched it to her chest and led the way downstairs.

Outside, I led her and Hunter into the backyard, then looked around for the place her step-dad had told me about. I finally found the patch of loose dirt and sent Hunter for shovels from the tool shed. Annabelle looked at me blankly but it was easier to show her than to explain.

Hunter and I dug together. It only took us a few minutes to uncover the suitcase and the sports bag, heave them up into the sunlight and shake off the worst of the dirt. Annabelle frowned at them, then opened them up.

I grabbed her hand, because I knew what she'd find.

Her clothes. Her purse. Her phone and its charger. All the things someone would pack, if they ran off to New York. Annabelle drew in a shuddering breath, squeezing my hand for strength. I understood: when her step-dad had told me this part, I'd nearly broken my promise. It was sickening, how well he'd planned it.

"No one would ever have looked for me," she whispered.

I pulled her into my arms and held her so close that I could feel her heartbeat. I didn't want to let go of her and that was the only thing that stopped me from marching into the house and killing the bastard for destroying her faith in mankind. .

Hunter backed off, giving us some space. I held Annabelle tight, the guilt filling me, choking me, until I couldn't take it anymore. I drew back and looked into her eyes. "I'm sorry I wasn't there," I blurted. "I'm sorry I didn't come back."

"I chose not to call you," she said. "I was keeping you for when I really needed you. And you came then."

I wanted to say something but I couldn't find the words. I could feel stuff stirring in my chest, shit I hadn't felt since I was a teenager, and I couldn't explain it. Not just wanting her. Not even just wanting to protect her. More than that. "I'll never leave you again," I said at last.

She swallowed, tears welling up in her eyes. "Promise me that," she said.

I nodded. "I promise." And then my hands were on those soft cheeks, my thumbs rubbing away her tears, and I was grabbing her and kissing her hard, kissing the pain away. My hands slid up her cheeks and I buried my fingers in her soft copper locks, unable to help myself. Every brush of that silky hair against the backs of my fingers was reassurance that she was *here, now,* and not back in those years of hell with her step-dad. And meanwhile her hands were under my cut, running over the muscles of my shoulders and back, clinging to me as if I was her link to the present. I don't know if I was imagining it or if her step-dad had dragged himself up off the bathroom tiles and made it to a window, but I felt like he was watching us. *She's mine now,* I thought viciously. *She's mine and you're never getting her back.*

When we finally broke, her tears had dried but she still clung tight to my hand as we stumbled across the uneven ground to get back to the road. It would have been quicker to cut through the house but neither of us wanted to venture inside again. Hunter was waiting for us by the bikes. He'd already strapped Annabelle's bags to them and was in the saddle, ready to go. I nodded to him to go on ahead. "We'll catch you up," I said.

He nodded and roared off, but not before giving me another of those reproachful looks. *Shit.* He was pissed I'd come out here solo, acting on my own again instead of involving the club. He'd tell Mac and he'd be pissed, too. I'd have to deal with that tomorrow.

I climbed onto my bike and Annabelle climbed on behind me. But when I sat there without starting the engine, she touched my shoulder. "What's wrong?"

I sucked in a deep breath and let it out. "Your step-dad didn't know anything. He never saw Volos's face. He never heard his real name. He overheard one of the fucker's bodyguards say something about *standing stock*."—I shrugged and shook my head in disgust—" must mean the other women they've bought, the ones they haven't sold on yet. But that's it. Nothing we can use to find him." I gazed back towards the house. "I should have killed him."

Her cool hands grabbed my cheeks, her skin soft against my stubble, and turned me to look at her. "No you shouldn't," she told me. "That would make you like him. Like Volos."

I lowered my head. "I already *am* like him."

She put her hand under my chin and made me look at her. "No you're *not*."

I stared into her eyes. She knew I'd done things for the club. She knew I'd killed. But she didn't know the worst of it.

She didn't know about the innocent life I'd taken.

"What?" she asked.

I shook my head.

"You read my diary," she said defiantly. "I should know *this*. Whatever it is."

I looked back at the house. "Reading your diary showed me the worst of *him*. Not of you."

She put her hands on my chest. "I want to know all of you. Even the worst parts."

But I shook my head. The memories were a sac of poison inside me, the toxins slowly dripping out and soaking through my soul. I'd gotten used to that bitter, dark taste but I didn't want it touching her. I didn't want it touching what we had. I turned to face front and finally started the bike. As it roared into life, her arms slipped around my waist. But there was a tension between us, now.

I gunned the throttle and we left her old house behind forever. Her past was laid to rest but I couldn't get away from mine.

I wanted to be with her, body and soul. I wanted it so bad. And she was right: if you're going to really be with someone, you have to know them completely.

But I couldn't tell her about what I'd done...once I started, it would all come out. Briggs. Chicago.

My family.

I couldn't take telling her that.

But if I didn't tell her, I might lose her forever.

33

ANNABELLE

"Okay," I muttered. "There's something you don't see every day." I was looking up at a huge white banner that stretched between two trees. *Sixth Annual Hill Descent Challenge*, it read. And right in the center was a cartoon of an ox riding a Harley.

I looked down to where the real Ox straddled a real Harley. The cartoon looked sensible by comparison. I'd wondered how on earth such a big guy could ride a bike and the answer was, simply, *he has a very big bike.*

The Harley must have been custom-built for him. It was longer, wider, *meaner.* A rhino could have ridden it and not have looked out of place. Ox just about fit.

The event was pretty simple. Ox rode all the way from the top of the twisting mountain road to the bottom at breakneck speed. There was a sweepstake with prizes donated by local businesses: the winner was the person who guessed closest to the exact time. After six years, it had gotten pretty serious, with a big digital clock linked up to the Sheriff's speed trap hardware at the finish line and hundreds of sweepstake entries. Mom sold hot dogs and there were commemorative t-shirts, too. All the money raised went to the kids' ward at the medical center.

"And he organizes all this himself?" I asked Carrick.

He nodded, sliding an arm around my waist. "We all help out, but it's a *him* thing, not a club thing." He looked at Ox. "I know...he doesn't seem like the type. But he likes kids."

I smiled. I was enjoying getting to know them. Mac, Hunter, Ox, Viking...the bikers who'd scared me so much when I first walked into the clubhouse were starting to feel like friends. And with Mom around, it almost felt like a big, weird family. "Gentle giant with a heart of gold, huh?"

Carrick gave me a look. "Not so gentle when he gets riled. Don't ever make him angry." He used the arm around my waist to hook me around so that I was facing him, then pushed the hair back from my cheek. For a second, he just looked at me. I could feel myself flushing. I still wasn't used to the way he looked at me: those intense blue eyes eating up every detail, drinking me in like I was the best thing he'd ever seen. Then the lick of raw heat that let me know he was imagining stripping me, hurling me on the bed and roughly taking me, his stubble scratching my cheek as he pounded into me from above or his breath hot in my ear as he slammed into me from behind—I swallowed, a wave of heat racing down my body to pool in my groin.

When he looked at me like that, with those eyes as clear and blue as the sky, it seemed like everything was perfect. But inevitably, his eyes would cloud with pain. Something he was remembering, something that was eating away at him from the inside. That thing he'd done that he thought made him irredeemable. The one he still wouldn't share, the one that meant there was still distance between us.

He slept like a baby in my arms each night but, if I woke and went to the bathroom, I'd sometimes return to find him in the midst of a nightmare, face so contorted in hate and disgust that my chest clenched up tight. But when I woke him, he'd refuse to talk about it.

Mac passed us, his cell phone clamped to his ear. "One minute!" he announced. "They're all ready at the finish line!"

Carrick glanced at him and I saw his face tighten. He and Mac had had a shouting match just after we returned from my old house. Mac had been mad that Carrick had gone off on his own again and Carrick had snapped that he'd do what he wanted. It had been three days and they still hadn't made up. I'd seen how close the two of them were. It must be killing them to be at each other's throats. And I knew that I was part of the cause.

At least there'd been no more attacks by Volos. Everyone was waiting for the other shoe to drop but there were enough armed bikers attending today's event that I felt safe. Even the Sheriff's department was there, since they'd had to close the road. Sheriff Harris had been looking into Volos for us but so far had drawn a complete blank: no one had any information on the guy.

Ox started his bike, sending plumes of blue-gray smoke into the air. Its massive engine made the air throb and the pavement shake. The crowd whooped and roared.

"Ten seconds!" yelled Mac.

Ox revved his engine. The crowd cheered and started a countdown. "*Ten! Nine! Eight!*"

Carrick leaned in to kiss me before the start. For a moment, our problems were forgotten. It only needed a brush of those hard Irish lips against mine to make me forget *everything.* He kissed me hard, then teased me. His tongue licking along my upper lip...and then he sucked it into his mouth and nibbled it in a way that made my whole body lift and quiver.

"*Seven!*" yelled the crowd. "*Six!*"

Carrick's hands slid down my shoulders, down my sides and grabbed my ass, pulling me closer, my body fitting so neatly against his, like we were designed to fit together. What had started as a quick kiss became something else: his hands were possessive, locking me against him, and there was nowhere I would have rather been in the world.

"*Five! Four!*"

His tongue found mine and we kissed open-mouthed and hungry, my hands running over the muscles of his arms. God, I wanted this man. I *needed* him. Why wouldn't he let me know that final part of him, the part he hated so much?

He reluctantly released me as the crowd yelled, "*Three! Two! One!*"

I opened my eyes and turned to look just as Ox roared away in a cloud of tire smoke. Everyone else coughed and turned away but, me being me, I inhaled it like it was nectar. *Burnt rubber. Oil and gasoline. And—*

I blinked. And then tore away from Carrick and ran to the start line as Ox disappeared into the distance. He caught up to me as I squatted down right where Ox's bike had been and fingered the ground. "What is it?" he asked.

I wiped the clear liquid off the pavement and put my fingers right under my nose to check I was right. But I knew that smell anywhere. I'd smelled it when we'd been working on Hunter's bike, checking the oil and the tranny fluid and the—

"Brake fluid," I croaked in horror. I grabbed Carrick's wrist. "*Someone messed with Ox's bike!*"

34

CARRICK

I ran for my bike. Annabelle was smart enough that she didn't ask to come with me. She knew I'd ride faster on my own. But even going flat-out, could I catch him?

My bike was parked at the side of the road but it had been swallowed up by the crowd. I had to yell and curse at people before they jumped back out of the way. Then I had to start her and get her pointed in the right direction. *Come on! COME ON!*

I tore off down the mountain road, crossing the start line and whipping past a terrified-looking Annabelle. Her face was begging me: *please.*

Please don't let Ox die.

Because that was what was going to happen here. He'd pick up more and more speed going down the mountain, trying to beat his fucking record. And then he'd reach for his brakes and nothing would happen and he'd slam into a tree doing ninety.

My stomach tightened. *Not Ox.* What had Annabelle called him? A gentle giant. Well, maybe she didn't know him like I did but he was a far more decent guy than I was. *Not Ox. Please not Ox.*

I sped around the first corner as fast as I dared. My heart was thundering in my chest. The enormity of what I had to do was just sinking in: Ox was *racing,* trying to get down the mountain as fast as possible. His bike was more powerful, faster on the straights. And he had a head start. The only way I could catch him was to go suicidally fast on the corners.

I leaned the bike all the way over for the next bend and sped round it doing fifty. The spectators lining the route looked up, astonished, then gave me a cheer.

I could still smell Ox's exhaust in the air but he was still out of sight. *He can't be that far ahead,* I told myself. *Please. Maybe he's slow this year.* Then I rounded the corner and caught a glimpse of him: five turns ahead and going faster than I would have thought possible. *"OX!"* I yelled, and honked my horn. But I knew he wouldn't hear me over the bellow of his engine.

He knew the road better than I did, knew every twist and incline. The only way I stood a chance was to take chances he wouldn't. I twisted the throttle and flew around the next corner at nearly seventy.

I could feel the bike fighting me like a nervous horse: the speed was just too much for the tight bends and downhill grade. And every cell in my body, every hour in the saddle I'd racked up, was screaming at me to *slow down!*

I sped up.

Each corner was a nerve-shredding, tire-squealing slide, now. Cold sweat was creeping down my neck, soaking my t-shirt. *Jesus, this is insane.* But I wasn't going to let him die. Not Ox. I could feel that psycho Volos's presence looming over the mountain. He'd done this. He was trying to rip our club apart in the most painful way possible, by murdering one of our brothers. *No. Not Ox!*

Slowly, very slowly, I started to reel him in. I could smell the rubber I was leaving on the road as the bike fought for grip and I was leaning so far over on each bend that my knees almost brushed the asphalt.

Then I cut a corner a little too tight and the wheels hit loose dirt. The handlebars went light and my stomach lurched into my throat. I went sideways towards one of the crash barriers: I'd smack into it, cartwheel and fall a hundred feet down the mountain before I hit anything else—

Then the tires found purchase and I shot forward. And now I was close enough to call to Ox. Panting and shaky, I yelled as hard as I could. "*OOOX!*"

He turned and, even from that distance, I could feel him frowning. I was messing up his time.

I raised my hand and frantically mimed slashing my throat. "*STOP!*"

I saw him hesitate...and then throttle back. I powered forward and came alongside him, but we were still doing almost eighty. "Your brakes!" I yelled over the wind. "Someone messed with your brakes!"

I saw him squeeze the levers...and the sick dread on his face when they did nothing at all. I looked ahead. The next bend was a sharp left-hander and there was no way we were going to make it at this speed. I could brake but Ox would plow straight off the road and into one of the massive fir trees.

There was only one thing to do. "Bail!" I yelled. "Bail!" At least he might have a chance.

The trees were rushing up to meet me. I slammed on my brakes and Ox seemed to shoot forward, out of my reach. *Bail!* I thought. But he was staying on as long as possible, trying to lose speed before he jumped. Only a few seconds from the trees, I finally saw him heave himself off the back of the bike.

I winced as he hit: at that speed, you basically become a sack of meat with nothing but physics to determine your fate. He had his arms up, protecting his head, but he was bouncing and rolling with sickening speed. His bike slammed into the trees, its momentum carrying parts of its mangled frame ten feet in the air. Meanwhile, Ox was rolling and spinning off to the side. I screeched to a stop, jumped off my bike and *ran*—

And saw him slam to a stop as his head hit a tree.

35

ANNABELLE

Within seconds of Carrick blasting past the start line, I'd yelled to Mac and Hunter what was going on and we were all tearing down the mountain in pursuit. I don't know if Hunter had expected a passenger but I leapt on the back of his bike before he could argue. I was scared for Ox but I was terrified of what risks Carrick might have taken to save him.

I had my phone back, now. I whipped it out and called 911, yelling to be heard over the rushing air. Maybe someone had gotten word to the Sheriff and they'd already called an ambulance, but I wasn't taking any chances.

We found them almost halfway down the mountain. The first thing I saw was Carrick's bike, slumped over on its side in the middle of the road. Then I saw the remains of Ox's bike, mashed into trees just ahead of a bend.

And then I saw Carrick, on his hands and knees over Ox's body. As one, we ran to them.

"No," Carrick was saying over and over. "No, no, *no!*"

Ox was lying on his back, arms battered and bloody from where he must have scraped along the road. His head was against the trunk of a tree and a lake of blood was spreading out from under it.

"Get—Get an ambulance," said Mac, his voice catching.

"On its way," I croaked. I couldn't take my eyes from Ox. He was so *still.*

A siren wailed in the distance. Carrick looked up and his eyes caught mine. I could see it in his eyes: *this is my fault.*

No, I thought bitterly. *It's mine.*

36

CARRICK

Annabelle and I rode with Ox in the ambulance with everyone else following on their bikes. Ox was rushed straight into surgery and the waiting room gradually filled up with black leather as members arrived. A few moments later, Mom screeched up in her station wagon and my chest went tight as we told her the news. Mac, Hunter and I gathered her into a hug as she began to sob.

Volos. Volos did this. All I needed was two minutes alone in a room with that motherfucker. I didn't care how much money and power he had. But all of my rage had nowhere to go. I still had no idea where to find the guy. Sheriff Harris and every one of Hunter's contacts had drawn a blank, too. The guy was a ghost.

Hours went by with no word on how the surgery was going. I needed air. I marched towards the exit. Annabelle grabbed my arm.

"You did everything you could," she told me. "If you hadn't chased after him and warned him, he wouldn't have even stood a chance."

I nodded, but without much feeling. This was all on me. I should have ended this at the Blood Spiders' bar, in Teston. I should have killed every one of them and Volos, too. Then this never would have happened. The guilt was eating me up. "Give me a minute, okay?" I said.

She nodded and stepped back, but she kept hold of my arm until the very last second. The realization hit me with a sickening lurch just as I pushed through the exit doors: *Shit. That sounded like I was brushing her off.* I hadn't meant it that way. *She's upset, too.* I cursed and shook my head. *I'm no fucking good at this relationship stuff.*

I looked over my shoulder but Annabelle had already turned away. I promised myself I'd apologize as soon as I went back inside.

It had started to rain: lightly, for now, but it was gathering pace and the whole sky was turning gray. I turned my face up to the heavens and let it soak me. *Why Ox?* I asked whoever was listening. He was a part of the club in a way I could never be because he relied on them. His whole life was the club—he and Mom held it together like glue. I'd die for the club but I'd never been able to trust it with my soul. That's what Mac didn't understand. I let them lean on me but I couldn't lean on them because....

Because I couldn't lose a second family.

The rain coursed down my face like cold tears. If Ox died, the club was done...but Volos would keep coming and coming until either we were all dead or we gave up Annabelle. *Goddamn you! Come at me! Leave the rest of them alone!*

A sudden, shrill sound from the depths of my cut. My phone. Who the fuck was calling me? Everyone I knew in the world was ten feet away in the waiting room. Was there news on Ox?!

I ran to the nearest overhang to shelter from the rain. It was getting heavy, now, and lightning was lighting up the clouds. I pulled out my phone, then frowned. I didn't recognize the number. "Hello?"

"Heard about what happened," said Agent Trent.

I wanted to hurl my phone at the nearest tree. But that didn't stop me listening.

"I did some digging for you," Trent told me. "This guy Volos is one *serious* fuck. Obsessive, some people say. When he decides he wants a woman, he doesn't quit. There was a case down in Mexico where he wiped out an entire Hacienda: and I mean the family, their staff, even the fucking gardeners, just to get this one girl." Again, Trent sounded almost impressed. "*He will break you.* He doesn't have mercy. He's not interested in a fair fight. He's playing with you."

Playing with us. I couldn't stop seeing Ox's head hitting the tree.

Trent's voice grew softer. Compelling. "I'm staying right here in town. We could do a deal and I could have you and Annabelle in a safe house *tonight.* All your buddies would live. Isn't alive better than dead? You'd be saving them."

Saving them...or saving myself by becoming a rat? Everyone would go to jail.

But they'd be *alive.* The decision was ripping me apart. Neither choice was what I wanted. I just wanted my club back. My friends back. I wanted this bastard Volos off our backs. I wanted everything to go back to the way it was—

Except that wasn't true. I *didn't* want things to go back to how they were before Annabelle called me. Not even for a second. Because then I wouldn't have her.

Trent was listening patiently to my slow, furious breath. "O'Harra, I'm not gonna pretend I know what it's like to be in your shoes," he told me. "But I do know this: sometimes you gotta do the shitty thing to do the right thing. If you really love your friends, you'll take the deal."

I pulled the phone away from my ear and stared at the screen. I wanted to crush it in my fist. I wanted to tell him to fuck the fuck off. I wanted to scream that I'd never, ever betray the club.

But what if betraying them was the only way to save them?

"Am I interrupting?" said a voice.

My head jerked up. Mac was standing in the rain not six feet from me. I hadn't heard him come out. How long had he been standing there?

I stabbed the button to end the call and shook my head.

We walked towards each other and met in the rain. It was really coming down, now, soaking our clothes in seconds. Mac nodded back towards the medical center. "Annabelle's pretty upset."

I nodded. That was next on my list.

Mac stopped close by...but not quite close enough to touch. "We need to talk. This isn't the time for us to be fighting."

I nodded slowly. Mac was like a brother to me. I hated fighting with him.

He put his hands out palm up, rain pounding down on them. "You've got to stop all this lone wolf shit. We're a club. But first you ride off to Teston and rescue Annabelle, all by yourself, and start this whole thing with Volos. Then I have to put a gun to your head to stop you blowing away a rival president. Then you take off again and nearly kill a guy." His face tightened. "Now I find you standing out here on your own in the rain, on the phone."

Shit. He suspected.

"I'm just trying to fix it," I said bitterly. "I started this. It's my problem."

"It's not *your problem!*" snapped Mac. "It's *our problem!* When are you gonna learn that?" He sighed. "Why won't you ever let us help you? This is your club as much as it's anyone else's! We're here for you!"

I met his eyes. Rain was streaming down both of our faces and there was a crash of thunder from overhead. That was what he'd never understood: I couldn't take their help. It had to be a one-way street.

I didn't *deserve* their help. Not after what I did to my first family. And I couldn't risk losing the club like I'd lost them. I shook my head.

"Goddammit! *Talk to me!*" yelled Mac. "What aren't you telling me?"

This was it. This was when I should tell him about Agent Trent, if I was going to. I could come clean, never having made the deal, and he'd trust me again.

But then the deal would be off the cards.

And Volos would wipe out the club.

I had to fix this myself...somehow.

I pushed past him. And felt something between us break. It hurt like a motherfucker but I didn't see any other way.

Inside the medical center, I stood with water streaming from my rain-slick cut and pattering onto the tiles. More water was running out of my soaked hair and getting in my eyes and I had to keep brushing it away. But even when my vision was clear, I couldn't see Annabelle anywhere amongst the army of black leather.

I grabbed Viking's arm. "You see Annabelle?"

"She got a cab," he said. "Said she was going to your place."

I frowned. That wasn't like Annabelle. She wouldn't leave us all here, worrying about Ox, and sit home on her own. And she knew better than to take off on her own when Volos was still after her.

I found Mom and gave her another hug, telling her I had to go. "I need to find Annabelle," I muttered.

She grabbed my arm as I moved to go. "You're damn right you do," she told me, fire in her tear-stained eyes. "Don't let that one slip away, Carrick."

Slip away? I didn't understand women but Mom did and her words started a sick churning in my stomach. I nodded and ran for my bike.

The rain had slowed traffic to a crawl but I threaded my way through, going as fast as I dared on the slick streets. It was only early evening but the sky had turned so dark overhead that it felt like twilight. I had to flick my lights on as I roared up the street towards my house.

I hurled open the door. "Annabelle?"

Nothing. Why on earth would she come here and then leave again? Unless Viking had been wrong and she'd never come here at all. Or....

Shit.

With a sudden sense of dread, I stalked into the bedroom and threw open the closet doors. The bags we'd brought back from her step-dad's house were gone. The clothes I'd bought her since were gone. She'd run.

I called her phone. My heart sank as I heard her ringtone coming from the living room. I walked through and found her phone sitting on the coffee table.

I raced out into the rain and stood there, chest heaving, looking wildly up and down the street for some clue: a cab's lights disappearing at the end of the street, maybe. But there was nothing. She was well ahead of me and I had no idea where she was going.

You idiot! I'd been so busy blaming myself, I hadn't considered that she'd be doing the same thing. It was her Volos was after so she was convinced she was responsible for what happened to Ox. She probably blamed herself for the fire, too, and anything that Volos did in the future. She was trying to protect the rest of us by getting out of town. *Shit! Why didn't I see this coming? Why didn't she talk to me?*

Because I was an asshole.

Because I'd spent so many years on my own, doing the club's dirty work, I didn't understand this stuff.

Because I'd refused to share my past...and if I wasn't going to talk to her, of course she wouldn't talk to me.

I'd lost her.

I stared down the street, the rain sliding down my face almost blinding me. *Maybe it's better this way. Maybe she's better off without me.* She was smart and resourceful and she had clothes and money, now. If she ran far enough, maybe Volos wouldn't find her.

I shook my head, my hands tightening into fists and crushing the raindrops. *Fuck that. Maybe* wasn't good enough. I wasn't going to leave her out there on her own. I'd made a promise that I'd be there when she needed me. She needed me now, whether she knew it or not.

And it wasn't just the danger she was in. I wanted her back. I needed her back.

I ran to my bike. Where would she go? How would she get out of town fast?

The bus station.

This time I rode even faster, fantails of water kicking up behind my wheels as I roared through the streets. But when I pulled up outside the bus station and checked the schedule, I cursed.

Two buses had left in the last half hour. One went south, towards Sacramento, San Francisco and LA. The other went north, towards Portland. Opposite directions. And the minutes were ticking away:

soon, the buses would make their first stop. She might get off at some small town and check into a motel and then I'd have lost her forever.

I stared at the two routes and tried to think like Annabelle. Which would she have picked?

South, right? The bright lights of LA, or at least San Francisco. Sunshine. Everybody loves sunshine. Nobody wants to go to Portland.

I revved the engine and pulled out onto the street, heading south....

And then I slewed to a stop right in the middle of the street.

The guy behind me angrily honked his horn. I twisted around in the saddle and growled at him and he meekly held his hands up in apology.

I was thinking about Annabelle and how well I knew her. *Everybody loves sunshine.* Except Annabelle. She loved Haywood Falls, with its warm breezes and shady spots. But the further south you went, the hotter it got. In LA or even San Francisco, her gorgeous pale skin would fry.

I swung the bike around and roared north. And prayed I had it right.

37

ANNABELLE

I'd taken my sneakers off and was sitting with my feet up on the seat, hugging my knees and trying to thaw my soaked, numb toes with my hands.

"I *hate* rain. Don't you hate rain?" asked the woman sitting next to me. She was painting her nails a violent shade of pink.

"Mmm," I murmured noncommittally, staring out of the bus's window. The rain matched my mood. But there was so much water streaming down the glass, it was difficult to see anything.

It didn't matter. One road looked much like another. I figured one city would look much like another, too. And one cheap diner certainly looked much like another. That was the sort of place I'd need to waitress at: somewhere that was happy to pay me in cash, off the books. I wasn't sure how far Volos's reach extended but I wasn't taking any chances. I'd try to stay completely off the radar. I'd even deliberately left my phone at Carrick's house, in case Volos could somehow track it.

That wasn't the only reason, though. Walking out on him had been the hardest thing I'd ever done. This way, he couldn't call me and try to talk me round. I had to do this. It was the only way to put things right. I'd already put too many people in danger. I had to get the hell away.

"When we get to LA," said the woman sitting next to me, "I'm gonna lie on the beach *all day.*"

"Mmm," I muttered, not really listening. I rested my chin on my knees. It felt as if my heart was made of paper and someone was slowly, agonizingly, tearing it in two. *Goodbye, Carrick.*

38

CARRICK

The rain was pounding down so hard that the road was actually running with it, the tires surrounded by a halo of spray as they cut through. A few times, I felt the steering go light. But I had to catch that bus. *If I get her back, I swear I'll tell her everything. Every last detail.* She'd know me, poison and all.

Finally, I saw the bus's lights up ahead. I powered past it and checked my mirror. Yep: *Portland.*

I slowed until the bus was dangerously close behind me. The driver honked his horn. "Pull over!" I yelled, gesturing wildly. "Stop the bus!"

The driver shook his head. He looked terrified.

That's when I thought about what I looked like. A Hell's Princes biker, riding up out of the near-darkness, yelling at him. No sane person would stop. Hell, he'd probably call the cops. Just for once, I wished I didn't look so scary.

I dropped back so that I was alongside the driver's window. *"Please,"* I yelled, as diplomatically as I could. "Emergency!"

I don't know what did it. I don't know if it was something in my voice, or if he just figured that no one would be dumb enough to be out there on a bike in those conditions, chasing down a bus without a damn good reason. But after several seconds, he slowed and pulled over. I pulled in behind him and then ran, bursting through the doors as soon as they scissored open. "Annabelle!" I yelled as I bounded up the steps. "Annabelle!"

I scanned the sea of curious faces. She wasn't there.

She was on the bus to LA.

I felt my whole world disintegrate. I'd been frantic, desperate...but until that second, until that moment of actually losing her forever, I hadn't realized just how deep she'd gotten. I hadn't let myself admit that I had completely fallen for her.

And then I saw a cloud of copper hair rise from what I'd thought was an empty seat. She'd been hunched down low, out of sight. She stood, her eyes locked on me, but she didn't speak. She waited for me to.

I swallowed. She was near the back of the bus and I was right at the front, so I had to speak up. "I'm sorry," I said. My voice didn't sound like my own. Deep, sure. Irish, of course. But it had lost some of the gruffness. I was open, now. Exposed. "I didn't think...I'm not *good* at this fucking stuff."

She just looked at me with those big, moss-green eyes, blinking back tears.

"I should have realized...it's not your fault, okay?"

She squeezed past her seatmate and out into the aisle, but she didn't walk towards me. "It is," she said.

"It's *not!* This is him, this is Volos. It's on him, not you."

She swallowed. "Ox—"

"We knew what we were getting into. We said we'd protect you and we will." All around me, people were looking back and forth between us, following the conversation and trying to figure out what the hell we were talking about.

She sniffed. "If I go away, you won't be in danger anymore. The club won't be in danger."

I started marching down the bus towards her, boots clumping on the metal. "If you go away, I can't protect you. And I made a promise."

She swallowed again as I reached her. Her voice caught. "Is that— Is that the only reason?"

I shook my head savagely. "I need you to stay...because I'm in love with you." I pushed my fingers up her cheek and into her hair, leaving wet trails across her skin.

She took a big, shuddering breath. "I can't love you if you won't let me know you."

I felt that black, oily sac of poison inside me throb and glisten. I'd been hiding it away from her, terrified I'd lose her if she saw it. And partially, I realized now, scared of how much it would hurt, to split it open. But if I didn't do this, I was going to lose her for sure. And that would hurt way, way worse. I took her hand and knitted my fingers with hers. "You come back with me," I promised, "And I'll tell you every fucking thing."

She looked up at me, eyes swimming...and nodded. And then we were kissing, raindrops falling from my hair and splashing onto her face. We brushed lips, tasted, then kissed hard and desperate, hands coming up to entwine in each other's hair. The iron band that had been constricting around my chest since the hospital finally snapped and I could breathe again. I drunk her in in big, hungry gulps.

"If he's local," said the woman who'd been sitting next to Annabelle, "I can see why you put up with the rain. They don't make 'em like that in LA."

Annabelle turned, flushed and grinned all at the same time. Then she bit her lip. "I hate to tell you this, but I think you're on the wrong bus."

39

ANNABELLE

When the slightly reproachful driver had opened up the luggage bays and I'd retrieved my bags, when I'd pressed a $10 bill into his palm for all the trouble and the bus had driven off, I turned to Carrick.

We were in the middle of nowhere, halfway between Haywood Falls and the next town, nothing but a two-lane road with thick greenery on each side of it. The rain, if anything, had gotten even heavier and we were both soaked. Volos was still out there somewhere, plotting against the club.

And I didn't care about any of it. Carrick was in love with me. And I was—my whole chest lifted as I let myself think it for the first time —I was in love with him.

He grabbed me under the ass, hands squeezing the rain-soaked denim and the warm flesh beneath. Then he swung me up into the air and clasped me to him with my groin grinding against his abs. He started kissing the rain from my neck and then my bare shoulder, pushing my wet hair away and kissing up my cheek to my ear. I sighed and twisted, squirming against him as his lips laid trails of heat along my chilled skin. I kissed his forehead, his cheekbones, bent to kiss his jaw line. And finally, our mouths met and we kissed full on the lips.

It was even better than before. Raw and unrestrained because he wasn't holding anything back, now. His lips, dripping with rain, hard and bold as he kissed mine, savage against my softness. The slight scratch of his stubble as we twisted and pressed, the brush of his tongue as he swept it across my lips.

His tongue pressed for entry and I welcomed him in, dancing with him, panting together as our bodies began to move in rhythm with the kiss. His hips began to rock and my thighs squeezed in response as my groin ground against the hardness of his body.

Cars were tearing past us, their headlights painting our bodies white. I was so caught up in it, I barely thought about the people watching us. But when a truck tore by only a few feet away, Carrick walked us off the side of the road and into the trees, where we'd be safe.

The next thing I knew, my ass hit something hard and Carrick was pressing between my legs, wedging me between him and whatever was behind me so that he could use his hands. I wriggled my shoulders and felt rough bark.

Carrick's face was inches from mine. "I can't wait," he told me and that rich seam of Irish in his voice was like a ribbon of silver, whipping my mind and sending a deep rush of heat straight to my groin. "I need to have you right here."

Then he was kissing me again, warm hands on my cheeks, lips coming down and owning me. I closed my eyes. Thunder rolled overhead as his hands slid down my body and found the hem of my soaked tank top. He dragged the wet fabric up over my breasts and then pushed the bra up to follow it. I began to pant as the cold, wet air hit my breasts, nipples standing out like pebbles. Then his warm hand and furnace-hot mouth captured one, fingers squeezing as his tongue lashed across my sensitive flesh. I cried out: every stroke of his tongue made me writhe against him, my breath hitching faster and faster.

He lifted his mouth for a second. "*Jesus,* you've got beautiful breasts," he growled. His mouth took possession of the other one: long, hot sweeps across my aching nipple. My ass rasped against the tree, my back arching: I was almost climbing it, the feelings were so intense. He straightened up and his hard pecs rubbed against the slickened softness of my breasts. We kissed again, twisting and grinding. Rain poured down our faces but it couldn't find a chink between us, we were so tightly locked together from lips to groin.

Then I felt his hands at the belt of my jeans. As he worked the buckle, my hands grabbed the bottom of his t-shirt and dragged it up his body, baring his abs and chest. I couldn't get his cut off but I needed to feel his bare skin against mine. As soon as I pressed forward and his abs stroked my stomach, I went wild. My arms went around his waist and then rose, sliding over the muscles of his back, feeling the power there. I felt my jeans loosen and then his hand was going down between our bodies, scooping under the elastic of my panties—

Ah! Two fingers found my clit, gliding either side of it in an upside-down Y, teasing it, making me helplessly circle my hips. Then he was moving lower, down over my lips. I was already wet for him. He only had to rub once, twice and then...*God!* Two thick fingers spearing up into me, slow but unstoppable.... He began to pump me like that, growling in my ear. "You're *mine,* Annabelle. Not just my lover but my fucking *love."* The way he said *love* changed everything. In his accent, it became a whole new word, a new role. Not poetry and flowers but something hard and enduring, forged in fire and blood.

He drew back just enough that he could look into my eyes. "Say it."

His fingers never stopped pumping me and I could feel myself tight and hot and *God* so wet around them. With every satiny push I caught my breath and squeezed my thighs together. I realized I was going to come, right there in the rain, up against a tree. "Your love," I rasped.

His mouth went to my ear, his fingers driving faster, harder. I was grinding my ass against the tree now, the orgasm rushing towards me.

"Forever." Another foreign word. *Forever,* with his accent, wasn't something said on a whim. *Forever* was a promise.

I panted. *"Forever."*

He put his lips so close to mine I could feel every syllable. "I love you," he told me. And kissed me just as I exploded. I clutched him tight, panting hard against his lips as I levered him against me as tightly as I could. I wanted to absorb him, to become one with him. I wanted to never stop feeling those rugged, warm shoulders under my hands. I felt myself spasm around his fingers as the orgasm rippled through me, my whole body rocking again and again until I slumped weakly, only my grip on his shoulders holding me up.

He looked down at my half-naked body. I could feel the bulge of his cock through his soaked jeans. He wanted me...but he must have come to the same conclusion I had: we couldn't do it here. Even if we could make it work against the tree, my legs were so shaky I couldn't hold myself up for long.

My solution would have been to get on his bike and ride back to his house. But Carrick wasn't that patient.

He bent, put his shoulder into the crease of my hip and lifted me. I yelped as I was hoisted over his shoulder. Then he set off, carrying me deeper into the forest.

40

ANNABELLE

I hung upside-down, half-naked and panting. My tank top and bra were still under my armpits, my naked breasts pressed against the wet leather of his cut. My jeans and panties were at mid-thigh, my naked ass upturned to the sky as I bounced on his shoulder. Part of me was thinking things like, *thank God there isn't anyone around* and *I should tell him to put me down.*

Part of me was thrilling to the feeling of being picked up and carried off, caveman style.

It was getting dark and, out here, that meant *really* dark. We were too far from the road for the streetlights or headlights to reach and the clouds meant there were was no moonlight. Were we even going to be able to find our way back to his bike?

Then he stopped. "This looks okay," he muttered.

What does? Where are we? I couldn't see anything. All I could see was the shadowy outline of his taut ass under his jeans and the gleaming silver of his chain belt. But we seemed to be moving into a clearing....

He slowly turned around so that I could see. I tossed my soaking hair out of my eyes and blinked through the rain.

It was a cabin, long since abandoned. One window was missing its glass and the roof sagged in one corner but it was mostly intact. And definitely drier than outside.

There was a flash of lightning and the rain pelted down even harder. That must have made up his mind because he turned to face front and marched through the door.

Inside, he still didn't put me down. I twisted, getting an upside-down view of a kitchen, a living room and finally a bedroom. It must have been a holiday place where some family came each year, because it hadn't been completely stripped of furniture. There were still couches and beds, even curtains at the windows, but it looked as though no one had been there in years. Probably, the bank repossessed it and then, when it sat unsold for years, it had been left to go derelict. *That's so sad....*

Then Carrick was bending his knees and flipping me off his shoulder—

I landed with a *whump* on a big double bed. The mattress was dry —the roof was intact in here, at least. It was almost silent: we were too far from the road to hear the traffic. The only sound was the rain beating on the roof and my own fevered panting. I looked up...and saw Carrick slowly stripping off his cut.

Outside, in the rain, we'd both been desperate. Now we could take our time. He peeled off his soaked t-shirt, revealing those glorious washboard abs and the deep centerline that ran up his body.

"Take your clothes off." That blend of scalding, molten Irish silver and the hard rock beneath it.

I swallowed. I'd never undressed for anyone before. At the motel, I knew he'd secretly watched my reflection as I changed, but this different. This was deliberately stripping off for my lover.

No. My *love.*

I knelt up on the bed and slowly peeled my sodden tank top the rest of the way off. Then I unhooked my bra and tossed it aside.

Carrick said nothing. But his eyes gleamed in the darkness as he watched me.

As he stripped off his boots, I lay back on the bed and hooked down my jeans and panties, pushing the wet fabric down my legs and prying off my sneakers and socks at the same time, then letting the whole bundle fall beside the bed. Naked except for the shamrock necklace, I sat up, legs together and knees tipped over to one side. I watched as he pushed down his jeans and boxer briefs, his cock springing out as he released it.

"Lie back." I'd known he sounded more Irish when he was angry. I hadn't known, until now, that his accent thickened when he was really turned on. The hard *ck* of *back* was like ice shattering as it met the prow of an icebreaker, huge and unstoppable. I swallowed and lay back on my forearms, my feet towards him.

"Open your legs."

I slid the soles of my feet along the mattress and spread. I could feel my wetness as I opened to him.

I heard the rubber sound of a condom going on and then he was climbing onto the bed, the mattress sinking as his knee pressed between my legs. He moved up over me and I gasped as the hot length of his cock hit my thigh.

It was almost completely dark in the cabin, now. My heart sped up: there was something about not being able to properly see him that made him seem even more dangerous and darkly exciting.

He shifted a little and the head of his cock nudged my folds. I caught my breath. I felt his hands plant on either side of my head, the size of him making the mattress flex. Then his head lowered between my breasts and I gasped as he kissed the soft skin between them and the necklace that hung there. The gold shamrock pressed into my skin, the metal silky smooth and so warm from my body that it felt like a part of me. Then he traced upward with his lips, following a path between my breasts and up my throat, tilting my head back. When he reached my lips, he stopped and stared down at me.

"Once I found the club," he said, "I never needed anything else in my life. I never needed any*one* else. But I need you, Annabelle. You're like nothing else on God's earth. When we were in that motel, I thought maybe you'd been sent to tease me, because I couldn't have you." His voice was soft but loaded with weight. It boomed into me, the vibrations moving through every inch of me and turning to a warm glow. "But now I've got you." His thumbs rubbed slowly across my shoulders as if to prove it. "And I think maybe you were right. Maybe you're meant to save me."

He leaned down and kissed me, a feather-light touch, as if he wanted to kiss me without any risk of changing me at all. But I wanted to tell him that he already had changed me: that somehow, even with everything that was going on, I was happier now with him and the Princes than I'd ever been.

Then he was pressing into me and I arched my back as his thickness spread me, throwing out fluttering silver pleasure that turned hot and dark as he filled me. He plunged right up inside me until the glossy curls at his base were against my body, and I caught my breath at the feeling. I could feel myself tight around him, every heartbeat he stayed there triggering new waves of heady sensation.

As he began to move, I ran my hands over him, exploring him in the darkness. My palms slid from the wide shoulders that dwarfed mine down the muscles of his back to the hardness of his ass and I clutched him there. I could feel his ass flex as he pushed deep, pulled back and drove into me again.

The darkness was total, now but I didn't need to see him. I've never felt so close to a person. I was aware of every little detail: the slight roughness of his calloused hands when he pushed my hair back off my forehead; the stroke of his chest against my breasts, my nipples achingly stiff; the push of his thickly muscled hips between mine, holding me open and pinned.

He began to speed up and I went wild, tangling my fingers in his hair and drawing him down into a kiss. As his lips met mine he started to pound me, just as I'd imagined that night in the motel, his hips slamming me into the bed. The pleasure went from silver to white-hot, everything narrowing down to the feel of him inside me and his urgent possessive kisses. He owned my mouth, ravishing me with his tongue and then sucking my top lip into his mouth and biting it just a little. His hips never stopped rising and falling and now he began to twist them as well. I wrapped my arms around him, clutching him tight as my climax approached. "Carrick!" I panted through the kisses. *"Carrick!"*

The whole bed was rocking. His thrusts built and built, speeding me towards my peak. My fingers dug deep into the muscles of his back as I felt the pleasure spiral tight, ready to burst—

I found his cheeks in the darkness, his stubble rough against my palms, and drew him down for one last kiss. Our tongues met just as I exploded and my climax came out as a long, muffled moan. A second later, he groaned and I felt him shoot inside me.

When we'd recovered, he gathered me into his arms and rolled us onto our sides, my head against his chest. I still couldn't see him but it almost felt more intimate, that way. Thunder still rumbled overhead, but it seemed to be moving away and there was nothing, nature or human, that could hurt me when I was with him.

As our breathing settled and we lay there cuddling, the mood changed. I think it was the darkness. It made it easier for him to visit the places he hadn't wanted to go back to.

"It starts with my dad," he said at last.

41

CARRICK

"I was born in Ireland. The North. My mom was over from the US on business, met my dad and fell for him. She wanted to be with him but it was a pain for her to find work in Ireland and a pain for my dad to work in America. So there was a lot of travelling back and forth, when we were kids."

"We?" she asked. "You have brothers and sisters?"

"Brothers," I said. "Four of them." An iron band tightened around my chest. *Or maybe just three, now.* "We spent some time in the US, some in Ireland. Moved schools a lot. But we were a happy family. I spent more time with my dad than the rest of them: he used to have this motorcycle he'd ride on weekends and sometimes he'd take me out on it. He wasn't a *biker,* not like I am now, but he taught me to love bikes." I swallowed, remembering the smooth metal and chromed exhausts, the grin on his face as he looked round at me to check I was okay.

"Anyway," I told her, "we're spending a summer in the US. My dad's traveling for work and we're pretty close so I miss him a lot. I spend a lot of that summer brooding and maybe that's why I don't see what's going on." I could hear my voice going tight. Annabelle must have been able to hear it too because she pressed against me, her soft body calming me.

"She had these friends," I said. "That's how she introduced them to us. We'd all be packed off to another room and she'd have five, six hour talks with them. Really intense. A few times I listened at the door and it was like...I don't know, it was like a therapy session crossed with a bible meeting, only it didn't sound like, y'know, *the* bible. Just a lot of stuff about guidance and confessing and them helping her to find the right path."

I inhaled but breathing was difficult, my rage at my own stupidity filling my chest. "I was just a kid. She seemed happy—in fact, she seemed happier every time they came around. It didn't occur to me that grown-ups could make bad decisions. I didn't realize they were indoctrinating her."

I felt Annabelle's chest swell as she drew in a slow, horrified breath.

"By the time we figure out something's wrong, it's too late. I tell my dad and he starts making his way home. But by now, things are getting really scary. I hadn't noticed some things until then, like the way some of her *friends* who came to our house would look at us. Not nasty or angry but...like they were grading us. Assessing us like we were *things*."

"Oh Jesus," breathed Annabelle. I found her hand in the dark and squeezed it. I knew that she'd experienced that, too.

"My brothers had put it together before I did, Kian especially. He'd done some asking around and he'd heard things about these people. He figured out it was a cult. One where kids were—" I swallowed. "Where kids disappeared."

Annabelle was silent but she gripped me even harder.

"We could all feel it sliding out of control. We tried to talk to my mom, to warn her, but she was too far gone: I think they'd been feeding her drugs, in those meetings. If we criticized her friends, she'd get mad. All the rumors we'd heard about the cult were wrong, she said, propaganda by its enemies. And then she tells us that one of my brothers, Bradan, is going on a 'special trip' with her friends. She gets him in the car. We're all clawing at the handles, trying to get the doors open. Bradan's screaming, hysterical. And she drives off."

I drew in a shuddering breath. I could feel the most difficult part bearing down on me and I wanted to get it out while I still could. "Then my dad gets home. We try to explain what's been going on. My mom gets back and he tries to talk her down but seeing him sends her over the edge. I guess the cult knew my dad would come between her and them, at some stage, so they'd filled her head with really evil shit. She's convinced that he's a monster, that he's going to take her boys away from her, that only the cult can save us. She says she's going to take the other three of us 'to safety.' Tells us to get in the car. When my dad tries to stop her, she grabs a knife—"

Annabelle's whole body went stiff. I was just as rigid next to her, my mouth the only part of me moving. The darkness made it easier to talk but harder to stay distanced from the memories. I could see it all unfolding in front of my eyes. "There's a struggle. My mom and dad are down on the floor. We're all screaming. My dad has to get her to let go of the knife so he hits her head against the tiles...."

"And that's how my dad killed my mom."

42

ANNABELLE

I was glad it was pitch black. I don't think I could have stood to see the pain in his eyes. I tried to imagine what it must have been like but I couldn't even come remotely close. To lose one parent just as another turns into a killer...*God!* I clung to him for all I was worth.

He was trying to keep his voice neutral and detached: the only way he could get through it. "We couldn't find Bradan. He'd just vanished. The police came and took my dad to jail. Turned out, the cult had friends in high places, people who didn't want to see it investigated. They spun my mom's death as a murder, painted my dad as a drunken Irishman who'd come home and beaten his wife to death. The authorities put me and my brothers into care." He swallowed. "But...."

He took a breath. Another. Building up the courage to say it.

"I *ran*. I couldn't stand the thought of living with some strange family so I ran. Right when my brothers needed me, I disappeared. When we'd lost our parents, when we all needed to lean on each other, I vanished."

Suddenly, it all started to come together. Why he'd wound up in the MC. Why he was so insistent that he had to give but never take from them. He was still trying to repay the debt to his first family.

"You were just a kid," I told him. "You couldn't be expected to hold everything together. You just would have gone into care too."

I felt him shake his head. "I should have *tried.* Aedan tried. Got us to all get the shamrock tattoos, so we'd remember we were still a family. But the next morning, I ran."

"I went to Chicago and lived on the streets. Got by by stealing. One of my brothers, Aedan, had taught me how to fight so I could look after myself when I had to. But I didn't want to hurt anyone. I'd steal from parked cars, boost a TV from the back of a truck, anything but mug someone. I'd seen enough violence."

"A few years went by. I was on my own and I thought I was doing fine. My brothers were all with foster families but I don't know much about what happened to them after that. I felt so guilty about running...plus, there was a split down the middle. Kian and Sean couldn't forgive my dad for what he'd done. Aedan and I still loved him. I went to visit him in jail a few times: that's how I know that Kian went into the military as soon as he was old enough, because he had to get my dad to sign the forms. Sean, I don't know. Aedan wound up in New York, making money boxing. I reached out to him a few times, let him know I was in Chicago."

"But then things started to get too hot for me there. I'd moved onto stealing cars and I stole one too many from the wrong neighborhood, got some gangs after me. I had to run again and this time I hopped a goods train and rode it all the way to LA. And that's where I met Briggs."

"Briggs?"

"President of the Hell's Princes before Mac." Carrick sighed. "I'd literally just got off the train, was wandering the streets. Never been to LA before, didn't know where to go or which streets to stay away from. So straightaway, I got into a fight. Three guys have me backed up against a dumpster, I'm just about managing to hold my own but it's only a matter of time until they get me down on the ground and I get my ass handed to me. And then this Harley roars into the alley and a voice booms out, *Let the kid be.*"

Carrick drew a deep breath. "He was cool and tough and he

reminded me of my dad. He told me he needed guys like me in his club: I'd have to do my time as a hanger-on and then a prospect, but he could get me in, even though I was only seventeen. He took me back to Haywood Falls and that's how I found the club. Became a prospect and not long after that, I met you."

He went quiet. I wanted the story to end there: a happy ending. The guy who lost his dad found a new one. But I knew that wasn't how it finished. I could feel it in his body. I could hear it in his voice, a growing stain of bitterness as he talked about Briggs. Something bad was coming.

"I wanted to impress him," Carrick said. "And I'd do anything to help the MC. So when Briggs said he had a job for me, I jumped at it. He took me to a poker game someone was running on our turf and told me to smash the place up and teach the guy a lesson. And I did it. And I was good at it. And eventually, the club made me their enforcer."

"But then Briggs told me about this fed, a guy called Walker. He had some sort of grudge against the club and he'd faked evidence that we were dealing heroin. He was blackmailing Briggs: either he pay him or the whole club would go to jail. Briggs told me that the rest of the club didn't know, that we maybe had a rat and I was the only one he could trust. He said—" Carrick hissed air through his teeth—"he said I was like a son to him."

His voice was vicious now, sharp and toxic with the poison he was releasing. "I couldn't say no. I took an untraceable gun and a stolen car and I lay in wait for the guy. I ran him off the road and then, while he sat there bleeding and helpless in the wreck, I put a bullet in his head."

"And then, a few days later, I found out it was all bullshit. There was no blackmail plot. Walker hadn't been about to bring down the club. He had evidence against Briggs: *real* evidence, just on him. He was cooking up a drug deal behind the club's back. He'd conned me into doing his dirty work. And the FBI agent? Clean as they come. Had a wife and two kids." He swallowed. "I couldn't tell anyone: Briggs said he'd tie me to the murder if I did. Mac and the others eventually found out about the drug deal and Mac wound up killing Briggs over the border in Mexico. Mac took over as our new president. But no one ever found out about the FBI agent. No one except Briggs and me. And now you."

God...he'd kept this bottled up for years, trusting no one...until me. And I realized why he was able to tell me now, in this pitch-black cabin: he didn't want to see my expression. He thought I'd be disgusted. He thought I'd hate him. And he was willing to tell me anyway, to risk losing me, just so he could finally be straight with me.

I had to show him I still loved him. That I didn't think less of him, not for one second. He was lying there silently but I knew he was screaming inside, needing to know. I pushed him over onto his back and rolled on top of him. "Listen to me," I said urgently. "That is *not* on you. You didn't know. That's on Briggs, one hundred percent. He *used* you."

I could feel the battle going on in his body: half of him wanted to believe me but half had been living so long with the guilt that he couldn't let it go. "He used you," I said again, squeezing his shoulders. And after a moment, I felt his tension ease just a little.

"Doesn't bring the guy back though, does it?" he said bitterly.

"No." I was picking my words carefully. I knew it wouldn't help to lie. "It doesn't bring him back. But people can redeem themselves, Carrick. You saved me. That's got to be worth something."

His hands slid up my flanks, his palms smoothing over my skin. "Maybe," he said at last.

I covered my hands with his. "*Definitely.*"

And I felt his whole body slowly relax under me. I hadn't healed him, but I'd helped to open the wound so the poison could escape. "Come here," he murmured, and pulled me down into a tight embrace.

I woke to the sound of scampering. When I realized it wasn't a dream, I opened my eyes. Sitting on the floor next to the bed, looking up at us with huge eyes, was a chipmunk. It chattered once, then bounded across the floor and out of the door, probably wondering what the hell we were doing in its home.

I looked around. It was light and I was lying face-down atop Carrick, both of us utterly naked. His strong body had kept me warm all night.

When I checked the window, a clear blue sky was waiting for us outside. But when I woke Carrick, the blue I saw in his eyes was even better. I wasn't kidding myself that his past was dealt with and forgotten: you can't leave something like that behind you overnight. But I felt like I was on the inside, at last. We could deal with it together.

It was only six in the morning. "We could go to your place," I suggested. Curling up with him in a warm bed with actual covers sounded very, very good. I pulled on my still-wet jeans. *Eww.*

"I don't have much in the refrigerator," he said, pulling on his similarly-wet clothes. "Don't know about you, but I need breakfast."

He was right. I was starving. I hadn't eaten since before Ox's accident. *Ox!* That was a reminder that our troubles weren't over. Volos was out there somewhere, plotting. But we'd deal with that together, too.

"Let's go see Mom," said Carrick. "She's always up early and she always cooks breakfast for whoever's around. We need to stop by the clubhouse anyway to let them know we're okay. And we can get an update on Ox."

I nodded, pulled on my sneakers and we set off. The forest was completely different in the daylight, tranquil and beautiful. I could see why someone had built a cabin there.

Something was still bothering me, though, something I had to tell him while we had some privacy. As he climbed onto the bike in front of me, his cut and t-shirt rode up and I saw the shamrock tattoo, the one he'd talked about. "The club...that's your family now, right?"

He froze...then nodded.

I reached out and put my hand on the tattoo, smoothing my palm

across his tan skin. "Families look out for each other. The club wants
to help us. You should let them."

He didn't look around. "Yeah," he muttered in a way that didn't
mean *yeah* at all. I could see his shoulders hunching and knotting. He
was still too wrapped up in guilt over not being there for his real
family. I knew better than to push him. One thing at a time.

"You think you'll ever get back in touch?" I asked cautiously.

He shook his head and started the engine. "Some things should
stay in the past."

We were the first ones at the compound, other than Mom herself, so
we had to unlock the gate and pull it aside ourselves. We figured
everyone else had stayed at the hospital until late and was still asleep.

Carrick headed into the clubhouse to make some calls and find
out about Ox. I said I'd help Mom whip up some breakfast. As I
walked up to her trailer, my stomach was rumbling. *This was a good
idea.* Mom always had fantastic coffee and I was thinking bacon, with
eggs sunny side up on toast made from her homemade bread....

I stopped outside the door and frowned. That was weird. Mr.
Fluffy was outside, scratching at the door. Mom never shut him out at
night. And Carrick was right: she was always up early. So why wasn't
she letting him in?

I knocked. No answer. I pushed open the door.

And stepped into hell.

43

ANNABELLE

For a second I just stood there on the threshold, gaping. I couldn't process what I was seeing. That mistake nearly ended me. Hungry for the fresh outside air, the flames surged out to meet me. I heard the crackle as the loose strands of hair on my forehead singed. Just in time, I staggered back, choking on a cloud of black smoke and slapping at my hair.

I ducked low and tried to see through the smoke. The entire inside of the trailer was ablaze. The flames had covered the floor, leaving only narrow channels and islands not alight. It had scaled the walls, the wallpaper and drapes hanging down in charred, burning sheets. When I looked up, I saw the ceiling creaking and groaning: flames had spread up into the insulation and it was crumbling down in flaming chunks as big as my head. *Why hadn't we seen this from the outside?*

Then I saw why. Someone had taped black plastic sheeting over the windows from the inside. They'd turned it into a sealed box. If I hadn't knocked the door, we'd never have known. Beneath the choking smoke, I caught the stink of gasoline. The fire wasn't an accident.

I took a step into the room, trying to see through the smoke. Surely she couldn't be in here, but I had to check—

Fear clutched at my chest as I saw her. Mom was sitting on the floor by the sink, duct tape over her mouth. I started towards her, then realized what I'd forgotten to do. I leaned out of the door, looked towards the clubhouse and yelled *"CARRICK!"* as loud as I could.

He got there before I was even halfway to Mom. He looked as if he wanted to grab me and haul me out of there to safety, but he knew by now that I wouldn't have listened and he didn't waste time arguing. I loved him for that.

Together, we dodged and clambered around the flames to where Mom sat. Several times, I felt the flames lick my thighs as we cut it too close. The only thing that saved us was our damp clothes.

As we got closer to Mom, I saw she was conscious. *Why hasn't she moved? Is she hurt?* We hunkered down on either side of her. Embers had started her nightdress smoldering in a couple of places and I quickly slapped them out. Carrick ripped off the tape covering her mouth.

"Get out of here," she said immediately. "The propane tanks!"

My gaze snapped to the huge range cooker and then to the pipes that went down beneath our feet. *Shit.* She was right: as soon as the fire ate its way under the floor, they'd go off like a bomb.

Carrick and I started to haul her to her feet, ignoring her protests. We'd carry her over the flames if we had to. But before her ass even left the floor, she jerked to a halt.

That's when we saw the handcuffs. Her wrists were cuffed behind her and the chain was wrapped around the sink's waste pipe. *Oh, shit....*

He'd planned this. Volos, or one of his men. They'd set the fire, made sure no one would come to her aid and then left her to a tortuous death, choking and burning, knowing the explosion would come but not knowing when.... *The bastard!*

Carrick reached under the sink and wrenched...but the pipe was old, hard iron, not plastic.

"Get out," repeated Mom.

"No!" both of us said simultaneously.

"There's no time." She started coughing. "The tanks will go up any minute."

"There's an extinguisher in the clubhouse," said Carrick, and started to get up.

"It doesn't *matter*," rasped Mom. "The fire's already under the floor."

We looked down and realized she was right. The floor was starting to sag as the flames filled the dark spaces beneath the trailer, where dead leaves and other debris had been building for years. Even if we put out the fire inside, we couldn't stop that one, not in time.

"*Go*," said Mom.

"We're not leaving you!" snapped Carrick.

I reached behind Mom and squeezed her hand, tears in my eyes. When I looked at Carrick, he was searching my face. I frowned. *What?*

Then I got it. This was something that couldn't be fixed with brute force or violence. This was a mechanical problem...and so he was looking to me for a solution.

I took in a terrified gulp of scorching air. *I don't know!* I couldn't think of anything. But if I didn't, Mom was going to die.

I stared at the waste pipe and tried to force my brain to work. Could we cut through it? There might be an acetylene torch somewhere in the workshop but there was no time to learn how to use it. Bolt cutters on the handcuffs? I couldn't remember seeing any. There was a crash as another section of the ceiling fell in and I turned to look behind me, the heat searing my face.

My eyes fell upon the huge, purple couch. Too big to go through the door. *The boys took the whole side of the trailer off for me.*

I looked around at the blazing walls...and the whole structure came apart in my mind. Four walls, pinned together at the corners with bolts so that the same parts could be reused to make different configurations of trailers. And the plumbing, including the pipe Mom was cuffed to, was part of the wall, not the floor.

"Find some chain," I told Carrick, coughing. "Thick, heavy chain.

Fix one end to your bike and put the other end through the window. I'll pass it around the pipe. Then *go.*"

Carrick stared at the pipe. "That'll break the pipe?"

"No. It'll pull the whole wall off."

"*What?!*"

"Do it! Go!"

He hesitated. I could tell the idea of leaving me there killed him. But someone had to stay to do up the chain. He finally growled and ran off through the flames.

Mom coughed. "I never thought I'd see Carrick listen to reason. You've got that boy hooked good."

Another piece of the ceiling fell in, spreading flames across the floor towards us. I tried using a blanket to smother them but everything was too hot, too dry: the flames sprang up again as quickly as I put them out. Mom and I huddled by the sink, drew our legs up and squashed ourselves into the smallest space we could. She started coughing again and I hugged her tight, her long silver hair trailing over my hands. *Hurry, Carrick.*

I hear the roar of a bike outside and the clank of heavy chain. I threw open the window above us and Carrick passed the end of the chain through: old and grimy but as thick as my wrist. I looped it around the metal pipe and passed it back to him. He grabbed me by the wrist and stared desperately into my eyes, as if he wanted to haul me right through the window and away with him.

"I know," I said. "*Go!*"

He ran to his bike. I ducked down. "Hold onto the sink," I told Mom. "As tight as you can."

From beneath us, there was a horrible, metallic *creak,* the sound of pressure that's built too high. I imagined the propane tanks, their paint blistered and peeling, their metal sides bulging....

I heard the bike accelerate away and the rattle as the slack in the chain was taken up. I squeezed Mom tight. Would this work? Would the momentum pull out the bolts or would the bike just snap to a stop at the end of the chain, sending Carrick flying to his death? *Please be right.*

The sound of the bike got quieter and quieter as it sped away from us. Then there was a metallic *chink* that vibrated through the whole trailer as the chain snapped taut and—

It was like being in a car that's suddenly rear-ended. One second, Mom and I were clinging to a stationary object. The next, our arms were almost yanked out of our sockets as the sink, the cupboards and the whole wall were jerked away.

Cool, clean air and brilliant sunlight drenched us and there was an instant when we were flying through the air. Then the wall become the floor as it crashed to the concrete and we were being dragged along behind Carrick's bike like sailors clinging to a makeshift raft. I felt one of my sneakers come off and looked down to find one of my feet was trailing on the ground. I snatched it back to safety. If my laces hadn't been loose, I probably would have lost a foot.

Carrick cut the engine and we slid to a stop a hundred feet from the trailer, sparks flying where the wall scraped along the floor. I looked at Mom, then down at myself. My hip was bruised from when the wall had slammed into the ground and I felt like I might throw up, but both of us seemed to be okay.

Carrick ran over, crouched down, and put his arms around both of us. I grabbed his bicep and clung tight, panting with adrenaline. I stared at the trailer: the flames had completely filled it, now, the remaining windows shattering as the heat got too much.

I turned to Carrick. "We should call—"

I didn't hear so much as feel the explosion. I think it was just too loud for my brain to register as sound: I just felt the aftershock of pain and the hot gale against my cheek. I threw my arm up instinctively to cover my face and felt it pelted with scorching metal and glass.

When I looked again, it was like there'd never been a trailer. There was just a blackened, twisted mess of metal that had once been the frame and a ring of shrapnel around it, most pieces no bigger than my hand. Then I saw something moving through the smoke. Mr. Fluffy padded over to us, leapt into Mom's lap and settled down as if nothing had happened. I don't know where he'd been when the trailer exploded, but he must have used up at least one life.

Carrick mouthed something but I couldn't make out what. Bits of lighter debris started to drift down. I recognized scraps of purple fabric from Mom's huge couch. I put my arm around Mom and hugged her close. She hugged me back, then mouthed something at me.

"What?" I asked, frowning. Why did they keep miming? "Just say it!"

And then I realized they weren't miming at all. I just couldn't hear them.

I put my head on Carrick's chest and all three of us sat there, watching the debris drift down, until the first fire truck arrived.

44

CARRICK

Word got around fast. Everyone in town had heard the explosion and the compound was soon full of fire trucks, sheriff's department cars and bikers. Incredibly, no one was hurt, but fragments of Mom's trailer were found way down the street.

Our hearing came back after a few hours. Mom had some minor burns. Annabelle had escaped with some singed hair and a few bruises. After digging in the debris, she even managed to find the sneaker she lost and held it up proudly. I grabbed her and clutched her to my chest. *She could have been killed. They both could have been.* I could feel the rage start, deep inside me, a red-hot storm that grew and grew.

I had a hacking cough and it hurt like a motherfucker every time I took a deep breath: I'd inhaled a lot of smoke when I fought my way back out of the trailer to get my bike. The paramedics wanted to take me to the medical center but I shook my head. I helped clear some of the wreckage, hurling big chunks of blackened metal into a dumpster, but however much anger I vented there was always more inside.

I saw Mac having a heated argument with Sheriff Harris. The

explosion was way too big to cover up, especially after the fire at the warehouse. Either the FBI or the ATF would be starting an investigation into the club, even though we were the victims.

I stalked into the clubhouse but there was more bad news inside. Ox had come through the surgery but he hadn't woken yet. There was no way of telling if he would, or if there'd be permanent damage to his brain. My anger flared, white hot, my whole body trembling with it. *The whole club's being torn apart.* Just like Volos promised.

I got Mom moved into one of the spare rooms in the clubhouse. I made sure Annabelle was okay and then told her I needed to go for a ride to clear my head.

I passed Mac on my way out to my bike. He grabbed hold of my arm. "Where are you going?"

"I need to think," I snapped.

"You need to stay here. We got to figure this out as a club."

I snatched my arm away. "Fuck that! Mom nearly got killed, Ox is in the hospital, our warehouse is gone...what's next? You? Hunter? Viking?" I swung my leg over my bike. "*You* figure it out as a club." And I roared off before he could stop me.

Riding down Main Street, I could feel the eyes of the townsfolk on me. Sure, they'd always feared us...but that fear had been balanced by respect, even *need.* We'd always protected the town. Now we'd brought chaos to it: rocks coming through the window of the diner, a major fire and now an explosion right in the center of town.

They didn't trust us, anymore. And even an outlaw club can't operate unless its town is on its side.

I rode down to the lake and cruised along the road that skirted it. The sun was catching the waves, the sky was blue...everything was perfect, just like the day I'd first brought Annabelle here.

Except now, a thick, black plume of smoke rose from the center of town, spreading out and hiding the waterfalls. The picture postcard was ruined.

I'd started this, when I'd kept my promise to Annabelle. I'd brought this down on the town, on the club, on my friends. I had to fix it. And that meant doing the unthinkable.

I dug in the breast pocket of my cut and found the card Agent Trent had given me. And then I called him to make a deal.

45

CARRICK

When I got back to the clubhouse, Mac was waiting for me outside along with Hunter, Viking and the others. "We gotta talk," he told me.

I shook my head and pushed past him. Found Annabelle, grabbed her hand and led her out to my bike.

But Mac was standing in front of it. I could see his fists clenching and opening: he was hovering on the very edge of rage, just like me. "Brother, you've got to tell me what's going on. Where are you going?"

"I don't have to tell you that." I tried to push him aside but he held fast.

"Who were you talking to, last night at the hospital?"

"Get out of my way, Mac."

"Was it a fed?"

I froze. Which was all the answer he needed. He grabbed the front of my cut and slammed me up against the clubhouse wall. "Are you *fucking* kidding me?" he roared.

"It wasn't a fed!" I snapped. But I've never been good at lying. I heaved him away from me but he grabbed my arm and we spun around. Both of us went crashing through the doors of the clubhouse and we sprawled in the hallway.

He was up first, leaping astride me and driving a fist into my face. It hurt, but what hurt a lot more was when I glimpsed Annabelle through the half-open doors. She looked horrified...and disappointed. *But I'm doing this to save you!*

Mac was shaking his head. "You were like a brother," he spat. "I never figured you for a rat."

I snarled and threw him off me. He went crashing into the trophy cabinet, shattering several of the panes. The framed copy of the original set of club rules fell off the wall and smashed on the floor.

I jumped to my feet and pushed my way through the doors before Mac could stop me, grabbing Annabelle by the hand. But Hunter and Viking were waiting outside, standing in front of my bike.

I only hesitated for a second. They were my brothers. This was my club. But I had to end this thing.

I grabbed Caorthannach from its holster on my bike and pointed the shotgun right at them.

Annabelle grabbed my arm. "Are you *crazy?!* Think about what you're doing! Carrick, just *think!*"

"Get the fuck out of my way," I told them.

They slowly backed away, their faces like thunder.

I climbed onto my bike and felt Annabelle climb on behind me. Then we were roaring off and out of the compound, feeling their eyes on us the whole way. I blasted out of town and down to the lake, taking the back roads until I was sure they weren't following us. I finally slowed to a stop near a muddy trail that led right down to the lakeside.

I almost didn't want to turn around. I didn't want to face her. But I had to. She was crying, her eyes red, her cheeks shining. "What's going on?" she sobbed. "Just tell me!"

"We're going to meet an FBI agent," I told her. "We're doing a deal, so you can be safe." I climbed off the bike and led her by the hand.

She shook her head, hanging back. "No. *No!* I know what the club means to you. They're your family, you can't rat them out! I don't *want* to be safe, not if it means that!"

But I kept walking, towing her along. If I didn't hurry and get it over with, I might break down myself. Because this was going to be the hardest thing I'd ever done.

Agent Trent's SUV was parked in a clearing halfway down the slope. I could just see the lake sparkling in the distance. Trent was in the back seat and I could see a driver up front. Two serious-looking guys in suits—more agents, I guessed—were standing guard by the front of the car.

"You ready to do this?" said one of the guys as we approached. "We can take you to a safe location right now. The two of you can be in witness protection by the end of the night. All you gotta do is give Agent Trent what he needs to put the club away."

Annabelle spun to face me. "You *can't!* Carrick, this isn't right and you know it!"

I looked her in the eye and nodded. "You're right," I said softly. "It isn't right." I looked at the two guys. "That's why I'm changing the deal."

Immediately, they shook their heads. "No changes. You give us the club or no deal."

But the electric window of the SUV whined down and Agent Trent looked at me curiously.

I took a deep breath. "I can give you something even better." It took me another few seconds before I could bring myself to say it. I'd been keeping the secret for so long, until Annabelle helped me let it out. "I'll confess to the murder of FBI Agent Walker eleven years ago." I looked at Annabelle. "Annabelle goes into witness protection...and I go to jail."

46

ANNABELLE

"*What?!*" I could feel my face going white. Carrick ratting out the club would have been unthinkable but *this?!* Oh God, in his mind it made perfect sense: he'd save me, save the club...the only person who'd suffer would be *him*. "You can't!" I flung myself against him. "I won't let you!"

But Carrick was looking over my head, towards Agent Trent. I followed his gaze. Trent was trying hard to keep a poker face but I could see him weakening. He'd bring in the killer of a federal agent and solve a years-old case at the same time. He'd probably get a freakin' commendation. He nodded.

"*No!*" I almost screamed it. "Carrick, *no!*"

He looked down at me and shook his head. "It's the only way. You'll be safe. You'll get a new name. You can start again."

"I don't *want* to start again. I want—"—my voice caught—"I want *you* and *this,* I want Haywood Falls and the club—"

"Volos is never going to stop coming. Not until he realizes you're gone. This is the only way to keep everyone safe."

I clung onto him. I pressed my face between the cool leather sides of his cut and into the warm valley between his pecs. I could feel myself pressing the heels of my sneakers into the dirt, as if I could anchor him there if I only hung on hard enough. "No!" I said stubbornly. "There has to be another way!"

I felt that big chest twist as he shook his head. "There isn't. Not even you can come up with another way. Even with your big brain. This is the way it has to be." He bent over me, putting his lips to my ear. "All the pieces have fallen into place, Annabelle. Like one of your machines. This wouldn't work if I hadn't killed that agent. I'd have nothing to offer them. I've been living with this for years. You helped me deal with it and now it can finally do some good."

I thumped him on the chest. "*No!* It's Briggs who should answer for it, not you! He *used* you!" I looked up at him, panting and desperate. "*You promised you'd never leave me!*" I sobbed.

I'd changed him too much. The world didn't need men like him in jail. I had to make him see that before—

He leaned down and kissed me. At first, I tried to fight it because I knew what this kiss would mean. I tried to pull away but he put one big hand on the back of my neck and held me in place. And as soon as those hard Irish lips parted mine, I just crumpled. This was it. This was goodbye.

I slumped against him and gave myself up to it, tears rolling down my cheeks. My lips opened under his and I kissed him back, one last desperate attempt to make him see sense, to see what he was going to lose—

But it was no good trying to make him love me. He already did. That's why he was doing this.

So it became about us, about remembering, about drinking in as much of the other one as we possibly could because this was the last time we'd ever see each other. Every perfect press of his lips, every touch of his tongue, all of it had to be stored away forever.

He broke the kiss and when I opened my eyes I was looking up into clear blue, no sign of torment. He'd finally made peace with himself. My heart twisted. I was the one who'd told him people could redeem themselves, but I'd never wanted it to be like this.

He looked down at me as if there was so much he wanted to say. But in the end, he just put his palm against my cheek, kissed my lips one last time and said, "You're my love." And before the beautiful, Irish silver of it had fully faded from my ears, he was turning from me and presenting his hands behind his back, and one of the guys in suits snapped on a pair of handcuffs.

The other guy opened the rear door of the SUV. Agent Trent scooched over to make room for me and gave me a reassuring smile. He looked nice...normal. I knew he was only doing his job. But the thought of starting a whole new life, without Carrick, made my insides contract down to a hard little ball.

I climbed in and the guy in a suit slammed the door, then stepped back to stand with his buddy and Carrick.

Agent Trent took a deep breath and then let out a long sigh of satisfaction. He turned to me and spoke for the first time. "Don't worry," he said. "I'm going to take very good care of you."

I recognized that voice. For a moment, I was in the back of another car. Outside a bar. With a man in a mask.

I started to scream.

And Volos threw back his head and laughed and laughed and laughed.

47

CARRICK

It was her scream. The look in her eyes as she turned to me. Only one man in the world could scare her that much.

Trent is Volos.

I didn't even have time to process the *how* or the *why*. I just knew that I'd put Annabelle in a car with that psycho. I had time to lunge towards the SUV's door...and then the back of my head exploded in pain and I fell to my knees in the dirt.

Before the world had even stopped spinning, I was trying to struggle up to standing. But my hands were cuffed behind my back and the guys in suits leaned on my shoulders, putting all their weight into pinning me in place. I was bigger than them but without my hands I had no traction.

When I looked up at the SUV's window, Agent Trent—*Volos*—was leaning over Annabelle to gaze out of the window at me. That meant he must be pressed right up against her. The thought made my skin crawl. She was pressed back in her seat, face deathly pale, absolutely frozen with fear.

This can't be happening. This isn't possible. But...Annabelle had never heard Trent's voice, until just now. And she'd never seen Volos's face at the auction. And I'd never met Volos at all, only Trent.

"Are you even FBI?" I croaked. I thought at first that he'd lied about that. All I'd seen was a badge and badges could be faked.

But no. It was much, much worse.

"Oh, I'm the golden fucking boy of the FBI," said Volos. "They *love* me. Do you know how many people I've brought down?"

It all started to make horrible sense. Everyone had said that Volos was connected. *Protected.* Of course he was. Anybody who pissed him off went straight onto the FBI's most wanted list, courtesy of his alter-ego, Marcus Trent.

And of course no one could catch Volos. Of course he was a fucking ghost. He was sitting right there in the FBI office alongside the people trying to catch him.

"Why?" I shook my head. "Why do all this? You could have just rolled into town, shown your badge and taken her into protective custody. I never would have even known."

Volos leaned forward. Annabelle whimpered and tried to shrink even further into her seat cushion. He looked right into my eyes and that's when I realized what we were dealing with. People had thrown around words like *psycho* but I hadn't known, until that moment, just how broken he really was.

"Why?" Volos asked. "Because I had to *destroy you.* I wanted to see you tear yourself apart, agonizing over whether to save your fucking club or save your girl. I wanted you to watch your business burn. I wanted to see you grieve for your friends." He looked at Annabelle. "Because she's *mine.* And you stole her."

Oh Jesus. It all replayed in my mind, everything since we'd made the Blood Spiders back off. The fire at the warehouse: no wonder he'd shown up so fast. He'd burned the place and then offered me a way out. He'd put Ox in the hospital and then called me again. He'd tried to kill Mom and *known* I'd finally call him to make a deal. All just to torture me, like a kid pulling the legs off a spider.

He was a grade-A fucking psychopath. And I'd brought Annabelle right to him. I growled and managed to rise a few inches before I was slammed back down again.

Volos nodded to the guys in suits. "They're going to kill you, now.

But I want you to know this before you die, since you worked *so* hard to save your club. The state police are about to get a tip from the FBI that three pounds of coke is hidden in the club's compound."

"They won't find shit," I said.

Volos smiled politely. "Yes, they will." He nodded to his men again. "When they set the fire in the old woman's trailer, do you think that's *all* they did?"

Oh, Jesus. The whole club would go down. And the way I left it with Mac, they'd think—

"That's right," said Volos. "You'll have disappeared. No one will find your body. Your friends will go to jail and they'll think you planted the coke and ratted them out."

No! Jesus, no! I struggled again and got a gun butt to the back of my head. I slumped forward in the dirt.

The SUV pulled away. The last thing I saw was Annabelle's terrified face.

Then the cold barrel of a gun pressed into the back of my head.

48

ANNABELLE

E ver since I was a kid, I've needed to touch something. I've needed that physical grounding to fight back the monsters when I'm really, really scared. Maybe, if you asked a psychologist, they'd say it's because I lost my mom and then my dad. Maybe I'm just weird. But I clung onto Perkins and then I clung onto the necklace a biker gave me. And then I had one glorious week when I could cling onto something *real,* a solid, warm, badass man who I loved, who'd always protect me.

But now he was gone.

And I needed something. I needed it *so bad* because I knew what I was going to hear. I sat there next to Volos, eyes fixed on the seat in front of me, trying to somehow close my ears, trying to *not hear,* trying to—

The shot rang out behind us, an explosion that echoed off the trees. I gave a single, agonized cry, as if it had been me that had just been killed.

"And that's what happens to heroes," said Volos to himself.

It all came out, then. I cried: big, hacking sobs that shook my ribs and scalded my throat. I cried for myself, for the nightmare my future had just become. I cried for Carrick, the big Irish biker who'd just tried to do one good thing. I cried because our story was over and everything good that had happened since the auction had been undone.

Once, I'd thought I'd been lucky. A desperate phone call to the twelve year-old number of a near-stranger: it should never have worked. He should never have saved me. Now, I realized I'd gotten it all wrong. That chance in a million had made everything worse. I was right back with Volos, just as if Carrick had never come. Except Carrick was dead, Ox was lying in the hospital and the club was ruined. I'd cursed them all.

Volos took my purse, dug out my cell phone and dropped it out of the window. "Stop crying," he said absently.

I just turned and looked at him, incredulous. "F—Fuck you," I sobbed. I wasn't being brave. I was just broken.

He put his hand on my cheek, just like Carrick had. Then, with his thumb on my other cheek, he squeezed. He squeezed so hard my mouth distorted into a tear-stained pout. He squeezed so hard the inside of my cheeks scraped on my molars. He was terrifyingly strong: one of those men who aren't physically big but who get scary strong when they're angry...and his anger seemed to come without any warning. "Do you know where the name Volos comes from?" he asked.

I couldn't even shake my head. I just stared at him, panting in fear.

"Volos was a god. Of, among other things, cattle." He put his face close to mine. "Do you understand? That's what you are, now. That's what all of you are. *Cattle.* Don't get the idea I wanted you back because you're special. I wanted you back because *I bought you and you're mine.* You're livestock and if you don't do as I say, I'll hurt you. Understand?"

He released my cheeks so abruptly that I didn't realize what he wanted. I just stared at him.

He grabbed my face and rammed the back of my head into the

door pillar. I saw stars. While my face was still crumpling in agony, he pulled me forward again. "Understand?" he repeated.

"*Yes!*"

He released me and turned to face front.

And for the rest of the journey I sat there too scared to cry.

49

CARRICK

They say your life flashes before your eyes.

Most of mine, I'd relived enough times in my nightmares that I didn't want to see it again. My mum, changing into a different person. My dad hitting her head against the floor. Pulling the trigger and killing the FBI agent.

Maybe I deserved this. I certainly didn't deserve much better. What kind of happy ending had I expected, as a one-percenter?

But right at the end of that shitty life, crammed into the final seconds before the movie ended, there was something new, something that changed everything. A smart, sexy, lovable woman who saw things in ways no one else could, who saw things in *me* that I couldn't, who had hair the color of copper and pale, soft skin that made me crazy. And maybe a guy like me didn't deserve her. But that wasn't what this was about.

She was going to die, too. In a month or a year, when they had no more use for her. And her life until then would be a fucking horror movie.

Maybe I deserved this. But *she* didn't.

And her only chance, her only hope in the world, was me.

Behind me, I heard the trigger creak as the guy started to squeeze it.

I knew that, logically, there was no way I could win. I was handcuffed and they had me down on my knees with a gun to my head. There were two of them. I wasn't sure whether they were actual FBI too or whether they were just mercenaries Volos had hired, but either way they'd been trained and I hadn't. Logically, I was going to die.

But I was way beyond logic. I was into pure, angry, Irish bloody-mindedness.

I stood up.

It was the last thing the guy was expecting. Maybe he thought I'd beg or cry or piss myself, but he'd never known anyone to just plain *not cooperate*. He had the barrel of his gun pressed so hard against the back of my head that it got dragged along with me, tilting back and back towards the sky. By the time he remembered to pull the trigger the rest of the way, I was almost on my feet.

The gun went off. The whole back of my scalp erupted into blistering pain, like someone had thrown a pan of boiling water at my head, and I smelled blood and smoke. But I could still move, so I turned around. The guy was standing there gaping at me.

Now that the shock of the whole Volos revelation was wearing off, the rage was starting. I could feel it spreading and heating, an anger like I'd never known before. He'd fooled me. He'd taken my club. He'd taken my girl.

I head-butted the guy as hard as I could.

He went down straight down in a heap. The other one was trying to get his gun up so I lurched forward towards him. I didn't know what the bullet had done to the back of my head, but I was unsteady as hell. So instead of trying anything fancy, I just used myself as a battering ram. He hit the ground first and, a second later, my whole weight slammed down on top of him.

I lay there for a second, my head throbbing. I couldn't believe I was still alive. Given how much my head hurt, I wasn't sure how long

I'd be alive for. But if I was going to help Annabelle, I had to get out of there. Already, the first guy was starting to get up.

I levered myself to my feet. The sun was going down. My bike was up at the top of the hill and, even if I could get to it, I couldn't ride with my hands cuffed behind me. I had to get away first and somehow get the cuffs off.

Both guys were on their feet, now, and searching the ground for their guns. I turned towards the lake...and ran.

50

CARRICK

I've never been a good runner.

Aedan, the brother who got into boxing, used to tumble out of bed and hit the streets for five miles before breakfast. But I'm too big, too ungainly. I'm used to smashing through things, not running from them. And with my hands cuffed behind my back it was even harder.

Running with no hands was exhausting and terrifying. One slip and I'd go headfirst down the slope with no way to stop myself. I couldn't put my hands up to fend off twigs so I had to just close my eyes and let them scrape across my face.

But I couldn't slow down. I could hear the two guys in suits tearing down the slope behind me. Occasionally, a shot would ring out. I was far enough in front and the light was low enough that they'd missed so far, but twice I'd seen a bullet take a chunk out of a tree, scarily close. I was already out of breath but I had to push myself faster, faster—

I stumbled and had to crouch so I didn't go right over. I slid on my ass for a few seconds and then managed to regain my balance, panting. *Shit!* Now they were even closer.

And they were boxing me in. I'd been planning to skirt around the edge of the lake but they'd spread out so that, whichever way I turned, I'd be coming right at one of them. The only way I could go was straight downhill, towards the water, and that was a dead end.

The closer I got to the lake, the boggier the ground got. At first, my boots just slipped a little but soon I was running on a thin crust of leaves and moss on top of a thick, black quagmire. And as the light faded, I couldn't see where to put my feet. The ground would be solid, solid, then suddenly I'd go in up to my ankle and have to waste precious seconds getting free. It tired me even more, my legs throbbing and aching. And every single step jolted my injured head, sending fresh pain shooting through my skull.

Lungs burning and muscles screaming, I burst out of the trees and skidded to a stop. I'd reached the water. In front of me, inky-black smoothness extended into the distance, as if someone had laid a colossal sheet of glass. *Shit!* I looked left and right, my heart thumping in my chest. I couldn't see them but I could hear them scrambling through the trees towards me.

I bent double, heaving for air. I was dead. I couldn't go left or right or I'd run right into them. I couldn't make it back up the slope without my hands. That only left the water.

And I couldn't swim with my hands cuffed. *Fuck.*

Part of me almost gave up. I pictured myself just standing there, head bowed, waiting for them. A quick bullet to the back of the head and it would all be over.

But then Annabelle had no chance at all. My hands tightened into fists.

I started to wade out into the water. I didn't have a plan except to hide. But there were was nowhere *to* hide except under the surface and I couldn't hold my breath for long.

My boots sank into the thick mud of the lake bottom. The water crept up my ankles, my calves, my thighs, warm from the sun but still cool enough to make me shiver. Behind me, the guys had almost reached the shore.

I was immersed up to my chest, now. I threw myself forward to start swimming...and immediately started to sink. *Fuck!* I'd been right: swimming was impossible. My hands jerked uselessly at the handcuffs. I rolled onto my back and went completely under the water, gulping in a mouthful of it. *No!*

I kicked hard and my head broke the surface. I coughed and choked, blinking through the water. My toes could only just touch the bottom, now. I could tread water like this for a few minutes but I was dead as soon as they saw me. The only chance was to stay underwater.

By now the sun was so low that the surface of the lake was almost black. Simple, primal fear took over. No creature wants to drown itself. *I can't!*

But then I heard shouts, right at the shoreline. I took a lungful of air, pushed my legs out from under me...and slid under the water.

I couldn't see much but I could make out indistinct, moving shapes at the edge of the lake. They knew I'd gone in the water: that was the only place I could have gone.

My only chance was if they assumed I'd drowned and walked away before I ran out of air. For about thirty seconds, I thought maybe that would work. Then a beam of blinding light lit up the water in a huge fan shape above me. *Shit!* One of them had a flashlight. And they were going to make sure I was dead. All they had to do was to wait for a few minutes and I'd either have to show myself or I'd drown.

By now, my lungs were straining. When I dived, I'd still been out of breath from my run down the hill, plus my chest was still battered from inhaling smoke and red-hot air. My brain was screaming at me to breathe and it was harder and harder to fight the response to surface. If I surfaced, I was dead. But if I stayed down, I'd die anyway.

The flashlight beam swept over me again and again, back and forth. I was starting to panic, now, my wrists jerking at the handcuffs, the metal cutting deep. I twisted underwater, thrashing like a fish on a line. *Don't surface. Fight it. Fight it. Maybe they'll give up.*

But it was useless. They were professionals. They were going to make sure. The flashlight stayed on the water and I felt myself weakening. *Dying.* My vision darkened. My lungs felt as if they were going to burst. My whole body strained to take a breath—

Something scraped the back of my hand. Something plastic and hard. It had to scrape twice more before I figured out what it was.

The straw. The straw I'd kept from that fucking milkshake at the diner. All my thrashing had shaken it half-out of the pocket of my cut and now it was catching on my thrashing hands.

My chest burning and aching, I thrashed and twisted to try to shake the straw fully out of my pocket. When it was mostly out, I managed to knock it with my cuffed hands and it floated free. But I still had no way to get it to my mouth.

I had to chase it down to the lake bottom, lunging for it with my jaws and taking in mouthfuls of lake water each time I missed. It bounced off my lips twice before I managed to crush it between my teeth, swim up and poke it above the surface.

Of course, the thing was full of water. Blowing it out was the hardest thing I'd ever done: I had no air left to use. But I finally blew the water free and then I had no choice but to inhale: a huge, deep lungful. If I'd gotten it wrong and the tip was still below the surface, I was about to drown myself....

Air. Cool, sweet air. It felt like my tortured lungs were sucking up all the air in the night sky. It filled me up right down to my toes. Then I slowly exhaled, trying not to move the water at all.

The flashlight beam swept over me. I hoped the straw looked like a reed in the darkness. If not, they'd know exactly where to put the bullet. I hung there almost motionless, toes just scraping the bottom, head craned back, straw just above the surface....

And eventually, the flashlight went out.

I forced myself to give it another few minutes before I surfaced. When I was sure there was no noise from the shore, I waded out.

Once the night air hit me, I started to shiver. My jeans and cut, saturated with water and mud, felt like they weighed about a thousand tons. All I wanted to do was get under a hot shower and put on something dry.

But I had to warn Mac and the others. My cell phone was dead, drowned by the lake. I'd need to climb the hill, get to my bike and do it in person.

But first I had to do something about the cuffs. I couldn't do the climb without hands and I sure as hell couldn't ride with my hands behind me.

I'd seen people in movies maneuver their cuffed hands around from behind them to in front of them. It didn't look too difficult.

It *fucking* is. I'm not some lithe, ninja-trained, CIA contortionist. I'm built for strength, not gymnastics. I wound up on my back in the cold mud, trying to pass my tucked-up legs through my hands, and it took me at least ten minutes to pull it off. The whole time, I was picturing police kicking down the door of the clubhouse.

When my hands finally slipped over my boots, I let out a long sigh of relief and pushed myself to my feet. By now, so much black mud had been crushed into the back of my cut that the *Hell's Princes* logo wasn't even visible.

I struggled up the hill, grabbing onto roots and branches, straining to see through the gloom. There's never been so welcome a sight as when I saw my Harley gleaming in the darkness. I climbed on and started her up. Riding in cuffs was going to be interesting: I couldn't reach both clutch and throttle at the same time. But I'd make it work.

I rode for the clubhouse, pushing my bike as hard as she'd go. But halfway down Main Street, I could see the red and blue flashing lights.

I was too late.

I pulled into an alley across the street and watched, helpless, as Mac, Hunter, Viking and the others were led out in cuffs. They didn't see me, but even from the alley I could hear my name, again and again. *Irish.*

He fucking sold us out.

He's dead, if I ever see him again.

Volos had done it. My friends were heading to jail and they'd be there for years given the amount of coke involved. And they blamed me.

I slumped against the wall of the alley. The club was gone...and it was all my fault.

51

ANNABELLE

We drove for hours on back roads, way out into the country. There wasn't a street light or a lit-up house anywhere, just impenetrable blackness beyond the windows. I was too scared to cry, or ask where we were going, or do anything other than stare straight ahead.

After a while, he began to play with me.

I don't mean sexually. I mean, he started to fiddle and toy with me, like a guy with a new gadget. He shoved a finger into my hair, just behind my temple, and plowed towards the back of my head, watching the way the strands moved. He looked down my tank top but not in the same, leering way a normal man would. He hooked his fingers in the front of it and hauled it away from my body, tugging me a little forward in my seat, not caring if a few threads snapped, and simply raised his head to look down at my breasts. It was as if he'd bought a doll and wanted to see what was under its clothes.

And throughout all this, I didn't respond, didn't move or stop him. I knew that anything I did was likely to make him snap into violence again. I sat as rigid and passive as I could while my heart beat faster and faster. I prayed for the journey to end. Wherever we were going, it couldn't be any worse than this.

I was wrong.

When the car stopped, Volos hauled me out and led me up a hill towards a huge, dark building. I couldn't see any windows at all. It looked industrial but we weren't in an industrial part of a city...we weren't in a city at all, from what little I could see in the darkness. There were no lights, no traffic noise, just fields.

He took me through a door and into a room with long tracks on the ceiling, from which dangled hooks. Even at a time like this, the mechanics still caught the attention of my weird brain. There was something familiar about it but I couldn't remember what it reminded me of.

Volos pushed through some strange, soft, rubbery doors and—

The light was the first shock. Everything was painted white and every surface was being blasted by violently bright lights that hurt my eyes. The room was huge, cold and completely alien. There didn't seem to be a soft edge anywhere.

As I blinked, I saw shoulder-height metal rails. They made it seem claustrophobic even with the room's huge size. It was a little like being in a line at a theme park, the room designed to funnel you a certain way. Only where a theme park is all about fun and lightness, this room had been sucked clean of everything remotely comforting. Some rooms, like Mom's trailer, made you feel good. This had no feel *at all,* as if it wasn't even designed for people.

Volos stayed outside the rails but roughly pushed me forward between them. They guided me into a metal box barely wide enough to stand in. Doors closed behind me and, for a second, I was trapped. Then Volos heaved on a lever, cursing at its stiffness, and the metal doors in front of me hinged open. That's when I saw her.

She was walking towards me, but on the far side of the metal barrier. She was about my age, maybe a year or two younger. She had long brown hair that fell like mist, right down to the middle of her back.

She was utterly naked.

Every step was precise. As if she'd experienced what happened if you walked too quickly or too slowly and she never wanted to experience it again.

Her eyes were focused on the middle distance. She clearly saw me, standing almost right in front of her, but her eyes stayed straight ahead, not even glancing. I saw her chest rise and fall more quickly, though, and her lips tightened as she passed.

She was too scared to look.

And as my eyes adjusted to the harshness of the lights, I saw more women behind her. Seven, eight, ten, more. All naked. All following the first at neatly-spaced intervals.

Volos's hands pushed me forward. My sneakers squeaked on the floor and I saw it was black rubber, almost like a gym. *What is this place?!*

I turned a corner and saw a line of....

My brain didn't want to process it. *Cells.* I mentally branded them cells.

Except they weren't like a prison cell. They were too long, too narrow. Volos pushed me into one, slammed the door and secured it with a padlock, and left me there.

That's when I noticed the smell. It permeated the whole place, soaked into the walls and floor by years of use. Not a smell a person should ever experience. The smell of not just fear but absolute loss of hope.

I allowed it in, then. I couldn't shut it out any longer. I let my brain put together the pieces: the huge, echoey room, the guiding barriers, the rubber floor....

This wasn't a cell I was in. It was a stall, designed for a cow.

And this was a slaughterhouse.

52

CARRICK

When the cops had left, I sneaked across the street and into the compound, then into Scooter's workshop. And there, armed with a hacksaw, I finally managed to get the cuffs off. Then I used a spare rear view mirror to take a look at the back of my head. It was a mess: I had a powder burn from the gun going off so close, and there was a deep, bloody wound across my scalp where the bullet had grazed me. It wouldn't kill me but it hurt like hell.

I slapped a dressing on it—it was the best I could do, for now. I was soaked and exhausted but there was no time to rest. I had to move. I had to get Annabelle back. I headed for my bike—

And stopped.

I had no leads. I had no one to go to for help. I had nothing. I was just one guy.

My eyes fell on the line of Harleys parked in front of the clubhouse. A line of cold, silent steel when it should have been a row of growling, thumping engines and guys climbing onto them to do battle.

Annabelle's words came back to me: *families lean on each other.* I'd been trying not to lean on the club ever since I'd joined. I'd given and given and never taken back: not until she showed up. She'd been the one thing that I'd loved more than the club, the one thing that had gotten me to ask for help: to rescue her on the highway and to confront the Blood Spiders' president at the sawmill. And it had worked.

Then Volos had shown up and I'd pushed them away again. I'd been convinced I had to protect them, that I had to deal with this on my own. And look where that had gotten me.

I slipped off my cut and looked at it. Then I wiped my hand across the back, clearing away the mud until the Hell's Princes logo was visible again.

I needed the club. And since I was the only one left, it was up to me to get them back.

I climbed onto my bike and rode for the Sheriff's Office.

～

The Haywood Falls Sheriff's Office isn't big. Just a few rooms for paperwork, a parking lot out back and the holding cells. I knew the guys would still be there: no way the State Police would get off their asses and organize a prison bus to ship them all out in the middle of the night. But in the morning, they'd be gone.

If I was going to do this, I had to do it now.

If Annabelle had been there, she could have come up with some elaborate break-out plan: cutting steel bars, disabling cameras, all that shit.

Given that it was just me, I figured I'd better just do what I'm good at: brute force and intimidation.

I walked right in the front door and pointed Caorthannach at the guy sitting at the front desk. He gaped at me: at the shotgun, at my dripping, mud-stained body, at the expression on my face. "What the hell is this?" he asked, terrified.

"It's a bloody breakout," I told him. "What the fuck does it look like?"

Sheriff Harris came out of his office and saw what was going on. "*O'Harra?!*" He put his hands out to pacify me. "What are you doing?"

He looked from me towards the holding cells at the end of the hall. "I thought you made a deal! I thought it was you who—"

"I didn't make a deal," I snarled. "Get over here. Both of you, walk in front of me."

"Easy, son," Harris told the front desk guy. "Do as he says."

I collected up two more officers who were filing reports in the office and marched all four of them down the hall to the cells. To my relief, Harris made sure no one tried to be a hero: I didn't want to shoot anyone. As I came into view, a ripple went through the big holding cell where all the Princes were standing. "What the *fuck?*" muttered Mac.

I directed the Sheriff's staff into an empty cell and had Sheriff Harris lock them inside. "Now open up that cell and let my club go," I ordered.

Sheriff Harris shook his head.

I raised Caorthannach.

Harris angrily pushed the shotgun aside. "You're not going to shoot *me,*" he muttered.

He was right. I wasn't. Harris had been a friend of the club for years. He'd played along to protect his employees, but now it was just the two of us he was calling my bluff. I could feel myself losing control of the situation. "Let them out!" I snapped, desperate.

"I can't do it," said Harris. His eyes were sad. "I'll do a lot for the club but there's a limit. I can't just let an entire cell full of suspects walk out of here. I'd lose my job."

Shit. All the bluster drained out of me. I lifted Caorthannach again...then lowered it. That gun had scared plenty of people over the years but it didn't scare him. Intimidation wasn't going to work. Not this time. It was over.

"I don't know what's going on," said Harris softly. "But the best thing you can do is turn around and walk out of here. Keep to the back roads, you might make it out of the state."

He was offering me a way out but that wasn't what I needed. I needed my club. And it was going to take more than scaring him to get them back.

I dug down deep, feeling for all the things I'd locked away a long time ago, the things Annabelle had reawakened. My voice softened. "He's got my girl, Sheriff. A real evil bastard. I got to get her back. And I need my club to do it."

Harris looked into my eyes for a long time...and I saw him slowly soften. He let out a long sigh, then lowered his voice. "You gotta hit me."

"What?"

"It's the only way the feds will buy it. It's gotta look like I fought you. So hit me. Hard. Then take the key. It's in my pocket."

I blinked at him, dumbstruck. Then I rotated Caorthannach so I could hit him with the wooden stock.

"Don't get the face," he said quickly.

I nodded. And swung the shotgun at the side of his head. He crumpled and I caught him and lowered him to the floor. Then I dug in his pocket, pulled out the key and unlocked the holding cell's door.

No one moved. Mac and the others just stared at me, eyes narrowed.

"I didn't rat out the MC," I told him. And I filled him in on Trent and the deal I *did* make, and how Volos had tricked me. When I reached the part about him planting the coke, I saw Mac's hands tighten into fists.

"He has Annabelle," I told them, looking from face to face. "I don't know where. I don't even know where to start looking. I need your help." I drew in a long breath. I needed them to go into this with their eyes open. "But you walk out of that cell, you're all increasing your sentences. Everyone's going to be after us: cops, feds. We'll be fugitives. They'll shoot first."

The MC all looked at one another. Then Mac spoke. "We do this," he said, "you're *with* us. No more lone wolf shit. No more keeping things from us. Family."

I nodded again. Quickly, because I could feel a fucking *lump* in my throat.

Mac stepped out of the cell and pulled me into a hug. "I missed you, brother," he told me.

Back at the clubhouse, we picked up our bikes and then got the hell out of town. We didn't know how long it would be until Harris woke up, or the next shift arrived and raised the alarm. We headed up along the mountain road until we could look down on the town, then pulled over to discuss our next move. As soon as we cut the engines, the night was almost silent. The stars were out and there was so little wind the lake below was like a second sky.

Everyone looked at me. "I don't know," I said helplessly. "He took her off in an SUV. They could be anywhere. For all I know, he's taken her out of the state. Out of the *country*." I thought about Annabelle drugged unconscious and loaded onto a jet and I nearly threw up.

Mac put his hand on my shoulder. "Easy, brother. We'll get the bastard."

Hunter had climbed off his bike and was staring off into the distance. He knew the land the way Annabelle knew machines. And he had years of experience tracking down psychos as a bounty hunter. "He does this a lot, right?" he asked. "I mean...he buys a lot of girls."

I felt sick to my stomach. Mac squeezed my shoulder. "Yeah. Everyone says he's a big timer." I frowned, trying to remember. "He sells them to some European guy."

"So he's a middleman," said Hunter, still not looking at me. He was going into full-blown detective mode, now, off in his own little world. "Probably goes all over Northern Cali, buying from people like the Blood Spiders. He'd need somewhere to keep the girls until he shipped them to Europe. And not all that far away. When you called him to set up the deal, how long did he need to get here?"

"An hour or two," I said. The more I thought about Volos's sick business, the angrier I got. He must have done this to tens of women, maybe hundreds. *And he has Annabelle.*

"He'd want it to be remote," said Hunter, still thinking aloud. "Not in a town. It'd only take someone to hear one scream—"

"Hunter," said Mac in a warning tone.

Hunter glanced at Mac and then me. I realized I was glaring at him as if ready to throw him off the mountain.

"Sorry," muttered Hunter.

"It's okay," I said in a strangled voice. "Do your thing." I didn't care how angry it made me, if it worked.

"Somewhere remote," said Hunter. "A big place, out in the country. What else do we know? Did you get anything out of her stepdad?"

I shook my head. "Nothing."

"*Anything,*" Hunter pressed. "Even if it seems like it's useless."

I sighed. "*Nothing!* He overhead Volos's goons talking but they were just bitching about the women they'd bought. Said the standing stock was a pain in the ass." My face twisted. "That's how they talk about women. *Stock.* Fucking *inventory.*"

"You sure that's what he said?" asked Viking. "*Standing stock?*"

We all turned to him. "Yeah," I said.

He shook his head. "*Standing stock* isn't anything to do with inventory. It's a machine. It's what they have on ranches, to trap cows in while the vet's working on them. I worked at a place like that, for a while."

I'd jumped to completely the wrong conclusion. All this time, I'd had a clue and not even known it.

"A ranch would make sense," said Hunter. "Out in the country, lots of privacy."

Mac dug out his phone and we made a list of every ranch within a two hour drive. "We'll split up," said Mac. "Take a few each." And he started dividing them up. A few minutes later, I was on my way to my first one. *Hold on, Annabelle.* She had to be in one of them.

53

ANNABELLE

For the first hour, I was beyond thought. The fear took over and I sat against the bars of my stall, eyes closed, arms hugging my knees. The place was too clinical, too hard, too *white*. You couldn't even look at it without despair taking over.

But the blackness behind my closed eyelids wasn't any better. Everything comforting I found there was gone. And it was all my fault. Mom's trailer? Destroyed. Ox, the gentle giant? In hospital, maybe with brain damage. The MC? In jail.

And then there was the biggest loss of all. Carrick was dead.

No one was coming to save me. I was right back to the nightmare I'd been in when I made that fateful phone call...except I'd gotten Carrick killed and ruined countless lives. It was too much. The panic rose up inside, overflowing. I opened my eyes but that was even worse. The slaughterhouse rose around me, huge and merciless. This was a place designed to process animals and now I was one—

A man dressed in coveralls came to my stall. He couldn't have been much older than me, with sandy-blond hair. "Take off your clothes," he told me. "Fold them at the back of your stall."

I gaped at him. Then I saw the stick hanging on his belt, like a slender aluminum baton with two shining metal contacts at the end. An electric cattle prod.

I took off my clothes, hiding my body as best I could, and folded them at the back of my stall. He showed no interest in me sexually, even when I was naked. "And the necklace," he said.

I looked down at the gold shamrock: my last connection to Carrick. My hand closed around it protectively.

The guard stepped forward, his hand on his cattle prod.

I slowly pulled the necklace over my head and dropped it on my pile of clothes.

The guard turned and walked away.

"Wait!" I called after him. "I need to use the bathroom!"

He didn't even break his stride. "Use the bucket."

I turned and saw the metal bucket in the shadows. My stomach turned and, suddenly, I was crying. Weirdly, it was the total lack of privacy that tipped me over the edge, more than the nudity. I closed my eyes and clutched the bars. *Why? Why not just take us to the bathroom? There must be a bathroom for employees. Why make us undress but leave our clothes with us?* I was losing it, panic breathing between my sobs. I didn't understand anything and every question increased my fear, made me feel even more like weak, warm, animal flesh in the middle of this huge machine—

And then, at the very height of my terror, I saw it.

This was a machine. It had been a machine when they built it, one designed to turn cattle into meat. Now it turned women into prisoners...docile, obedient prisoners, too scared to fight back, like the woman who'd refused to even look at me.

I opened my eyes. I was staring at my pile of clothes and the gold necklace that lay on top of them. I grabbed it and closed my fist around it.

This place was a machine designed to break us.

I wasn't going to let it.

If it was a machine, I could understand it. I could learn its secrets and find its weaknesses. And I could figure out how to beat it.

I squeezed my fist tight around the necklace. And over the next four hours I *watched.*

They wanted to depersonalize us. They could have let us keep our clothes on but stripping us naked, when the men were clothed, made us feel weak. Inferior. As did the bucket toilets and the stalls. We were no better than animals, stripped of our pasts. Except I had a secret: the necklace, gathered up and clutched in my fist. It reminded me who I was.

The slaughterhouse had a second, more terrifying impact. All around us were reminders of the fate cattle had once had here: the bolt guns used to kill them, the hooks and overhead track that lifted and transported their bodies, the hose-down floor that had once run with blood. *We used to kill animals here. You're an animal. Don't misbehave.* The slaughterhouse, I was sure, had been a deliberate choice by Volos. It worked in ways an abandoned factory or office building never could. But whenever the fear threatened to paralyze me, I squeezed the necklace tight, feeling the shamrock pressing into my palm. They'd taken him from me. No way was I going to let them win.

There was no night and no day. The lights never went off: we just huddled down on the floor of our stalls and tried to sleep whenever we could. Every four hours, they'd open the stalls and have us exercise by walking several circuits of the massive floor, our bare feet slapping the cold rubber mats. The barriers directed us, just as they had the cattle. The men, with their cattle prods, made sure we kept moving.

Food was a gray-green slop, served in a bowl with no spoon. It tasted disgusting but I forced myself to eat slowly and try to figure out what I could taste. Oats, definitely. Vegetables...maybe kale and broccoli? It had a milky smell that might have been protein powder. It was probably incredibly healthy: they wanted us to look good when they sold us. Anyone who didn't finish their bowl was threatened with the cattle prod.

The men guarding us were a mixture of ages and had the look of ex-cons. For the first few hours, I expected them to grab us: we were naked, after all, and there was no one here to protect us. But none of them tried anything. Watching them closely, I realized they were afraid, too: afraid of Volos. And I realized that was another reason for all the efforts to depersonalize us: making us into slop-eating, mindless animals helped remove temptation for the guards.

There were eight women there currently, including me. But from whispering to a few of the others, I learned there'd been as many as twenty, sometimes. One woman had been there for two months. Only the newcomers would talk to me and then only a few words, checking for a guard the whole time. The ones who'd been here more than a few days wouldn't talk at all. They'd been broken. I learned the most from Cassie, a slender blonde who was in the stall next to mine. She'd arrived just one day before I had.

Most women seemed to stay at the slaughterhouse for a few days. Then they'd be sold to a buyer, either a specific client or a trafficker in another country. Some women had heard things about Europe: there was some guy there who Volos shipped a lot of women to.

I couldn't believe the scale of it. A new woman arrived every few days. Well over a hundred women a year. How did the FBI not know about this? But then I remembered the story Volos had agreed with my step-dad. *She moved to New York with some guy.* My bags, packed and then buried. The other women would be the same. No one was looking for us.

I clamped down on my rising panic. I couldn't beat the system on that level. If I thought about how powerful Volos was, how untouchable he was with all that FBI knowledge and influence, I'd go crazy. I had to focus on the things around me, the stuff I could touch.

I examined the padlock and chain that secured my stall. It was something they'd added when they repurposed the place—the latch had been enough to stop a cow. The chain was heavy duty but the padlock was just a simple, store-bought thing like you'd use to lock your tool shed. That was my way out. A lock was just a machine. A lock could be picked.

What I needed was some wire. When we next exercised, my eyes searched every surface for a lost paperclip or a piece of electrical wire but there was nothing: everywhere was kept ruthlessly clean and free of clutter. By now, I figured it was late morning although I was rapidly losing track.

I slept a little. I ate. I exercised. I dug my nails into my palms to keep from crying.

It was when I was next trying to sleep that I thought of it. I had my head on the little pile of clothes I'd made and I sleepily pushed one item off it because it was digging into my cheek. I lay there with the thing in my hand for several minutes, idly fingering it, before I opened my eyes.

My bra. My bra had underwiring.

I sat up and started trying to extract the wire. What would have taken seconds with a pair of pliers took a full half hour. But eventually, I had a short length of springy, bendable wire I could slot into the padlock's keyhole.

I'd never picked a lock. What I really needed was a good book, with diagrams. But as I probed and twisted, I started to build up a picture of what was going on in the mechanism, the shining parts separating in my mind. If I'd been in jail, I could have worked on it all night but here there *was* no night: every ten minutes or so, a guard would walk past and I'd have to pretend to be asleep and then start all over again. The frustration was unbelievable. But one thing I had on my side was time.

An hour after I started, the lock finally clicked open. I stared at it for a moment, tracing the shining hasp with my finger. *Should I just go now?* The temptation to just pull the door open and run was unbelievable.

But I had no plan: they'd recapture me instantly. And I knew the guard would be back any minute. I'd have to relock it and trust I could do it again later, now I had the technique. I took a deep, shuddering breath and squeezed the padlock closed, imprisoning myself again. A few moments later, I heard the guard's footsteps approaching and quickly lay down.

This time, though, he didn't pass by. He stopped in front my stall and threw a bag through the bars. "Get dressed," he said. "Fix up your face. I'll be back for you soon."

I was forcing myself not to stare at the padlock in horror. *I should have gotten out!* "What's going on?" I asked in a strained voice.

"You're off to Europe," said the guard as he walked away. "You've been bought."

54

CARRICK

The sun was going down and I was ready to kill someone.

We'd been searching all night and all day. We'd checked every ranch in the area but there wasn't any sign of anything suspicious. Mac had even called in the chapters in the neighboring counties and had them out searching, but no one could find her. Meanwhile, someone had found Sheriff Harris and discovered our escape. An APB had gone out for all of us. There were fewer cops out here in the sticks but we knew it was only a matter of time until we were spotted.

We'd all met up at the final site on the list, a former ranch that was now nothing more than crumbling wood and knee-high grass. We'd hidden the bikes in the old stable block so they were out of sight from any passing patrol cars. But now, standing around in the gloom, no one had any ideas. *"Fuck!"* I yelled, and kicked at the rotting stable wall. My boot went straight through, fragments of sodden wood flying into the air.

"Could be I was wrong," Viking offered. He ran his hand over a cage-like device of rusting metal—the standing stock that had brought us here.

I felt the exhaustion sweep over me. The previous morning,

waking up happy with Annabelle in the cabin in the woods, felt like a lifetime ago. "You weren't wrong," I said stubbornly. I didn't want him to be wrong. If he was wrong, Annabelle was lost forever.

"We tried everywhere," said Hunter. He put a comforting hand on my shoulder but I shook him off. I didn't want comfort. I didn't want to hear what they were trying to tell me.

They wanted her back just as much as I did and they wanted revenge on Volos for what he'd done to the club. But it was over.

She's gone, a little voice inside me said. *She's lost. You had her and you lost her forever because you made the wrong choices.* I thought of how scared she must be, right now, and the rage roared through me, making every muscle tense and ache. If I got my hands on Volos, he wasn't going to jail.

I saw now that we'd been locked in battle from the first moment I'd walked into that bar. Two men, warring over the same woman. Except I wanted Annabelle as a gorgeous, bright, smart woman; he wanted her as a *thing,* as inventory to sell. A product—

I blinked and jumped to my feet. I grabbed Viking by the front of his cut. "Standing stocks," I said. "Do they use them anywhere else? What about where they cut up the cows? A slaughterhouse?"

Viking thought about it. "Probably. They've still got to control them, examine them. Yeah, I guess."

Everyone got their phones out and started searching for slaughterhouses. Mine had been wrecked in the lake so all I could do was muscle in and look over shoulders. "There!" I stabbed at one on Hunter's screen. "Right out in the middle of nowhere. And it's the right distance from Haywood Falls."

The mood changed. We had a target again. "Saddle up," said Mac savagely. "Let's ride."

55

ANNABELLE

I stared at myself in the hand mirror. I was dressed again and I'd put on lipstick, some mascara and a little eye shadow. I'd brushed my hair, too, and dabbed on the perfume that had been in the bag. The whole process made me fell ill: the last thing I wanted to do as to make myself more appealing to these bastards. But they had to think I was following their orders. I needed them to let their guard down.

Just as I finished, I hear footsteps approaching. Not just the guard, this time. Several men. And something about the confident footfalls of the man in front made my chest close up in fear.

Volos turned the corner and walked right up to my stall. Four men were with him, all in suits. I recognized two from the auction and two from when we'd met him by the lake. "We're taking a trip," he told me. "Ever wanted to see Europe?"

My stomach knotted. Once I was out of the country, there'd be no hope.

"Give me your hand," he said, his tone almost friendly.

I hesitantly put one hand through the bars, wanting to keep him happy as long as possible.

He grabbed my wrist and yanked. I was jerked forward and my

forehead slammed against the bars, bringing tears to my eyes. The men laughed. I was still reeling when I saw the needle.

No. No!

But he still had hold of my wrist. And before I could stop him, he was pushing the needle into my upper arm and squeezing the plunger. A clear liquid shot into me, burning and throbbing.

He let go of my arm. "Lie down," he told me. "Wouldn't want you hurting yourself when you fall asleep." He jerked his head at the others. "Get everyone together. I want to brief people on what'll be happening while I'm away."

They sauntered off. I jerked my arm back through the bars and rubbed at the sore spot. *Shit!* What had he given me? Some sort of sedative? Once it took effect, I'd be helpless.

I looked at the lock. It had taken me an hour last time. How long until they came back for me? How long did a briefing take? Ten minutes, twenty?

I dug the piece of wire out of my jeans, slid it into the padlock and frantically went to work.

56

ANNABELLE

I could feel the drug coming on. It was subtle but it was there, a sort of thickening of my thoughts. As if ideas had to swim through oatmeal instead of water. My hands started to slow, my head lolling.

Then a hand gripped my arm. I looked up to see Cassie reaching through from the next cell. She squeezed my arm in encouragement and nodded.

I forced myself to keep going. *Focus. Just...feel for the last...pin and then...twist....*

The lock sprung open. I blinked and stared at it for a few seconds before it really sank in. Then I very gently lifted the padlock from the loops of chain, trying not to make a noise. Getting the chain off the bars was even worse: the heavy links made clangs that that seemed to echo around the entire building. I lifted it free as gently as I could, wincing with each sound. When I looked up, all the other women were staring at me with huge eyes.

I inched open the gate and peeked out. For once, the entire massive floor was empty. The guards must all be having their briefing with Volos.

I glanced around for the nearest door: way over the other side of the room. But at least for once, I could duck under the barriers and go straight across instead of threading my way back and forth. I ducked under the first one—

Everything went simultaneously black and red. I stumbled backwards, dizzy, and very nearly brained myself on the metal barrier behind me. *Whoah.*

What's the opposite of a head rush? That's what had happened to me. Just ducking down had almost put me on the floor. The drug was starting to really hit me.

Moving more carefully, I ducked my way under the barriers until I reached the exit. I wrapped my hand around the heavy steel handle: locked. And it looked like it'd be much harder to pick than the padlock.

I looked desperately around. I didn't want to head towards the front of the building, because that's where Volos was having his meeting. There was another door at the back, behind a stack of boxes. I headed for that...but before I'd even gotten halfway, I heard a door open and voices coming my way. The meeting was over.

I searched around for a hiding place but there was nowhere. And I was in the worst possible place, the killing floor. It was just a big, white-tiled expanse with the meat hooks above and slightly sloping floors below to drain the blood....

I looked down and followed the slope of the floor. It led down to a big metal drain cover.

Oh Jesus, no. I can't.

The voices were getting closer.

I knelt down, which made me woozy again, and levered up the drain cover. The pipe below was big enough to crawl in: *just.* I lowered myself into it, slid the cover back into place and held my breath.

Footsteps filled the room as the guards returned to their positions. No shout went up, so no one had seen me. I took a second to look up and down the pipe. Thankfully, no blood had drained down there for years but it still stank and the walls were covered in slime. There were smaller grates every ten feet or so which let in enough light to see by. I could see side tunnels branching off. The pipes must run under the whole building.

At that second, I heard a yell from over by the stalls. As everyone ran over there, I followed them through the pipe, using their pounding footsteps as cover. By the time I got there, Volos was staring into my empty stall, a murderous look on his face. He reached through the bars of the stall next to mine and grabbed Cassie by the throat. "Where did she go?" he yelled in her face.

I held my breath. She'd probably watched me get into the pipe. Would she grass me up to save herself?

Cassie opened and closed her mouth a few times. Then, "I didn't see," she whispered.

Volos cursed and flung her aside. "Find her," he muttered. "Find her quick."

Very quietly, I crawled away. The drug was really starting to hit, now: thinking was like trying to walk through thick, glutinous mud. I had to find another drain cover. Somewhere near the edge of the building, or even outside. Through the grate above me, I could see guards running back and forth. If one of them so much as glanced down as I passed under a grate, if I made even the slightest sound....

I crawled until my jeans were soaked with slime and my knees were bruised. And just as I was about to give up hope, I found the only other drain cover big enough to climb through.

I crawled right under it and looked up. And saw a pair of legs in tailored suit pants.

Volos was standing directly above me, so close that I could have reached up and touched his shoes. He was shouting orders to the guards: that was the only reason he hadn't heard me approach. But just at that second, he went quiet.

I froze. I was in an awkward crouch, head craned back to look up through the grate, but I didn't dare move a muscle.

If I moved, he'd hear me. If I stayed there, sooner or later he'd glance down and see me.

I still had the necklace clutched in one fist. I silently slung it around my neck and fingered the shamrock.

I needed a miracle.

57

CARRICK

"This is it," I said. "This is the place." I could see Volos's red SUV parked at the bottom of the hill. Up at the top, the hulking shape of the slaughterhouse was silhouetted against the moon. I cocked Caorthannach and stormed up the track that led to the main door.

Mac caught me when I was halfway there and slammed me up against a cattle shed. "*Wait!*"

I snarled and lunged at him, getting right up in his face. After a whole night and day without her, I was going crazy. She was in there: I was sure of it. I had to get her back. That was all I knew.

But Mac didn't flinch. He just stared at me with those sad, understanding eyes and I eased back a little. There's a reason he's our president. "Do you even have a plan?" he asked gently.

"I'm going to boot in the fuckin' door and start hitting people," I muttered.

The others caught up to us. Mac squeezed my shoulder. "Let Hunter go take a look." And he nodded at Hunter, who disappeared into the darkness like a wraith.

Minutes passed. I kept glancing between Mac and the

slaughterhouse. It killed me to wait but he was right: the way to do this was as a club.

"We'll get her back, brother," Mac said quietly.

I looked at him, then at the rest of the club. Even if we rescued Annabelle, we were all still wanted by the cops. Most likely, we'd be in jail by the morning. But instead of skipping town, they were helping me. I couldn't find any words so I just nodded.

"Four—" said a voice an inch from my left ear.

I jumped about a foot in the air. "*Jesus!*" I hissed. Hunter had reappeared out of the darkness right next to me. The guy was uncanny.

"Sorry," he said, sounding not sorry at all. "Four guards plus four of that psycho's guys in suits, plus Volos himself. So nine. Volos and his guys look like they're carrying. The guards...." He glanced at me and then looked away.

"What?" I asked.

This time, he did sound apologetic. "They have cattle prods."

My hands balled into fists. *Oh, you son of a bitch, Volos....*

"Can we get in the back?" asked Mac. He was talking quickly because he could see I wouldn't hold back much longer.

Hunter shook his head. "Fire doors are all heavy steel. Only way in is the front."

"How many women are in there?" asked Mac.

"Seven that I could see," said Hunter. He looked at me. "I couldn't see Annabelle. Sorry."

My chest tightened. What if we'd missed her? What if she was already on a plane? "Let's go," I said. And we started up the hill.

58

ANNABELLE

I crouched there silently in the pipe, the slime seeping through the knees of my jeans to chill my skin. Volos was still standing directly above me and it was too quiet to risk moving. But my legs were cramping up and I could feel the drug draining the strength from me. Soon, I'd just slump to the floor of the pipe and he'd sure as hell hear *that*.

But then fate or chance or whoever was looking down on me granted me one tiny, golden shred of luck. A shrill bleating came from Volos's pants pocket. He sighed and pulled out a cell phone.

I crawled backward, away from the grate, lifting each knee with painstaking care.

"Everything's fine," said Volos into the phone. "We might be a little delayed getting to Vienna."

I took another careful step backward.

Volos started to pace, stepping off the grate and taking a few steps away. He ran a hand through his hair: it was the first time I'd seen him looking anything but confident and assured. The idea of someone who could make *Volos* nervous sent a chill down my spine.

I drew back a little more. I was nearly out of sight. Another step would do it.

"You'll love her," said Volos. "Red hair, pale skin. She's—"

He turned a little and his eyes fell on me. Both of us froze.

"She's perfect," he said into the cell phone. "I have to go."

He ran for the grate. I flung myself backward just as he heaved the cover away and lunged for me. His straining fingers brushed my tank top but closed just too late. "*Here!*" he bellowed. "She's in the drains!"

I turned around and crawled for my life but I knew it was useless. There was only one other grate and by now the guards would be running to block that one. They had me trapped like a rabbit in its burrow.

Volos was chasing me as I fled through the pipe, glaring down at me through every vent I passed. "I told you what would happen if you disobeyed me," he spat. "I can hurt you in ways that don't leave marks."

I was hysterical, now, almost in tears. Then I pulled up short: I'd hit a dead end. I was up against one of the walls, I could even see an exit through the tiny vent above me...but I had no way to get to it. I was trapped. I stared up at Volos, panting in fear.

"You!" he snapped, pointing to someone I couldn't see. "Stay here and keep an eye on her."

A guard ran over and stood directly above me, glaring down at me through the vent.

"Someone go in and drag her out," said Volos as he led the others away. "You. Use a cattle prod on her if you have to—"

There was a crash of metal that reverberated through the whole building. Everyone looked towards the entrance. An instant later, there was a boom that could only be a shotgun.

But not *any* shotgun.

"Fuck!" yelled one of the guards. "It's O'Harra!"

59

CARRICK

I was beyond rage.

Before I'd even made it fully through the door, the anger had taken hold. As soon as I smelled the stink of human fear, as soon as I glimpsed the place where they'd been holding my Annabelle, I forgot any notion of plan or strategy. The place had been chosen by that psycho to make women afraid. He deserved to die and so did anyone who'd helped him.

Two men in coveralls ran toward me. I raised Caorthannach and pulled one of the triggers. When the cloud of gun smoke rolled away, they just *weren't there* anymore. A third guard rounded the corner, gun raised, then staggered to a stop as he saw the blood on the floor. He hesitated long enough for me to reach him, lift him by his collar and hurl him into a wall.

Behind me, the rest of the MC were flooding through the door. Some with guns, some with brass knuckles, a few with baseball bats. They were finally face-to-face with the people who'd devastated their club and they were *pissed*. Outside, Tailor was calling the cops. If it didn't go our way, we wanted to make sure someone was there to get the women to safety.

We slowly fought our way through to the main slaughterhouse

floor. I used Caorthannach's other barrel to take out another guard and then switched to my fists, yelling in fury as I punched guards to the floor. I couldn't see Volos anywhere. But I saw the women locked naked in stalls and my stomach knotted. *Where's Annabelle?*

That's when I saw a guard standing off on his own, near one of the exits. He had his gun out and was glancing between the battle and a vent in the floor. He was guarding something.

Something valuable.

I put my head down and charged at the guy. He swung around and saw me but it was already too late. My head hit the middle of his soft stomach and he folded around me as we went down to the floor. One hard punch to his face and he was out cold.

I leaned over the vent, hardly daring to breathe. *Please let it be her!*

Big green eyes looked up at me. Copper hair gleamed in the darkness. She was in some sort of pipe, her clothes stained with black slime. But she was alive. All the emotion welled up inside me. I'd thought I was never going to see her again. And from tearful expression, she'd thought the same.

She put her fingers between the bars of the vent. I snatched them and entwined mine with hers. "Are you okay?"

She nodded but her head lolled a little. The bastards had drugged her. I wrenched on the vent but it was built into the floor and far too small for her to get through. "How do I get you out?"

She sniffed back her tears. "There's a grate." She pointed. "Over there. The exits are locked. We need the keys."

I looked at the guard I'd knocked down. There was a whole bunch of keys on his belt. I grabbed it. And I could see the grate Annabelle had pointed at and there was no one near it: all the guards were fighting.

But the battle was starting to turn. We'd taken them by surprise but now they were regrouping. I winced as I saw a bullet graze Mac's shoulder. Then Hunter went down, clubbed over the head with a cattle prod.

"Go help them," Annabelle said.

My eyes snapped to her. *No!* I'd finally gotten her back. I wasn't going to leave her again.

"*Go!* Just give me the keys. I can make it."

I glared at her, torn. She needed me. They needed me.

Annabelle looked up at me and gave me a brave nod.

I passed the keys through the bars. "I'll meet you outside," I told her. "By the cattle shed. Thirty fuckin' seconds."

She nodded. "Thirty fucking seconds." She squeezed my fingers and then she was off, crawling down the pipe.

I turned towards the battle just as Viking staggered and fell. My friends. My club.

I put my head down and ran to help them.

60

ANNABELLE

Cautious elation had pushed back the worst effects of the drug. *He's alive!* And all I had to do was get out and we'd be together again.

I crawled like all the hounds of hell were after me. When I reached the grate, I peeked up through it cautiously but it was still clear. I slid the cover off, climbed out and, for the first time in what felt like hours, I could stand up straight.

The exit was just a few feet away, behind a stack of boxes. I ran over to it, legs aching and cramping from all the crawling. I started trying each key on the key ring. *It can't be this easy,* I thought. But the third key turned and the door swung open, cool night air sweeping in.

I staggered back a little, almost hitting the boxes. It was *night?* I'd lost all sense of time. I'd been in the slaughterhouse more than twenty-four hours.

Taking a deep breath, I stepped out and pushed the door mostly closed behind me. It was like slipping into a cool, calming bath. After the endless brightness of the slaughterhouse, the moonlit night was a blessed relief. I hadn't realized how much my eyes had been aching...or how much they wanted to close. Now that I was safe, the adrenaline was fading and the drug was winning. All I wanted to do was lie down and go to sleep.

And soon I would. I was home free. I could see the cattle shed Carrick had mentioned: all I had to do was stumble down the hill and hide behind it. I could see the MC's bikes parked by the side of the road: the whole club must be here! And I could hear the distant wail of sirens. They were still a long way away, but they were coming. Volos and his men were going to jail.

I was about to step away when I heard Volos's voice from inside. I froze instantly. The door was still open a crack and I could see him talking to one of his guys in suits.

"It's going south," Volos told the guy. "The cops are coming. We can make this look like it was all the MC but not if those women are around to give statements. Get rid of them, fast."

They both marched off in opposite directions. I stood there with my heart thumping in my chest. My head was swimmy and I knew I was minutes from passing out. I was in no shape to help anyone. But that guy was going to murder Cassie and the other six. And there was no way to warn Carrick.

I looked down the hill towards the safety of the cattle shed.

Then I inched open the door and crept back inside.

61

ANNABELLE

I skulked along the very back of the slaughterhouse, staying as low as I could. My legs kept wobbling and I had to clutch at the wall to stay upright: I was only staying conscious by sheer force of will, now. The fight was raging at the other end of the massive room: I could see Carrick whirling and punching, plowing through guards like they were toy soldiers. As I watched, he pulled Viking back to his feet. Mac had his teeth gritted in pain, clutching at his wounded shoulder, and Hunter was bleeding from the scalp. But now that Carrick was back, things seemed to be turning in their favor.

Ahead of me, I could see the guy in a suit. His attention was on the battle and then, as he neared the stalls, he took out his gun and checked it. My stomach twisted. *Checking he has seven bullets.*

I looked around wildly for a solution. I couldn't get to the women before he did. I couldn't fight him: he had a gun and he was way bigger than me. *Shit!* He'd reached Cassie's stall. She saw the gun and shrank back against the far wall.

There was a fire extinguisher on the wall next to me. Through the haze of the drug, my mind did its thing: I saw pressures and forces, the deadly speed a screwdriver could fly out of the nozzle if I could adjust the valves—

Only there was no time. The guy raised his gun. I frowned in drugged desperation. *What would Carrick do?!*

I grabbed the fire extinguisher, swung it back and brought it down on the guy's head with all my strength. He crumpled to the floor and I stood over him panting, adrenaline coursing through my body.

Sometimes, simple is best.

I started trying keys in the padlocks. "Come on," I told the women. "We're getting out of here."

A few minutes later, I was leading all seven of them back the way I'd come. When we got to the exit, they stopped and stared in wonder. Some of them had been there for a month or more: the idea that they might finally be free was too much for them to take in.

"*Go!*" I told them. "Hide behind that cattle shed. The cops will be here soon." And they ran, bare feet padding down the slope.

I was the last one out. I was just slipping through the door when a hand grabbed my arm. *Shit!* I pulled as hard as I could but the grip was like iron—

I turned and looked down. The arm wasn't clad in an expensive suit. It was bare and tanned, thick with muscle.

I looked up into Carrick's blue eyes.

"You're meant to be out by the cattle shed," he growled.

I wilted against him, all the exhaustion and stress and the effect of the drugs hitting me full force. "So are you," I mumbled. I pressed my cheek against his chest and wrapped my arms around him. "Oh *God* it's good to see you!"

He brushed his hands through my hair and down over my cheeks, then tilted my head back. His lips came down on mine: a quick, hard kiss to reclaim what was his. And I knew everything was going to be okay. I closed my eyes, opening under him and relaxing into it. But then he grudgingly pushed me back and shook his head.

"Come on," he said, nodding down the hill. "First, let's get you out of—"

His words were cut off as if someone had thrown a switch. And suddenly his whole huge body was falling, torn from my grip. He went down hard, slumping on his back on the floor. And as he fell, Volos was revealed behind him, panting in rage. He was holding a cattle prod like a baseball bat, ready to swing again.

"*Run,*" croaked Carrick from the floor. And he launched himself at Volos's legs. But Volos brought the cattle prod down again and Carrick went limp.

I launched myself through the door and ran into the night.

62

ANNABELLE

I could hear Volos charging down the hill behind me. I knew he was going to catch me. There was no way he couldn't. The drug he'd given me had been held back until now by adrenaline but my body's supply had run dry. My muscles ached, my lungs burned and my vision was going blurry.

I saw the cattle shed ahead of me. But the last thing I wanted to do was led him to the other women. I veered and headed down the steeper side of the hill instead.

That decision saved me. I stumbled and fell, rolling headfirst down the hill in a limp tangle of limbs. I picked up some bruises and felt like I was going to throw up but, when I picked myself up near the bottom, I'd gained a little ground on him.

It didn't matter, though. In front of me was the road and across that an empty field. There was no place to hide. He'd be on me in seconds. Unless—

The MC's bikes were right in front of me, gleaming in the moonlight just like Carrick's bike had, twelve years before. Monstrous, chromed beasts out of my dreams.

The drug was coming on fast, now. I was woozy and getting worse and my fall down the hill hadn't helped. *This is a bad idea.* I could only just control one of the big bikes when I was at my best. But I didn't have a choice.

It took me two attempts to get my leg over the nearest bike. Then I frowned at the controls. I knew this stuff...but thanks to the drug, I might as well be trying to fly an alien spaceship.

Footsteps pounding closer, off to my left. *Think! Don't look at him —think!* I hit the starter button and the bike roared into life. But as the engine settled down to an idle I could hear Volos again, even closer.

What's next? I flipped up the kickstand, almost overbalancing. Then I twisted the throttle....

The bike didn't move. Volos's feet didn't sound like they were on grass anymore. They were on asphalt, running across the road towards me—

I stared at the bike in drunken bewilderment for another second. Then, *put it in gear, you moron!* I toed the lever and felt it click.

Volos's hand clapped down on my shoulder and tugged, trying to pull me off the bike.

I twisted the throttle as hard as I could and the bike leapt forward like a startled horse. If I hadn't been gripping the throttle so hard, it would have shot straight out from under me. Volos's hand kept hold of my shoulder for a split-second...and then slipped free and I was roaring off down the road.

63

CARRICK

Volos threw down the cattle prod and sprinted after Annabelle. I groggily climbed to my feet...then fell hard on my ass again, the room tilting and spinning. *Fuck!* I'd taken way too many hits to the head in the past week.

But he was after Annabelle. She needed me.

Grunting, I hauled myself to my feet and set off down the hill after them. My stomach lurched as I saw him closing in on her. But then she got on Hunter's bike and roared away. *Atta girl!*

Volos stared after her for a second and then ran to his SUV. *Shit.* By the time I reached the road, he had it started and was tearing after her. I scrambled onto my bike and gave chase.

Annabelle had a good head start but she was still new to riding and she didn't dare push the bike as fast as it could go. Volos started to close the gap, inching closer to her rear wheel. I twisted the throttle hard, surging up behind him. He saw me in his rearview and started weaving from side to side, refusing to let me get alongside him.

We reached the road that led up the mountain and started to climb. Volos was creeping slowly closer to Annabelle: his headlights lit her up and I saw her twist around and look back, her eyes wide.

That made her bike veer dangerously and my stomach leapt up into my throat. There were no crash barriers here, just wooden fences. Miss one corner and you'd fly out into space and pinwheel down the mountain.

We climbed higher and higher and still I couldn't get past Volos. Annabelle's bike was no match for the power of Volos's SUV, on these inclines, and he closed right up behind her...and then came alongside. He swung sideways, aiming to ram her back wheel, and I heard her panicked cry.

She veered out of the way but that took her off the asphalt and into the dirt. The bike skidded sickeningly, sending gravel flying. My heart almost stopped as she skidded towards the edge...but she regained control just in time and straightened out. It had taken everything she had: I could see her hanging limply over the handlebars, completely drained. And Volos was opening the space between them, getting ready to swerve again and drive her off the edge.

Now.

I twisted the throttle as hard as it would go and pressed myself low on my bike. Just as Volos opened a gap, I raced through and came between him and Annabelle. She was grimly clinging to the handlebars, her face pale and her eyes struggling to stay open. I swung my bike as close to hers as I dared and held out my hand. She looked at me with wide, terrified eyes.

"I won't let you fall," I promised.

Volos saw what I was doing and started to swerve across the road towards us.

Annabelle took a deep breath, pushed off from the handlebars and threw herself towards me. Her bike fell sideways and she barely got her legs clear in time, but then she was clinging to my shoulders and I had one hand on her ass, clutching her to me as I twisted the throttle—

We shot forward. Volos's SUV missed our rear wheel by inches and drove over Annabelle's bike. The front wheels came off the ground and I saw Volos wrenching at the wheel as he lost control of the steering—

And then there was a crash and shriek of splintering wood as the car plunged through the barrier and off the edge of the mountain. A few seconds later, we heard the crunch of metal as he hit and rolled for the first time. The noises took a long time to stop coming.

I hit the brakes and pulled up. Annabelle was clinging to me like a limpet, her eyes closed and her breathing weak. "Annabelle?" I cupped her cheeks and pressed her gently back so I could look at her. "Annabelle? Say something!"

She half-opened her eyes and looked at me. Groggy. Shaken. And just as determined as that night I'd first met her. "Don't let go of me until I wake up," she said, her voice insistent.

I pulled her into my chest and folded my arms around her. "I promise," I said softly.

EPILOGUE

Annabelle

One Month Later

"You're *sure* the crane can take the weight?" Carrick asked, looking up and shielding his eyes from the sun.

"Oh, yes. Actually, it's really interesting: I was talking to the crane driver earlier and he was saying how as long as the arm isn't *fully* extended, the load's mostly taken by the—" I glanced sideways: his eyes were glazing over. "*Yes,* it can take the weight."

I could see why he was nervous, though. The doublewide trailer looked enormous as it swung over the compound's fence. But as we all held our breath, it settled gently into place atop the supports I'd built for it. Mom's new home had officially arrived.

"Needs a lick of paint," said Mom from beside me. "And some plants." But she was grinning. Behind us, the new couch—even bigger than the last one but just as purple—was already waiting for us to unbolt one of the trailer's sides and carry it in. Mr. Fluffy was curled up in the very center and would probably stay there throughout the whole process.

"I'll get the propane hooked up," said Ox. He'd awoken from his coma after three days and found himself with a metal plate in his head, a broken arm but no long-term damage. I was already working with Scooter to custom-build a new Harley for him. We'd also built a new outhouse to store the propane tanks. If there was ever another fire, Mom wouldn't be sitting on a bomb.

As the sun started to go down, the guys got the oil drum barbecue going and music began to pour out of the clubhouse. The nights were getting cooler now and I could feel my arms getting gooseflesh. But then Carrick's muscled body pressed against my back and his arms wrapped around my waist, hugging me to his warmth. I sighed and snuggled back against him.

I saw Mac looking on approvingly. Things had gotten much, much easier for the club in the last month. When Carrick and I had first arrived back at the slaughterhouse, we'd found the cops trying to arrest the entire MC. But as soon as the guy I'd clubbed over the head with a fire extinguisher learned that Volos was dead, he abandoned his story about the MC being responsible and told the police everything he knew. Suddenly, the whole thing turned into a much bigger investigation. Several very senior, very embarrassed FBI agents descended on the town to find out how one of their own had fooled them for so long. And once it came out that Volos had had one of his men plant the coke, the MC were released.

Everyone wanted to talk to me, especially when I told them about the phone call I'd heard between Volos and the guy in Vienna. There were rumors of an Austrian guy who controlled a whole worldwide network trafficking in women: Volos's boss, essentially. He was so shadowy the FBI didn't even have a name and he'd only been glimpsed once, when he came to Texas to try to buy fake passports. *"Tell the Sisters of Invidia about this,"* I overheard one FBI agent mutter to another.

Who the hell were the Sisters of Invidia? It sounded like a band.

Mom took charge of looking after the women who'd been imprisoned in the slaughterhouse with me. While the FBI handled interviewing them and getting them counseling, Mom made sure they were fed, clothed and given rooms at Haywood Falls' one hotel until they could contact their families. She was fiercely protective of them, even telling the FBI to back off when the endless interviews got too much. Of the seven women, five went home to their families in other parts of California. Two—Cassie and a woman named Francesca—were in the same situation as me, sold by a family member. Those family members—along with my step-dad—were arrested and the women began to build new lives: Francesca in LA and Cassie in San Francisco. Both promised to visit as soon as they were settled.

The reputation of the Hell's Princes gradually started to heal. It helped that the local press hailed them as heroes who'd helped bring down a corrupt FBI agent. And Sheriff Harris had helped broker a deal with the FBI to cover some of the cost of the warehouse fire, since it was one of their agents who'd started it. Money would be tight for a while but the club would survive. Mac was already looking around for a new legitimate business to invest in.

And me? I'd found my place. It was in the club's workshop, helping Scooter repair, customize and tune. He was overjoyed to find someone who talked his language and we got on well despite his grumpiness. He was even making noises about me taking over when he finally retired. I'd never been happier and would work late into the night until Carrick came and pulled me away from the engine blocks and into his arms.

Tonight, though, I was taking a break. Tonight, I just wanted to be with my man. The compound and the clubhouse, once so intimidating, had come to feel like home. And Haywood Falls was turning out to be a great place to live...maybe even a great place to raise a family, one day.

Carrick lowered his lips to the back of my neck, brushing my hair out of the way. He still couldn't seem to get enough of my hair, always sinking his fingers into it as he kissed me or sweeping it forward to fall over my breasts as I rode him in bed. Now, though, there was a new twist: when he pushed it back off my bare shoulder it revealed his name, picked out in black ink. I wanted the world to know that he was my love. Forever.

He'd got one, too, on his right bicep. My name in curling, elegant script, the letters riding the wings of a brightly-colored butterfly. When I asked why the butterfly, he mumbled something about thinking about me that way. For a hard man, he could be sweet as hell once you drilled deep enough.

His kisses traced a line around my neck, working their way towards my lips, and I twisted to meet him, tilting my head back and gasping as those hard Irish lips met my soft ones. What started slow and gentle quickly turned hot. He squeezed me closer and my breasts crushed against his chest. His tongue played with mine and the kiss turned open-mouthed and hungry.

"Everyone's watching," I panted, breaking the kiss for a second and flushing red.

He glanced around, then shrugged. "Don't care." And he pulled me even closer. My body molded against his as he kissed me long and deep. I closed my eyes and willingly gave myself up to it, kissing and grinning at the same time. There would be other challenges for the club and for us. I didn't kid myself that life with an outlaw would ever be simple. But we felt *right* together, like two parts of a machine that mesh perfectly and work in beautiful, rhythmic harmony.

Carrick

The Next Day

"Keep 'em closed," I told her, leading her by the hand. I checked and she was doing it, her eyes squeezed closed despite all the logs and branches underfoot. She trusted me completely and that made my chest open up in a way I hadn't been expecting. This relationship stuff was going to take some getting used to.

When we eventually arrived, I put my hands on Annabelle's shoulders and guided her until she was in the perfect position.

"Okay," I said. I could hear just a trace of nerves in my voice. "Open them."

She opened her eyes. The sun was just coming up, drenching the place in pinks and golds. The dew was still fresh on the greenery around it. It had meant getting up at the crack of dawn to ride out here and Annabelle wasn't a morning person—I'd have to feed her coffee and pastries when we got back to town. But it was worth it to see the place like this...I hoped.

Annabelle blinked a few times. "It's where we spent the night," she said slowly. "It's beautiful." Then she frowned. "The door looks new. Is someone living here now?"

I just turned to her and smiled.

Her jaw dropped. "You *bought* it?!"

I shrugged. "Turns out, they didn't want much for it, 'cos it'd been empty for so long. We can live at my place but, when we want to get away from town, maybe on a weekend...."

She flew at me and *whumped* into my chest, red hair tickling my nose. "I *love* it!"

"It needs a lot of work," I warned.

"That's the best part!" She was almost bouncing up and down. I could see that mind of hers going to work, already planning all kinds of things. "Can we stay here tonight?"

"If you're okay with sleeping bags and a lantern for light...yep."

She hugged me again. "Thank you."

I kissed the top of her head. And then picked her up, tossed her over my shoulder and carried her inside, just like I had the first time.

That night, we sat out on the cabin's porch looking up at the stars. Both of us were naked, our bodies still heated from sex but cooling in the night air. Annabelle was between my legs, her ass against my groin and her back pressed to my chest. I had a blanket wrapped around our shoulders to keep the chill off. Through the trees, I could just catch glimpses of the lake, a million points of light reflected in its surface.

I was thinking about family.

Not starting a new one with Annabelle. Maybe kids would happen, someday, but that was a long way off. And not the family I'd reconnected with here in Haywood Falls: Mac and Hunter, Ox and Mom.

My first family.

All the mistakes I'd made with the club—hell, everything since I left Chicago—had happened because I'd been trying to make up for running out on my brothers. There was only one way to really put things right.

"How would you feel," I asked slowly, "about a road trip?"

We took it slow, stopping at motels and enjoying the scenery. It took us almost a week to reach New York. And then it took us another few days of asking around before we found the underground fighting circuit where I thought Aedan would be.

But everyone we asked shook their heads. Aedan was gone.

We eventually got the story from a guy called Connor at the gym Aedan used to train at. Maybe he took pity on me because I was a fellow Irishman. He said Aedan had gotten into trouble with a shady fight promoter. There'd been a woman, too, named Sylvie, and her brother, Alec. And when it was all over, Aedan had left town for good. No one knew where he'd gone.

I turned to the punch bag that was hanging next to me and slammed my fist into it. *I wasn't there for him.* I'd been off on the other side of the country when he needed me most.

Annabelle thanked Connor for me and towed me away. At the diner across the street, she bought me coffee and got me calmed down.

I glanced moodily around. The place was some sort of haven for boxers: there were photos of guys in gloves all over the walls, some of them black and white. It was the sort of place Aedan had probably come, when he was here. Fighters, just like bikers, are predictable.

I stared into my coffee, seeing my reflection in the surface. Aedan had skipped town because he was in trouble. But wherever he wound up, he'd still be a fighter and he'd still join the local circuit. I could find him, if I prowled places like this for long enough. But only if I knew which city to look in.

That's when Annabelle squeezed my hand. "You came here because, the last thing you heard, he was in New York...right?"

I nodded.

"So...doesn't it make sense that he might go where he thinks *you* are?"

I thought on that for a while. I hadn't talked to Aedan since I left Chicago. As far as he knew, I was still there. Would he have fled to Chicago in the hopes of finding me? It seemed like a long shot. But it was all we had.

"Okay," I told Annabelle. "Chicago."

Four days later, we were at a tiny little boxing place in the heart of the city. It had less than a hundred seats around the ring: the equivalent of playing in a dive bar. But it was a legitimate fight, not an underground one. There were even posters.

And the posters showed my brother.

I drew in my breath as I watched Aedan step into the ring. When he turned to put in his gum shield, I saw the tiny shamrock tattoo between his shoulder blades. He'd picked up a few new scars since I last saw him but if anything he was bigger and more muscled than I remembered. He'd been training hard.

And something else had changed, too. I saw a woman hug him just before he stepped into the ring: a tiny, dark-haired thing. *Sylvie?*

For the next three rounds, I watched him stalk his prey, learning the other guy's weaknesses. His opponent was good: fast *and* strong. He even got a few good hits in.

But he didn't stand a chance. Aedan waited until the third round...and then he annihilated him. It was like watching a town be swept away by a tidal wave: the guy was driven back, back, and then lifted right off his feet by the final punch. The crowd cheered so loud that we couldn't even hear the ref count the guy out.

We pushed our way backstage: when security tried to stop us, I growled in their faces. And in the dressing room I found Aedan.

He was sitting on a table and the dark-haired woman was between his muscled thighs, kissing him, her hands running up and down his sweat-slick back. Neither of them saw us and Annabelle and I were left standing in the doorway, unsure whether to interrupt. *I'll just wait until they're done,* I decided.

Then Aedan's hands slipped under the woman's top.

Annabelle coughed to announce our presence and the woman spun around. Aedan looked at us over her shoulder...and his jaw dropped.

It's funny how you can be planning a moment in your head for weeks—maybe years—and yet, when it finally arrives, you have no idea what to say.

The woman glanced at Aedan and something in his expression must have told her what was going on. She nodded and stepped aside. *She knows who I am,* I realized. *He's talked about me.*

Aedan slid down from the table and walked towards me. He was still fresh from the fight, sweat rolling down him, muscles pumped and hard. I wasn't sure if he was going to slug me for abandoning the family, or for being out of touch for so many years. But I was ready to take it, whatever he had for me.

He stepped closer...and suddenly grabbed me and pulled me into a bear hug to rival any of Ox's. I could hear his breath shuddering as he held me. I realized I was doing the same thing. I wasn't ready for the sudden upwelling of emotion.

I had my family back: the first member, at least. And as soon as I thought that, I knew what I had to do.

We had to find the other two: Kian and Sean. And then, together, we had to find out what happened to Bradan. If he was dead, we needed to bury him. If he was alive somewhere, maybe still with the cult...then we had to get him back.

It was time to put our family back together.

THE END

Thank you for reading.

Five of my books feature the O'Harra brothers. The order you read the first four in isn't too important because they're all standalones, but you should read *Brothers* last.

The story of Aedan, the bad boy Irish boxer, is told in *Punching and Kissing*.

The story of Sean, the sledgehammer-wielding badass who teams up with a good girl to save her sister, is told in *Bad For Me*.

The story of Kian, the bodyguard who winds up protecting – and falling for – the President's daughter, is told in *Saving Liberty*.

Carrick's story you've just read.

Finally, *Brothers* brings all four O'Harra brothers – and their women – together to search for their missing brother.

Read all of my O'Harra books? Try *Lying and Kissing,* the story of a geeky CIA analyst who's ordered to seduce and spy on a billionaire Russian arms dealer.